Happy Reading

Lu McAllister

SQUAW DANCE

SQUAW DANCE

by
Lee McAllister

Reno, Nevada

DEDICATION

For the Navajo Code Talkers with hopes that this story will raise the reader's appreciation for their unique contribution.

And for John.

Death had come as a surprise. His dark eyes stared, wide and glazed, as much in disbelief as in the horror of his last seconds. His jaw hung from its hinges, his mouth gaped. One could envision his last words as the essence of life had spurted from the deep slash along his left carotid artery while he prayed someone would hear him proclaim that he was dying . . . really dying.

In a deep pool of dark blood his hands had slumped from his throat and now lay alongside his right cheek in their macabre bath. Blood caked his dark hair and had trickled down to the running path.

Standing several yards away, Inspector Jim Matheson of San Francisco's Homicide Division bit off the tip of his cigar, spat it away from the scene and flipped open the engraved Zippo he carried in memory of another cop, his father. He lighted the thick roll from Tampa, puffed it until the end glowed red, then spoke around the protrusion as he turned to his partner.

"Well, Lindy, it looks like he ran into someone waiting for him . . . someone quick and efficient."

Inspector Linda Hansen glanced again at the body surrounded by crime scene technicians collecting evidence. Having tripped over him in her morning run, she'd seen enough of the dead youth. She swallowed to still the panting that had yet to ease, not from physical exertion, but from slipping in the slime of death and landing almost nose-to-nose with the victim. The body had been pulled just far enough under a large cotonester to delay its discovery. Looking again at the blood stains on her gray sweats, she gulped in revulsion and wished more than ever for a long, hot shower. But that would have to wait until the technicians had completed every detail of the crime scene, until after the reports had been filed and after the decision when she could be excused.

"You so concerned about job security, you were running around hoping to bump into a case?" teased Matheson.

Groaning, she rubbed her scraped palms. "Very funny, Jim."

His broad shoulders shook along with his middle-age paunch. "I'll suggest the Lieutenant assign you this one."

Her eyes scanned the plastic yellow ribbons that cordoned the crime scene. Beyond, had grown a crowd of curious public, stretching in morbid fascination to get a better view.

"I never said you owed me."

Matheson blue a puff of blue smoke, which spiraled into the crisp June morning air. "You never say much of anything. I guess that's what I like best about you. You just get to work."

She pulled the red terry sweatband from her head and raked her fingers through short, black hair, then drew the back of her hand across the beaded moisture of her forehead. Only her round, cornflower blue eyes distracted from her Native American features. Producing a feeble smile, she returned "That's why I'm here."

"Inspector Matheson!"

The Homicide inspectors turned toward the man approaching them.

"What have you got, Adams?" asked Matheson.

Sergeant Keith Adams produced a worn, leather wallet. His face was a mask of black jade as he unfolded the maroon eelskin. A Social Security card and California driver's license showed through the plastic inserts.

Matheson took the wallet, then muttered, "Chris Cortez. Seventeen." He shrugged. "Anything else?"

Adams shook his head. "Not so far. No signs of a struggle."

Matheson scratched the back of his neck. "My guess is he had a meeting to make a buy. The killer kept the dope and skipped with the money. Only an idiot would be alone in the park when it's dark." He looked at Lindy and grinned. "Nothing personal."

He was right, of course, she knew. But the running paths of Golden Gate Park offered the closest soft running surface in her neighborhood. The sidewalks were too hard on the joints, and she *did* have her revolver holstered at the small of her back under her sweatshirt.

"Well, Lindy, what do you think got the kid killed?"

She glanced one more time at the terminal look of shock on the dead boy's face. "I think I'll wait for some evidence."

"And *I* think," Matheson said, "I'll call in his identity." He lifted his shoulders. "Who knows?" Somebody might be missing him."

"I wish *I* had," Lindy mumbled as much to herself as to her partner, now ambling toward his car.

Adams looked over as Matheson began a conversation with a voice crackling over the radio, then turned back to Lindy and pointed to her blood-stained sweats. "Looks like you really jumped into this one."

"Slid into it is more like it." She lifted the stiffness

of her sweatshirt away as an expression of disgust rose on her face.

"Well, we haven't had a body turn up in the park for over a month. We were due. Last one was missing his head. Were you in on that one?"

"No. I missed that opportunity."

"Rumor control claims it was a cult killing . . . Satan worshippers."

"So I heard, but the D.A.'s looking at it as plain and simple murder. He says it was a sicko or someone with a big ax to grind."

"Makes an easier case to sell a jury." Adams snorted his repugnance. "They always look for nice, tidy cases to sell juries. Gives them a better track record. You ever get tired of bustin' your tail so they can plea-bargain."

Lindy turned back toward the on-lookers. She refused to become entrapped in the frustration of a system that too frequently sullied the memory of a victim and crushed the souls of survivors.

"Lindy!" Matheson called from the car.

Abruptly, she excused herself and joined her partner. She leaned against the driver's door as he slipped the radio's handpiece into its holder.

"The kid was called in as a missing person around two this morning," said Matheson. "Lives in the Richmond District. He was last seen yesterday afternoon when he left another kid's home on Haight Street . . . seventeen hundred block." He ripped a page from his notebook and handed it to her. "Lieutenant says the case is ours. *I* say you can start right here and right now."

"Did the Lieutenant say I could grab a shower first?"

"Yeah." He chuckled. "And he said I could wash your back."

"A ride home will do."

"My pleasure. Hop in."

Lindy walked around to the passenger door, opened it and slid in as Matheson turned the key in the ignition, firing the engine to a ragged start.

"Say, Lindy," he asked as the car begin to roll, "if you're really an Indian, where did you get those blue eyes?"

She grinned. "From an ancestor."

He chuckled around his cigar. "From a tepee creeper would be more my guess."

Just over an hour later, Lindy eased her Blazer against the curb on the seventeen hundred block of Haight Street. She liked driving a carryall and appreciated its convenience. As she swallowed the last bite of her banana, she turned off the ignition. Eating on the run was part of a detective's job. Within days of becoming an inspector, she realized the value of carrying fruit and muffins instead of grabbing the handiest fast food which quickly settled in her stomach like a rock. A final swig of the peach-flavored Canadian sparkling water washed down the banana. After locking the driver's door, she stepped onto the curb and belched the carbonation of the bottled water. A whiff of cinnamon from a bakery two doors down instantly overcame the satiety of the fruit, and she suddenly yearned for an obscenely delicious sticky bun.

Haight retained little of its infamous hippy legacy of the sixties and early seventies. In recent years it had evolved into a trendy district of thriving boutiques and artisans. An occasional artist lived above his or her business. At seven thirty-eight on Friday morning, the street had yet to fill with the rush of people going to work.

The address was boldly printed in a calligraphic scroll above the name, *MARIA'S NATIVE AMERICAN ARTS*, etched on the display window.

As she approached, Lindy saw a slender, bronze arm supporting a wide, ornate silver and turquoise open bangle bracelet reach and place a piece of pottery in the display. This bowl was Pueblo, small and round, its designs defined in textured and glossy black.

Gently, Lindy tapped on the window. A woman's face, whose age Lindy guessed to be in the late thirties, bronzed and framed with long, straight black hair, lowered to peek at her early visitor. The woman shook her head and pointed to the sign: *OPEN 10 A.M. TO 6 P.M.* Lindy produced her I.D. The woman nodded and retreated. She smiled tensely as she opened the door.

"Can I help you, officer?"

"I'm here about Chris Cortez."

Genuine concern flickered in the woman's black eyes. "Come in," she invited, standing aside as she opened the door further. "My name is Maria Sawyer."

"Inspector Hansen." As Lindy entered Mari Sawyer's establishment, she was immediately struck by the stunning Native American art. Besides the pottery in numerous designs were Navajo rugs, paintings in all media, silver, gold and copper jewelry and countless other objects. One painting drew Lindy's attention instantly: a large acrylic by the Cherokee artist, Virginia Stroud, depicting the gentility and innocence of the Native American woman in her daily life as was characteristic of the artist's work. The warmth and happiness Lindy knew very well from her first eighteen years and promised herself that she would one day have a Stroud original of her own. Dream on, she thought, then turned back to Maria.

"Is Chris all right?" Maria asked. "We've been worried out of our minds. His parents called us just before midnight, but Chris left here yesterday afternoon before I closed the gallery."

Lindy shook her head.

Maria Sawyer instantly knew. "Chris is dead, isn't he?"

Lindy nodded. "I'm sorry."

Maria pressed a flattened palm against her breastbone. "My God! What happened?"

"I hope you can help us find out."

"How . . . how did he die?"

Lindy selected her words carefully, hoping to spare the grisly details. "A knife wound. He was found in Golden Gate Park this morning."

As the horror of reality descended, Maria began to tremble. "Have his parents been told?"

A police chaplain is with them now."

"Terrible. This is really terrible. Delmer . . . he's my son . . . he's Chris' best friend. This is going to be really hard on him."

"Mrs. Sawyer, I realize this is a bad time, but I need to ask you a few questions."

Maria nodded. "I understand."

"Exactly what time did Chris leave here?"

"Around five-thirty. We didn't know he was missing until his parents called."

"Do you know where he was going?"

"He was *supposed* to be going home."

"But he didn't," a third voice stated firmly.

Abruptly, Lindy and Maria turned toward the deep voice. A man stood at the base of the stairway in the rear of the gallery. He was of medium height and stout but not fat. A bright yellow shirt was tucked into his jeans. A heavy silver and turquoise buckle fastened a tooled leather belt under a belly sagging with age. Black slanted eyes glinted from a heavily lined copper face. His black hair had few flecks of white despite his late years.

"What do you mean, Papa?" asked Maria.

"He went to find them," the man answered. "I told him not to, but you can't tell kids anything."

"Who?" Lindy asked.

"Excuse me," Maria interrupted. "Papa, this is Inspector Hansen from the police. Inspector Hansen, this is my father, Dan Paya."

"Who?" Lindy asked again.

"The black eyes narrowed fiercely. "Whoever is trying to build a bomb."

Sergeant Joe Barnett glanced up from the report in his typewriter and recognized his former partner entering the squadroom. Beneath his receding hairline, his brown eyes rounded to Muppet proportions as he stood. In a voice loud enough to turn the heads of the other members of the squad, he announced, "Oh God, circle the wagons!"

Lindy smiled and greeted Joe with a strong hug. "Hello, Joe," she said and leaned back. "How's life with the Bomb Squad?"

"A real blast," he returned, chuckling at his pun. "What brings you here?"

"Lieutenant Walker sent me over to introduce Mr. Paya to Lieutenant Sloan."

Joe looked over Lindy's shoulder and noticed the elderly man still standing in the doorway. His face tightened in chagrin over his initial greeting to Lindy in fear that the old man had taken offense. If he had, it didn't show. The older man stood quietly, waiting for his cue to move.

Quickly, Joe glanced over his shoulder, then tilted his head toward a door across the squadroom. Big black letters identified the office of *MATTHEW SLOAN, LIEUTENANT.* "Maybe you can put him into a better mood."

"Am I about to be sent to the wolves?" Lindy asked, grinning.

"More like an old bear with a scalded ass. It began when one of our teams went to check out a bomb threat at UCSF Medical Center this morning. One of those animal rights activists threatened to blow the place sky high. The moron pulled a gun and killed one of our bomb-sniffing dogs. Can you believe that? Blew a dog away over a bunch of rats! And he wounded the dog's handler before we could disarm him.

"Anyway, Sloan wanted to throw the book at the guy. The bureaucrats are moving slowly since it's such a sensitive subject. He spent the whole morning arguing with them. He's out numbered, but he's not through. Not by a long shot."

Lindy's eyebrow's lifted in twin raven wings. "I'm not sure I can change his mood, but I bet I can get his thoughts on something else."

Joe snickered and winked. "I just bet you can."

Laughing, Lindy said, "I stepped into that one."

"I forgot. You've never met my boss."

"I'm beginning to wonder if I ever am."

"Don't say I didn't warn you," Joe said as he walked to Sloan's door. He opened it, leaned in and muttered something inaudible. A few seconds later and still grinning, he returned to Lindy. "He's all yours."

Lindy turned to Paya. "If you'll follow me, Mr. Paya." She waited for the man to join her, then headed for Sloan's office. With a soft but confident knock on the door, she announced her arrival.

"Come in!" boomed from the other side of the door.

Joe had been right. Matt Sloan was in no mood for an appointment. This morning had left him with a good dog dead, a good man wounded and a chain-of-command that told him to cool his temper. If anything, the cautious handling of the situation had made his temper hotter. With one hand thrust deeply into his pocket, he ran the fingers of his other through his dark burnish hair. He sighed. What a day! At least it was Friday.

His green eyes stared out the window. The action on the street was hidden behind the vision of the morning's bomber gloating over his success. *All* bombers had a sickening gloat whenever they saw the damage done. Matt had seen it in Italy, Germany and France with the offshoots of the Red Brigade and the Baader-Meinhof gangs, and in Britain with the IRA. He'd seen it everywhere with the rising tide of Neo-Nazis, with the radical elements of the animal rights activists, the anti-abortionists and a host of others who decided they had a case. In his book, no matter who embraced it, the cause was the same . . . the power to disrupt and destroy regardless of the proclamations.

"Lieutenant Sloan?"

His head jerked around to the throaty timbre of the unmistakenly feminine voice at his door. Everything, he noticed instantly about the striking woman at his door, was unmistakenly feminine. Her casual dress in one of those blues, which designers always gave outrageous names, barely camouflaged her soft curves. Briefly, her gold loose-woven jacket parted just enough for him to get a glimpse of the weapon holstered beside her left breast. A .44 Special. A Smith & Wesson 24-3, one of only five thousand manufactured in the early eighties. The lady was obviously very serious about her business. Then he looked up and fell right into those magnificent blue eyes. His foul disposition faded so quickly, he had to smile at himself as all his chimes began to peal.

"Good afternoon," he greeted lightly as he extended his hand.

Her handshake matched her smile, professional but

warm and cordial.

"I'm Inspector Hansen."

"Please have a seat."

"Thank you. But first I want to introduce you to someone." She leaned out the door. After she said, "Come in," Matt saw the older man enter. "Lieutenant Sloan, this is Mr. Paya."

"Pleased to meet you, Mr. Paya," Matt said, offering his hand again.

Paya nodded as he accepted the greeting with a solid handshake while Matt noted the man's austere assessment. The black eyes missed nothing, and Matt realized that he'd just met one of the few men in his life who'd drawn an automatic respect. The day was turning into one surprise after another.

"Mr. Paya," Lindy said, gently placing her hand on his arm, "Lieutenant Sloan is an expert on bombs. I want you to tell him everything you told me." She gestured for Paya to take a seat, then settled into a second chair.

Matt rested a hip on his desk and extended his right leg over the corner.

"Before I begin," Paya said, leaning forward and placing his hands on his thighs, "I want you to know I have a reason to think I've come onto something."

Matt quietly waited for Paya to continue. The glint in the black eyes spoke authoritively and offered challenge to anyone not prepared to listen.

"From forty-three to the end of the war I was a Code Talker in the Pacific," said Paya. "Ever hear about us?"

Matt smiled and nodded. "In Military Science." Too bad, he thought, that knowledge of this unique group had passed through so few avenues of education. The Navajo communication skills in their native language prevented enemy interception of many Pacific campaigns. Thousand of men were alive today because of the Navajo Code Talkers and unfortunately had never known of their existence.

"ROTC?" Paya asked.

"West Point."

Paya's expression changed abruptly. He was impressed. His skepticism began to ease. "Not too many people in this part of the country know who we are."

"And what brought you to this part of the country, Mr. Paya?"

"My daughter insisted I move in with her after my wife died two years ago. Maria . . . my daughter . . . came out here seven years ago from Flagstaff. She has a good business selling Native American art to interior decorators and to the public." Seeing he had the Lieutenant's full attention, Paya shifted back in his chair.

"Since the war," he continued, "I've kept up with my radio. Got the highest license there is. My legs give so much trouble . . . the doctors want to put a tube in my belly to make my blood flow better, but I don't want them cutting on me." He waved his hand to dismiss the subject. "Well, anyway, I don't get out much. Most of the time I listen to my radio. Even my bodyguard and I keep in touch. The commanders assigned us bodyguards after several of us were mistaken for Japanese in Marine uniforms. I spent two days in one of our prisoner camps in Guadalcanal because a Marine corporal from West Virginia thought I was a Jap in a Marine uniform. Sometimes I sit up at night when my legs are bothering me and work the radio." The black eyes narrowed. "That's when I started hearing the transmissions.

"Just over three weeks ago I picked up the first one. They kept giving different call signs, but I knew they were up to something right away."

Matt wasn't sure what this had to do with the Bomb Squad, but he was definitely intrigued by his guest. He glanced at Lindy. By *both* of his guests. Also, he had a schoolboyish notion that he had just met a legend. "How's that, Mr. Paya?"

"First was because of their subject. They were

sharing secrets for venison jerky."

Matt frowned lightly. "Lots of men, including two of the men out there," he said, tilting his head to indicate the squadroom, "pride themselves in their venison jerky receipes."

"You don't hunt, do you?"

"I fish."

Paya's eyes locked directly with Matt's. "It's June, Lieutenant. No one makes venison jerky in June. They make it right after the hunt. That's in late fall. Early fall in some places unless they live on a reservation where they can hunt and fish all year."

Matt swallowed his humor at Paya's patronization. "I understand, sir."

"Second clue was their fists. That's radio talk for cadence or tempo. Everyone has his individual fist. Third was what they were putting in their recipes. Nutmeg, thyme, rosemary. They would wreck a good venison. So I began to copy the messages just to see what they might be up to. There've been twelve in all. This past Monday, I realized what was going on."

"And?"

Paya retrieved a small notebook from his pocket. "Got a piece of paper?"

Matt circled the desk, pulled a blank sheet from a drawer and stood back while Paya rose and leaned over the paper, turning it sideways.

"On May twenty-first, I picked up the first message. After the five parties had made contact, the messages all began with, 'Have latest success to improve venison jerky.'

"Then an ingredient is given. First was," he said, printing as he spoke, "garlic-one clove. The second message was oregano-half teaspoon and so on." Silently, Paya printed the rest: half teaspoon tarragon, whole coriander-one teaspoon, iodized salt-half teaspoon, nutmeg-one fourth teaspoon, no sodium beef broth-one cup, ice water-one cup, half teaspoon rosemary."

Paya straightened and stretched his back as he cast a glance to reassure himself that he had Matt's full attention. He did. Absolutely!

"My first thought was to look at the first letters of the ingredients. The G-O-H-W-I-N-N-I-H. In the Pacific we had to send messages phonetically when the word couldn't be translated into Navajo. Like with some of those Japanese names. But, as you can see, those letters mean nothing. Then I looked to see if it was an anagram. Still nothing. I looked again. I knew there had to be a clue somewhere, and I realized it was with the first message. If I hadn't picked up that first message, I'd have never figured it out." His finger tapped the paper. "There it is. The number one in the garlic-one clove. It's really an old form of code, called a Caesar code, but unless someone suspects one is being sent, it's likely no one will pick it up. Garlic begins with the seventh letter of the alphabet. But the *one* in the one clove renumbers *G* as the first letter. Now, watch this."

Across the lower half of the page, Paya printed:

ABCDEFGHIJKLMNOPQRSTUVWXYZ
GHIJKLMNOPQRSTUVWXYZABCDEF

Paya tapped the paper again, this time at the second ingredient. "O is the fifteenth letter. But if G is the first letter, the new fifteenth letter is U." His black eyes bore into Matt's with a challenge. "Now given that, you tell me what the rest of the letters are."

Matt lifted a pen from his pocket and smiled. "You're going to make me work for this, aren't you, Mr. Paya?"

A deep crease furrowed Paya's brow. "You'll learn something."

"I have no doubt," Matt said as he began a separate page. Within a minute he stared unsmiling at the new set of letters: G U N C O T T O N.

"Jesus!" he muttered.

"Does it surprise you that the next three letters are N-I-T?"asked Paya.

Still staring in disbelief at the letters, Matt said, "Not at all. And Mr. Paya, I'll bet you know exactly what those three letters stand for and what they're leading to."

Paya nodded. "Guncotton mixed with the right amount of nitroglycerine makes a form of plastique, that stuff everyone calls C4. It's very primitive, but it's effective enough."

Matt looked over at Lindy. She was quietly taking it all in. "When did you find out about this?"

"I met Mr. Paya three hours ago," she answered. "He has more to tell you."

Matt instantly realized more meant worse." Go on, Mr. Paya."

Paya returned to his seat. The strain was evident in the deepened lines of his face as he leaned back in his chair and laced his fingers over his belly.

"Tuesday morning I called the FCC office. The agent acted if I was some kind of crank. After I got nowhere with them, I called the FBI. Same thing. I should've gone over there and pounded on their desks until I got it through their thick heads. Now, I regret I didn't."

"What happened?"

"My grandson, Delmer is a ham too. Not many kids are getting into it anymore. But he and his friend, Chris, who also was a ham, got all excited about what I'd been hearing. When none of the federal agents listened to me, the two boys tried to play heroes. They set up two home-built direction finders without telling me. During Wednesday's transmission they identified one of the transmitters coming out of Golden Gate Park. Yesterday afternoon while Chris was over, the boys were very excited about something. It didn't take much for me to figure it out. I told both of them to forget about it. Chris has always been the more adventuresome of the two. It wasn't until his parents called us to say he never got home, that I realize he'd taken off on his own to look for the transmitter. This morning Chris was found in Golden Gate Park. His throat had been slit."

"Mr. Paya," Matt said gently, "you can't take responsibility for another person's lack of judgment."

"But in this case I do."

"I understand. I'm sure that if were I in your shoes, I'd feel the same."

"You think I'm onto something?"

"Absolutely. In fact, I'm going to start working on this right away." Matt looked at Lindy, "Have you taken a statement from him?"

Those round blue eyes, which had grabbed his when he first looked into them, still held their power, but it was now a different kind. Something in their depths said this case had become very personal with her.

"Yes," she answered, producing a page from her shoulder bag. "Here's a copy."

Matt smiled as he accepted the report. "Thanks." He looked back to Paya. "Mr. Paya, I'd like to ask you to give another statement to Sergeant Barnett. While you do, I'm going to see what strings I can pull to get the FCC involved. If someone's building a bomb in this city, I'm going to find him."

Paya's head moved from side to side. His voice began to show how tired he was from the morning's events. "It's not just this city."

"What do you mean?"

"These transmissions. They're coming through during the skip . . . the time for transmitting long distances."

"You're making my day, Mr. Paya."

"And it will get worse. It's going to be a big squaw dance."

"Squaw dance?"

"Code Talker talk. The Navajo language has no word for bombing area, so we called it a squaw dance."

Matt nodded. "Will you mind giving another statement to my sergeant?" After Paya assented, Matt stepped around him and called for Joe.

Joe's head appeared around the door. "Mr. Paya?"

Paya rose and began a careful walk out of Matt's office. At the door, he turned and said, "Thank you, Lieutenant."

"You're welcome, Mr. Paya," Matt returned.

Lindy stepped behind Paya but stopped when Matt called her name. She turned. "Sir?"

"Don't call me sir. I had enough of that in the Army."

"Yes, Lieutenant."

He was going to work on that one in time. "I'd appreciate a copy of the autopsy report of that boy's death as soon as it comes through."

She nodded, then followed Paya into the squadroom as Matt reached for the telephone.

At his desk, Joe sat across from Paya and readied himself to take a statement. Poised with pen and notebook, he looked at the older gentlemen and smiled. "Okay, sir. What have you got to tell me?"

Paya grunted. "Before I begin, I want you to know I have reason to suspect something."

Lindy smiled as she winked at Joe, whose eyes crinkled in acknowledgement, then she turned her head as she called Matheson. She was not surprised to sense the tension beneath his light "Hello."

"How did it go, Lindy?" Matheson asked.

"Fine," she answered. "Lieutenant Sloan bought Mr. Paya's tale. I should be able to take him home in about half an hour."

"Who? Sloan?" was followed by a fiendish but friendly chuckle. Matheson rarely passed an opportunity to slip one in.

She laughed. She knew his humor too well to let him rattle her. "Heard anything from the lab?"

Matheson's voice abruptly turned serious. "As a matter of fact, I did. Just a few minutes ago, Adams called about some strands of hair his team found on the bush the kid was lying under. Lindy, are you ready for this?"

"Fire away."

"It was a woman! Black hair. Ethnic."

Lindy frowned. "Sure it wasn't mine? The way I tripped, I could have hit the bush."

"Adams thought of that. He said, 'No way.' The hair strands were too long to have been yours. You think maybe we're after some gal who's acting out her hatred for men?"

"I think it should be so simple. Buckle your belt."

"Lindy, I'm too old for a bumpy ride."

Lindy glanced at Paya giving his statement, turned her head and lowered her voice. "How's the Cortez family doing?"

"Pitiful. The kid never caused them a bit of trouble. Honor student and all. He was planning to become an electrical engineer through Stanford. His old man swam the Rio Grande when he was fourteen. Worked hard to make something of himself. His son would have been the first in the family to make it to college. A cryin' shame."

"Yes, it is. Well, I'd better get back to Mr. Paya. His health isn't the best, and he's looking rather strained. See you later."

"You too, Lindy."

She cradled the phone and saw that Joe was rapidly gaining interest in Paya's background. It might be a long report, she thought, amused. She took a minute to think about the way the pieces were falling together. Each one seemed to make the puzzle more grim. Giving Paya a smile, she walked back to Matt's office and knocked again.

"Come in."

Opening the door, she saw him cradling the telephone. He looked up. "Lieutenant," she said, stepping into his office, "Inspector Matheson says the crime lab believes we're looking for a woman."

Matt's brow furrowed, and Lindy repeated Mateson's statement about the hair samples.

He tossed her words around for a few seconds before he said, "I just got through with the FCC. They're sending an agent over right away to talk with Mr. Paya. Can you do me a favor?"

"What's that?"

"This is your case, right?"

She nodded.

"Because explosives are involved, it's mine, too. I need you to keep Mr. Paya happy since he and the FCC haven't exactly started off on the right foot. We're going to need that old man. Any objections?"

Expressionless, she shook her head. "I want to find that kid's killer."

"And I want to find who's out to set off a bomb in this city and where and when. We need someone Paya trusts. He's a cautious old buzzard. But then, I guess Indians have a reason to distrust us."

She grinned. "Yes, we do."

Matt's brows lifted in self-conscious surprise. "Did I put my foot in my mouth?" Taking a stronger assessment, he suddenly recognized her heritage. She was still smiling. He swallowed a sigh of relief.

She laughed. "My great-great-great grandfather was a Danish settler in Humboldt County. Blue eyes aren't that all uncommon in some of the tribal families. I even have a brother with blond hair."

"Humboldt County," Matt repeated. "That makes you Hupa, right?"

"Right."

He smiled. "This is going to be a learning case for all of us."

"I believe it is."

Chuck Wilson was typical of what an office administrator would send over on a Friday. He was twenty-five and on his first tour with the FCC and bright with enthusiasm. With clean-cut auburn hair and horn-rimmed glasses, he looked crisp and fresh. Wilson arrived in Matt's office while Lindy treated Paya to lunch. By the time they returned, Wilson was eager to get to work. All thoughts of the weekend ahead became absorbed with locating the source of the transmissions. After he'd called a report to his supervisor, he sat with Paya and heard another account of Paya's exploits in the Pacific.

Paya's attention faded into a renewed energy as more and more people responded to him.

Thirty-seven minutes later, another man entered the squadroom. He was on the underside of fifty and dressed in a navy blue suit with a maroon tie accented with thin white stripes. He was friendly but intense. With a cordial smile, he introduced himself to Joe.

"Good afternoon. I'm Tom Kowalski, Special Agent-in-Charge of the FBI office. I'd like to see Lieutenant Sloan."

Joe was impressed. The ball could certainly start to roll when the right people pushed it. "He's in his office," he said, pointing over his shoulder.

Kowalski waved off Joe's offer to escort him across the room and headed straight to Matt's office. At the inviting, "Come in," he opened the door to see three men and a woman look up. He introduced himself and declined Matt's offer of his chair. After the round of introductions, he addressed Paya.

"Mr. Paya, for me to say that our office receives countless reports of one or another nature from the public is no excuse for the delay in listening to you. Mr. Wilson's supervisor called a few moments ago and filled me in on what's going on. I realize that you've had to tell your story several times by now, but I have to ask you to repeat it again."

Paya rubbed the ache in his cramped legs and grunted. He obviously wasn't impressed with the man in the blue suit. "I should have recorded it the first time."

Matt took the cue and lifted a small cassette recorder from a desk drawer. "Good idea, Mr. Paya." He set
the recorder on the desktop and pushed the *RECORD*
button.

Rubbing another leg cramp, Paya announced, "Before I begin, I want you to know I have reason to
think I'm onto something."

Lindy and Matt looked at each other, and each
quickly maneuvered a hand to hide a smile.

Another hour passed. It was official now. A joint
task force had received the blessing of the chiefs of
police and both federal agencies. Kowalski was to be
in charge through the weekend. He directed Wilson to
stay with Paya and identify the transmissions. If they
came on schedule, he hoped to have a location of each
within a day or two at the least. The Bomb Squad
would offer assistance if required.

Matt took note of Lindy's disappointment as she
watched Wilson escort Paya from his office. Wilson
was to spend the evening in contact with his office
while he waited for Paya to identify another round of
transmissions.

"Don't look so down," Matt said to her as soon as
Kowalski excused himself, "I got pushed aside, too."

"It shows, huh?" she said, her expression unaltered.

Matt smiled. "Like a neon sign."

"I'm never good at sitting in an office. That's not
where a killer is found. I keep thinking someone's out
there ready to kill again. And I keep seeing that dead
boy's face."

Matt recognized the anger in her voice. It was the
same rage he felt about people who set off bombs.

"That's always the hardest part . . . the waiting."

Lindy nodded and lowered her Styrofoam coffee
cup to her lap. Then she looked up and, for the first
time, recognized the personal interest in the green
eyes. Quickly, she looked back to her cup before she
betrayed the sudden realization that she liked what

she saw. A brief flutter teased her stomach as she asked herself if she really saw the undisguised interest, or was she looking for a reprieve from the horror she'd encountered that morning when she had first looked into the dead boy's eyes? Glancing up again, she had her answer. It was there, all right. A chemistry that would be interesting to explore when time and circumstances allowed. Her teeth sank into her lower lip to check her temptation to smile, Yes, it was there. And she liked it.

Matt settled into his chair, his memory retracing his initial impression of her. It hadn't changed at all. "So, Inspector Hansen, what got you into this business?"

Staring at her nearly empty coffee cup, she saw the brown liquid swirling. She stilled her hand and drew in a slow breath.

"I had just finished my freshman year at Humboldt State. I was planning to become a teacher and return to the reservation. Then one of those life-changing events happened. My best friend, Becky, telephoned me one evening. She was in hysterics. All I could get out of her was the address where she was babysitting. When I got to her, I found that she'd been raped by two men who'd jimmied the lock to the utility room and broken into the house. I called the police and did the best I could with her, which wasn't much, until they arrived. They were so nice to her. She would have never gotten through that ordeal had it not been for their kindness and understanding while I, her best friend, was practically useless. The following semester I registered my major as criminology. I never considered anything else."

Matt nodded. He had speculated that her reason lay behind something personal. "When did you get to SFPD?"

"After graduation I got a job with the Humboldt County Sheriff's Department. I was kind of a novelty to them, and all they could think to do with me was to send me on calls involving Indians in trouble off the reservation. A year of that, and I came down here and went through the academy." Her lips eased into an ironic smile. "And now, I'm back to dealing with Indians. But I'll admit that Mr. Paya is unique."

"He's an interesting man."

Her smile brightened. "He is at that."

"Matt?" Joe was leaning into the office and grinning from ear to ear. "We have a small problem."

"What's that?" Matt asked as if his day needed another.

"Mr. Paya refuses to ride in Wilson's Toyota because it's a Japanese car."

Laughing, Lindy rose from her chair. "I guess it's up to me to get him home."

Matt followed her out of the office. "Inspector Hansen," he said as she was about to bid Joe farewell.

She turned, the smile was still on her face as the telephone on Joe's desk rang.

"Keep me posted about Mr. Paya." Matt requested.

"I'll let you know the minute I hear something."

Joe cursed loudly and slammed the telephone into its cradle. "It's the Medical Center again. They think there's another bomb. This time in the emerency room."

Matt heaved a long sigh. "Let's get going."

After receiving report from the day shift, Elaine Judson, R.N. had made her customary rounds of the cubicles to check if anyone might have been omitted from her report and waiting for treatment. She had seen it happen before. A busy emergency unit can easily direct its efforts and attention to major trauma while a person with a minor injury is lead to a cubical and told, "Someone will be with you shortly," only to be overlooked in the hectic pace.

It had been relatively quiet for a summer Friday afternoon. That wouldn't last. Summers and Fridays were another description for the mayhem which would last through the weekend, especially through September. Every conceivable emergency would begin pouring through the door at any moment, and every cubical must be checked to see if it were adequately stocked with supplies.

Elaine was almost through with her fourth cubical when she noticed in the corner a worn, brown leather pouch protruding from behind a waste basket. Instantly, she recalled the report's account of the early morning incident in the research department. Struggling with her anxiety, she stepped quickly down the corridor to announce her discovery.

The entire department had been evacuated by the time Matt, Joe and the rest of the bomb squad detail arrived. Within seven minutes, a throng of curious staff members collected around Joe as he removed his protective head cover and held open the bag to reveal its contents and laughed.

"It seems that someone lost his bag on the way to give an anesthetic," Joe announced to the cluster around him.

"Anesthetic?" Matt asked as sighs of relief were expelled.

"Yeah," answered Joe as he set the bag on the cubicle's gurney and pulled off his vest. "I maintain my EMT license and work with these instruments all the time." His finger moved across the contents as he announced, "Bite blocks, endotracheal tubes, airways."

"Well, it's not one of ours," said Dr. Elkins, the physician in charge of the evening shift, as he moved forward. "All of our stuff is kept in the crash carts outside the cubicles. I can't imagine who that belongs to. I wouldn't be caught dead with a bag like that. It looks like something from the age of silver bullets."

Chuckling, Joe glanced again into the bag. "I don't believe there's any in there. Not even a rubber mallet."

"For heaven's sake!," Elaine Judson said, groaning her relief. "I must have aged another ten years, and it's less than an hour into the shift. I really believe the rest will be anticlimactic after this."

"I wonder if it's some kind of joke," Matt said. "Sometimes that happens after an incident like this morning's."

While everyone around him slipped into the laughter of relief, Matt saw no humor. *Nothing* was humorous about bombs or threats of bombs.

I doubt it," returned Elkins. "My guess is it belongs to one of the staff anesthesiologists. I'll check with surgery." He turned, took a few steps, then turned back to Matt. "Oh," he said as if it were an afterthought, "thanks for the quick response. Sorry about the trouble."

"No trouble," said Joe. "Trouble was what we had this morning."

"Yeah, I heard about that," replied Elkins. "How's your man?"

"Last report, good." Joe swung around to Matt after Elkins headed down the corridor. "What say I pay Norm a visit before we leave? Care to join me?"

Matt shook his head. "I'm sure he's still out of it. I'll finish up here while you're gone. With luck I'll have the report completed, and we can call it a day after we drop it off."

Nodding, Joe left while Matt scribbled a hasty account of the call. Since he and Joe had arrived in a separate vehicle, he dismissed the rest of the detail and waited idly for Joe. Thrusting his hands in his pockets, he leaned against the wall. The wait wasn't sitting well with him. He walked to the emergency waiting area and decided it was too noisy for his mood. Glancing up, he saw the friendly smile of a pretty, petite, redheaded receptionist as she gently instructed an older man with filling out a form. Reaching into his pocket, he brought out the small, spiral notebook to check for any unfinished business before he called it a day. He flipped through the last two pages of the day's notes. All items had been checked off but one. Inspector Linda Hansen and her telephone number had been his last entry. He smiled to himself, wondering if she might be available for dinner. Glancing at his watch, he saw it was twelve minutes before five. Her tour ended at four-thirty. He walked to the pay phone by the entrance and fished a quarter out of his pocket. The throaty voice on her answering machine said she wasn't home. He frowned at the idea of someone else occupying her time. He'd try once more after he got back to the squadroom. A smile replaced his frown as he remembered a similar determination to get to know a woman better. There hadn't been one since Cindy Simpson in high school. But that had been twenty years ago. and he'd been an over-confident, swaggering running-back on the A string and due to be taken down a notch. Cindy had done a good job of it. She dumped him for the quarterback.

As he strode toward the elevator that Joe had taken, he saw the doors part. Joe was exiting with an older man dressed in stained surgical attire covered by a white coat flapping behind him as he scuttled toward the emergency desk. Joe was laughing, but the man was obviously embarrassed as he reached the receptionist and whispered, "I'm Dr. Harris. My bag?"

The pretty receptionist giggled as she produced the battered leather bag. "Shame on you, Dr. Harris."

"Sorry," Harris returned sheepishly. "I spotted an old patient of mine this afternoon when I answered a cardiac arrest call. He was in to have a few stitches in his finger. Got himself with a hand spade while he was working in his flower bed. I guess I just absently set my bag down while we chatted and then forgot it."

The receptionist gave him a bright smile. "Dr. Harris, perhaps if you'd invest in a new bag, there wouldn't have been such a to do. Dr. Elkins said his kids' pony eats oats out of a better looking sack than that."

Harris patted his possession protectively. "Sentimentality, I guess. My wife gave me this bag when I first began my practice."

"Then you better hang on to it better than you did this afternoon."

"I'll make sure I do that." His smile could make anyone forgive him for the inconvenience of the afternoon. "Well, I guess I better get back to work. Have a nice day."

"You too, sir," she said, laughing as he returned to the elevator.

Joe chuckled when he reached Matt and pointed to the departing anesthesiologist. "Were all our calls as such. Boy, was he embarrassed. He was really catching it upstairs."

"How's Norm?" asked Matt.

"He's coming around, but he's not to have visitors outside of the immediate family until tomorrow. He should be able to return to work in a couple of months."

"Glad to hear it," Matt said. "Come on, let's get out of here."

"Don't have to tell me twice."

That evening the cadre of law enforcement professionals at the home of Maria Sawyer had grown to three besides Wilson. Kowalski and Lindy had been joined by Gary Seaton, the only agent in Kowalski's office who had a ham license. Seaton's expertise was in electronic surveillance. He was a blond California beach type with a tan fading from hours spent in a suit. He was as intrigued about Paya's tale as the rest.

Paramount for all was the sober air hanging over those whose lives had been touched by a violent death. One look into Delmer Sawyer's eyes would make anyone feel his torment. The death of his best friend was Delmer's first experience with premature death. It was also his first experience with violent death. He was quiet and withdrawn and had yet to pass the stage of denial in grief. As his grandfather and Wilson had ascended the stairs to Paya's small radio station, Delmer held back. What should be an exciting part of his young life had suddenly been stained forever by Chris' death.

Lindy was present at Kowalski's request to support him with Paya after she'd dashed home to change into jeans, pull-over and the usual running shoes she wore for casual work. Not wanting to add to the family's anxiety, her loose jacket covered her holstered weapon. She sat in the kitchen with Maria while Paya showed his radio room on the second floor to Kowalski and Seaton and described once more how he'd come across the transmissions.

Maria hadn't opened her business that day. Her full attention belonged to her son. "I knew he would take this hard," she told Lindy. "He's feeling angry and helpless. Just like Papa, he feels responsible for what happened to Chris."

"That's very normal," said Lindy. "At his age, they think they're going to live forever."

"I bet you see quite a bit of this," said Maria.

"I'm afraid so."

"How do you manage it?"

"By doing what I can to keep it from happening more often," Lindy answered.

"Rotten job."

"Sometimes."

The tea kettle whistled, and Maria rose from her chair, turned down the flame, filled two cups and delivered them to the table. A sealed bag of herbal tea sat on the edge of each saucer.

"Thank you," said Lindy. She peeled the teabag from its pouch and settled it into the steaming cup and listened while Maria eased some of her tension with talk.

"Delmer never knew his father. He was four months old when his dad decided the responsibilities of a family were too much for him. Delmer idolizes his grandfather." Maria cringed as a light smile floated across her face. "He's even thinking about making a career in the Marines after he finishes college." Her smile turned sad with the glint of pain in her eyes. "He's been planning to study electrical engineering." She sighed heavily. "After this morning, I doubt I could get him interested in changing a light bulb. I just wish there were something I could do to get him out of his shell."

Before Lindy could think of an answer, Kowalski

and Seaton were standing at the kitchen door.

"I need to ask your son a favor," Kowalski addressed Maria. "We'd like him to explain how he and his friend determined the location of last night's transmitter. I realize that he's already given Inspector Hansen a statement, but there's a chance that he might remember something else. Do you mind?"

"No," answered Maria, rising. "He's in his room. I'll take you up."

Kowalski turned to Lindy. "Please join us, Inspector Hansen."

Lindy smiled, nodded and stepped in behind the two men following Maria up the stairs.

Maria tapped on her son's door and announced, "Delmer, these gentlemen would like to speak with you."

When the door opened, Delmer met them with a mixture of curiosity and despair. His black, almond eyes looked from his mother to the two men, then to Lindy. He smiled uneasily. He stood back and held open the door. "Come in."

Entering his room, Lindy glanced around and saw it was much like many other teen-age boy's room. It was small. A trundle bed was parked against a windowless wall. His desk, constructed of a plain door supported by what looked like twin custom made filing cabinets of pine and simple brass handles, sat against another windowless wall. On the top, sat an IBM clone computer with a daisy wheel printer to its left. Above were shelves of brackets and planks holding three tiers of books. A small rocking chair sat by the window. The free wall space above the bed held the usual assortment of sports posters so popular with young boys. But more eye-catching was the wall covered with large maps.

"What can I do?" Delmer asked.

Kowalski introduced himself and Seaton, then said sincerely, "Delmer, I'm sorry about your friend."

Delmer's head lowered slightly; his words came

painfully low. "Thank you."

Softly, Kowalski said. "I'd like to ask you to show us just exactly how you and Chris determined where the transmission was coming from. We're going to find the person who killed Chris, and we need all the help we can get."

Delmer shrugged. "All right. Where do you want me to begin?"

"At the beginning. And no matter how small you think a detail might be, don't leave it out. You'd be surprised how many times the slightest bit of information makes a difference."

Delmer paused, then stammered, "I-I'll do the best I can." After his mother excused herself, and the others settled into the room. He sat on the edge of his bed. His shoulders slumped. His eyes were still clouded with pain.

"It was Monday," he began, "when Chris and I got the idea to start our own hunt. We belong to a club for radio amateurs and have done lots of hunting in the last two years. It's called fox hunting or sometimes bunny hunting. Chris and I have won most of the hunts we've entered. It's been a lot of fun.

"Anyway," he continued, "Monday afternoon, we went to a local radio station and got a copy of the relief and contour map their salesmen show to describe what territory the station reaches. We said we were working on a summer school project. They were really nice about it." He rose and walked across the room. "This is it," he said, pointing to the large map mounted on the wall. His finger indicated several areas circled in blue. "These areas are the ones for the best transmissions and receptions. If you think about it, there're really not that many in a large city. Too much interference from buildings, power lines and everything. Then we got to thinking. See these areas with the black marks inside the blue?"

His audience leaned for a closer look. A round of nodding followed.

"Chris and I decided if someone was really trying to communicate in code, especially if he were planning to build a bomb, he wouldn't want anyone to walk up on him. So, just from the process of elimination, we came up with the areas marked in black.

"That night, we constructed a couple of direction finding antennas." He moved toward his desk and stooped to retrieve a metal circular device approximately the size of a tennis racket's head. A flexible cable hung from the base. "This one's mine. If you take a coaxial cable and connect it to a portable short-wave radio, it's light enough to use while walking." He paused and picked up a small flat Sony all-band radio and connected the flexible cable. "All you need is for two people to station themselves far enough apart during the transmissions and rotate their antennas until the sound of the transmission becomes the weakest. Then each person takes a compass reading. See these two lines?" he asked, indicating a large X on the map. "Well Tuesday night while Grandpa was listening for the messages on forty meters, I climbed on the roof and picked them up. Chris did the same thing from his house, but Grandpa didn't know that. The next morning we compared our compass readings and here," he said, his finger tapping where the X had been drawn over Golden Gate Park, "is where the lines crossed."

Kowalski's brow rose as he looked at Seaton.

Seaton nodded his agreement to Delmer's conclusions. "It would work."

"It was the same on Wednesday and Thursday nights, Delmer continued. "Then Grandpa got wise to us and insisted we forget about it." His eyes narrowed in a tight flinch. "I really thought Chris had taken his advice when he left."

"I'm impressed," Kowalski said to Delmer. "I only wish my son used his time and talent for such innovation. Right now, he's going through his video game phase. At least, I hope it's a phase."

"Tom?" came Wilson's voice from the door.

"Yes," answered Kowalski.

"We're ready. As soon as Mr. Paya gives the signal, our stations'll start tracking." Wilson looked at his watch. "I figure we've got about three to four hours before any transmissions come through tonight." He stretched and yawned. "I'm starved. What do you guys think about ordering a few pizzas?"

Shaking his head, Kowalski said, "There's a restaurant three or four blocks down. Called 'All You Knead'. I always did like its food." He chuckled. "I just wish they hadn't painted over that mural of God having a glass of wine while watching TV. But that was from another era." He looked from Wilson to Seaton. "I guess that was before your time." Turning to Delmer, he asked, "How about you, young man? Think your mom and grandfather would like to join us?"

The strain of Delmer's day had kept him from eating little more than a few nibbles, but the last few minutes left him suddenly starving. "Great!" he said, his eyes finally widening with excitement. "But I thought you'd want to go out and look for tonight's transmitter."

"I'm afraid we'll have to relocate him . . . her."

Delmer's eyes grew wide in disbelief. "It was a woman?"

"Crime lab says the evidence indicates that it was."

"But," Delmer said, "I think I know where the next transmission might come from."

Kowalski glanced at the smiling Seaton, then back to Delmer. "How's that, son?"

Delmer's growing excitement raised his voice. "Like I said, he . . . she wants to be where no one is likely to get in the way. I've spent all day with these maps and thinking about where I would go if it were me."

"Where's that, Delmer?" Kowalski asked, checking his amusement that he might have unleashed a waterfall of ideas that would require careful scrutiny before spending valuable man hours investigating them.

Delmer darted back to his map and excitedly tapped a point on the east side of the peninsula. "Here! At the cemeteries in Colma! Nobody's there at night, and they're easy to get to."

Kowalski turned to Seaton again, and Lindy saw the muscles of his throat working at his continued amusement over Delmer's burst of enthusiasm.

Seaton smiled and shrugged. "Makes sense."

Kowalski looked back at the young hopeful eyes. He had procedures to follow, but checking out a lead never hurt. He also felt a lingering guilt that Paya's call to his office had received no response and now a boy was dead. His hand lifted to ruffle Delmer's hair. "All right, son. We'll all have a bite first, then Agent Seaton and Inspector Hansen can check out your idea. How's that?"

Matt groaned, then grumbled a curse at the ringing of the telephone. His face, stuffed into the pillow, turned enough to open one eye and see the red digital numbers *4:17* staring out of the darkness. He grunted as his hand fumbled for the telephone.

"Hello."

"Lieutenant Sloan?" asked a woman's voice, tense but free from the grogginess of sleep.

He groaned again and rolled onto his back.

"What is it?" he asked through a yawn as he rubbed his eyes.

"This is Officer Baker. I'm sorry to bother you, but we're calling in everyone off duty."

Rolling on his side, he looked again at the digital numbers. *4:18*. This was no dream. Most likely, it was a bomb call. "What's going on?"

Her voice rose a pitch, firing off a little alarm in the back of Matt's brain. The same little alarm that made his stomach tighten.

"Two officers are missing," she answered quickly. "A Fed and one of ours. Maybe you know her . . . Linda Hansen?"

"I'm on my way," Matt answered abruptly, not certain if his response was heard before he slammed the telephone into its cradle.

Virginia Pearson had been turning the nutrients into the soil at the base of her rose bushes for over an hour when she heard her neighbor's front door creak open. Stripping off her garden gloves, she rose and worked her fingers into the cramped base of her back before stretching to peer around the porch. At first, she failed to catch sight of Edna's white head and felt the grip of instant anxiety. She was worried about Edna. Sweet good hearted Edna, who found fault with nothing or no one. How a body could live to eighty-four, still live alone and not learn to be wary of strangers was completely beyond Virginia's realm of perception, leaving her determined to keep a close vigil over her neighbor.

Virginia stretched again and could see only the top of the screen door with the wood door behind it open. "Edna?" she called out. "Are you there?"

"I'm here," came Edna's musical answer.

"Here, where?" Virginia called again as she made her way around the wooden structure dividing their front porches.

"Here, feeding the cat."

Virginia sighed as she saw Edna's thin frame leaning down to pet the plump gray and white cat she'd adopted as a stray three years before.

Stroking the cat's back as it hungrily devoured its ration of tuna, Edna looked up at the approaching Virginia. The corners of her blue eyes crinkled with her smile. "I don't think Molly's had much luck catching mice. She's especially hungry this morning."

Virginia snorted as her feet pressed against the creaking wooden steps of Edna's porch. Her boney finger jabbed the air as it pointed to the cat. "Molly eats more than you do, including mice. And," she added, balling her hand into a fist and resting it on her hip, "she's been dumping her load in my rear window box. That's the second flat of cascading petunias in two months that I've had to replace because of that animal." Her finger pointed again. "I'm warning you this time, Edna. I've spread a whole box of cayenne pepper in the flower box. If that doesn't discourage Molly, I'll be forced to use poison."

Keeping her attention on the cat, Edna said, "Now Virginia, you don't mean that."

Tensing at the harshness of her own words, Virginia sighed and said, "No, Edna. I really don't. I just get upset when I get worried."

Edna looked up and smiled in acceptance of her neighbor's anxiety. "About what, Virginia?"

Virginia's hand swept back the long gray strands that had worked loose from her bun. "About us, Edna. We're just two old women living alone. It scares the bejesus out of me to think how defenseless we are. I even dropped my subscription to the paper because reading about crime every day got to where it kept me from sleeping. I don't like to listen to the radio or TV because of all the violence."

"You worry too much," Edna said, rising and wincing as the action challenged her arthritic hips. "Too much worrying is bad for a body. Let them put you in a nursing home. Then you'll know what worrying is really about. Believe me, the minute you surrender yourself to letting others take care of you it will be downhill from then on. Remember Hilda Kramer? It only took five months after she allowed her children to admit her into that nursing home, and she was dead within another three."

"Hilda had cancer!"

Edna shrugged. "Well, if it hadn't been that, it would have been something else. And if you keep on worrying about everything the way you do, it'll drag you down just like a sickness." Seeing Virginia unimpressed with her opinion, Edna said, "Come on in and have coffee with me. And for God's sake, let's talk about something positive. Virginia, I think what your problem really is is that you don't have enough to occupy your mind." Her arm waved toward the large wooden planters along Virginia's front porch. "Those roses are not enough company."

Virginia struggled with her increasing sulk.

"Come on," Edna said, opening the screen door. "After we have some coffee, we can walk to that new hobby store on Mission. There's a sale on sewing notions, and it's time to start thinking about what to make the grandchildren for Christmas."

"It's five blocks to the store! And uphill all the way back.

Edna giggled. "If you get too tired, I'll push you home in a shopping cart. Now come on in the house."

"All right," Virginia said and began mounting the steps.

"Oh, look," Edna said, looking over Virginia's shoulder, "It's the girls coming home. My, my it looks as if they had a hard night. They look so exhausted."

Virginia turned to see the two young women coming up the sidewalk. Dressed in navy coveralls, each held a large canvas bag, appearing very heavy from the downward slopes of their shoulders. As they walked, both kept their eyes downcast.

"Good morning, girls," Edna said cheerily and

waved.

Frowning, Virginia watched their faces rise and respond with tight smiles.

"Good morning, Mrs. Wallace," returned the one known as Rosa.

"Have a rough night?"

"Yes, ma'am," answered Rosa.

The shorter one, known as Luisa, said nothing, but the flare in her black eyes produced a chill in Virginia's spine.

"Edna," Virginia whispered, "that's another thing that worries me. I wish you knew more about the people you rent that apartment to. The way those two go out every night, how are you sure they aren't prostitutes or something worse?"

Embarrassed, Edna whispered back, "For Heaven's sake, Virginia! I've never seen such hard working people as those girls. It's really a comfort having them around. Now get into the house."

Virginia stiffened and marched through the door. "I don't believe for one minute that those two are here to work in their aunt's janitorial service. Mark my word, they're no good."

Shaking her head, Edna groaned and closed the door behind her.

Forcing themselves to get on with their job, the crime scene technicians avoided as much as possible looking into the back of the tan carryall. Lindy Hansen's vehicle, abandoned on Mission Street between Seventh and Eighth Streets, had been reported by a patrolman making rounds shortly after sunrise. In the back of the vehicle blood coated the interior. Around the carryall, a line of chalk-faced uniformed men and women made a tight circle along the yellow ribbons identifying a crime scene and detoured the early weekend traffic.

"Oh shit!" Joe cried. His face had drained of color when he first laid eyes on the back of the carryall. He sucked in quick breaths to fight the rising nausea threatening to empty his stomach. His only relief was that he hadn't had time for breakfast for he surely would have lost it on the street the minute he saw Lindy's Blazer. "I helped her pick it out just before I left patrol" He turned his head and blinked unashamed tears.

Absently, Matt pressed a supporting hand on Joe's shoulder. The strange emptiness he felt over the woman who'd so suddenly entered his life left him dazed. Recalling his initial reaction to that pair of blue eyes, he even felt cheated that life was going to rob him of the chance to explore the chemistry those blue eyes ignited. His selfishness produced guilt.

Kowalski was going on his twenty-seventh straight hour without sleep, his eighteenth straight hour concerning this case and his sixth straight hour absorbed with the disappearance of two members of his task force. He appeared to be using the last of his strength to refrain from flinging his temper at Matheson as his raw, croaking voice said, "I'm sorry, Inspector." His shoulders lifted in a heavy shrug. "I didn't give the Sawyer kid's theory much credit. In fact, I only sent Seaton and Hansen out to make amends for not listening to his grandfather in the first place."

"You son of a bitch!," screamed Matheson. "She was my partner. You sent her out to find a killer without a backup."

"Look," Kowalski said. "I lost a man, too."

Matheson's red face screwed up for another furious vent when the Chief of Police pulled at his elbow. The fury didn't ease as he looked at his superior.

"Take it easy, Inspector," said the Chief, his diplomacy firm in presence of the federal agents. "We haven't found any bodies yet. There's always the chance . . ."

"Take a look, Chief!" Matheson's arm flung out to the carryall. "It looks like a slaughterhouse in there. You and I both know that they were dumped after they bled to death." Matheson heard his words turning watery. "Oh Christ! In the twenty-eight years I've been a cop I've known a lot of them to go down but never like this." A rising tremor began to surge through him. His voice stiffened. "Look, I know I'm out of place."

"Don't worry about it," said Kowalski. "I'm not arguing with anything you've said." His head moved wearily from side to side. "Besides, you're nothing compared to the look in that kid's eyes when Seaton didn't return my radio call this morning. He and the old man had really gotten attached to her."

"She had a way of doing that to people," Matheson said after blowing his nose on his handkerchief.

"I've heard that several times this morning," said the Chief, looking as if he meant it. He also looked as if he'd been aroused to a police chief's worst nightmare, which he indeed had at two twenty-seven in the morning when Kowalski had called. "Inspector," he added gently, "take the rest of the day off."

"Like hell!"

"Come on, Matheson. That's an order. I promise that as soon as you're over the initial shock, I'll see you're part of this case." The Chief turned to Kowalski. "You have no problem with that, do you?"

"None at all," returned Kowalski. "We're going to need all the help we can get."

Calling over his shoulder to a patrolman standing quietly behind him, the Chief said, "Officer Golden, I'd like you to give Inspector Matheson a ride home."

"Sure thing, sir," said Golden, stepping to Matheson's side.

"Ah Jeeze," Matheson said. "You're treating me like a baby."

"I lost a partner once myself," said the Chief. "I wasn't worth a plug for days much less worth anything to the job."

Matheson nodded and let Golden guide him toward the patrol car. When he saw Joe, his face sank lower into grief. Without a word, he stepped forward. The two exchanged silent embraces, then Matheson drew back and slapped both hands on Joe's shoulders. They exchange nods, and Matheson followed Golden and climbed into the passenger seat of the patrol car.

Joe's hand rose in a final wave as he heard the voice of Keith Adams, crawling from the back of the vehicle. Adams held up a large silver chain resembling a man's necklace. A link had been broken. From the chain dangled a worn, blood-stained suede pouch. "Anyone recognize this?"

Joe shuddered again as a low, hissing gasp escaped from his throat while Matt and everyone else, it seemed, felt the weight of cold, stark reality as they stared at the stained pouch swinging lightly from the broken chain. The blood had to be Lindy's.

Kowalski shook his head with another miserable sense of defeat. "Yeah," he answered, his voice at last trembling to the point of almost choking, "I do. Paya insisted Hansen wear it before she went out last night. Said it was given to him by his Navajo grandmother to protect him against evil spirits when he joined the Marines. I told her to go ahead, at least for the night."

"Lieutenant Sloan," the Chief called.

Matt's head snapped as his superior's voice pierced what he felt to be a nightmare. He stepped forward. "Yes, sir."

"You stay a part of Agent Kowalski's group until we find whomever is thinking of setting of a bomb in this city. As for the press, this is a case of two members of a task force formed to investigate a narcotics ring. There might be a chance that we didn't spook the maniac that did this." He turned to Kowalski. "Do you agree?"

"I do."

"Got any news from the FCC? Did they pick up anything last night?"

"To tell you the truth," Kowalski answered, "I've been totally absorbed with finding Seaton and Hansen. But I requested Wilson inform me as soon as he knows anything. So far, there's been no word from him."

"God, I hope they came up with something. I don't like the feeling in my guts. It's bad enough losing a cop, but I'm afraid the worst is yet to come."

"I'm afraid you're right," Kowalski agreed.

"Now," continued the Chief, "I'm going to take a ride down to Colma and see what they're making of the scene there. Sloan, you come along."

Matt nodded.

The Chief shook his head, sighed and looked around. "There's got to be some reason why Hansen's rig was left here. It doesn't make sense to do away with two cops in Colma and park this rig practically under our noses. It's only four blocks to the Hall of Justice. Whoever it is is awful dumb or cocky as hell. Like thumbing their noses at us." Wearily, he turned again to Kowalski. "Got somebody to take over for you?"

"In a while," Kowalski answered. "I'm going to check out Colma first."

"Want a ride?"

"I'd appreciate it."

Minutes later, Candlestick Park had just appeared on their left as the Chief's driver steered his private car south on Bayshore Freeway when the radio crackled.

Her eyes glued to the road ahead, the solemn, pretty blonde reached for the radio mike.

"I got it," the Chief said, and the driver's hand returned to the wheel and gripped it beside her other one.

Sitting in the back, Kowalski and Matt glanced at each other when the message came across.

"Sir," a man's voice on the radio announced, "Seaton's body was found floating outside the San Bruno Canal. A fisherman sighted it just after sunrise. The San Mateo Sheriff is at the scene. He says he's calling in all his deputies."

Without a word from the Chief, the driver flipped on the siren, pushed down hard on the accelerator and whipped into the fast lane.

Kowalski turned his head toward the window but didn't appear to notice the traffic giving way to the siren.

"Shit," he muttered.

* * *

The press had already begun collecting in the small industrial area at the end of Haskins Way. Two white San Mateo Sheriff's patrol cars kept the clamoring reporters at a distance while the Chief's car was waved through. The driver pulled to a stop among the official vehicles crowded in a paved turn-around just inside the entrance to the canal. Beside the Medical Examiner's van, a group huddled around a bagged body being strapped to a stretcher.

The driver remained with the radio as the Chief, Kowalski and Matt climbed from the car and were greeted by the San Mateo County Sheriff.

"Hell of a way to begin the weekend," said the Sheriff.

"No shit," returned the Chief. "And thanks for the assistance."

"Don't mention it."

"This is Agent Kowalski, FBI," the Chief introduced the man coming up on his right. "Seaton was his man."

Kowalski and the Sheriff exchanged handshakes as Kowalski asked, "What have you got so far?"

The Sheriff turned and glanced at the body now being lifted into the M.E.'s van. "We didn't make his I.D. till half an hour ago. All we know is that somebody did a hell of a number on him. There's a crevice in his neck you could drive a truck through. Doc thinks he bled out before hitting the water."

"Any sign of my officer?" asked the Chief.

The Sheriff shook his head. "I called in my cruisers as soon as the I.D. was made. I just finished briefing them a few minutes ago. They're fanning out to look for her." He turned and pointed inland. "Our guess is that they were dumped into the canal during high tide. If so, she may be back there or in the bottom of the canal. We may have to drag it. Even call in the divers. I was just about to call for a chopper check."

"I'll take care of this one," offered Kowalski, his face hardening. They knew he referred to the ex-

pense. It always came down to a matter of budget. "I
sent them out. I'll pay for it. In the meantime, I'd like
a ride to Colma and see if anything's come up there."

"Sure thing," said the Sheriff. "I'll have one of my
patrol cars take you."

Turning to Matt, the Chief instructed, "Head up the
canal and see if they're coming up with anything. I'm
going to call in some more help."

Matt nodded. As the Chief and the Sheriff continued talking and ambled their way toward the
Medical Examiner, Matt began his own slow journey
to the west.

Keeping to the narrow gravel path, Matt studied the
terrain along the canal. The grisly thought came to
him of how much the area truly resembled a dumping
ground. Refuse, natural and man made, lay everywhere. Old tires were strewn along the shore. More
rose out of the water, their dark gray rounded edges
ignoring the soft slapping of waves from the morning
tide easing back to the bay. To his left, the barnacle-
crusted axle of an unidentified car stretched across
the silt. Twenty yards beyond, the cab of an early fifties Ford pickup truck stood with canal water at mid-
door level. Sections of concrete conduits, some upright and others propped on their sides remained
from construction projects. The deeper he strode into
the industrial area, the more of its waste littered the
ground. Pieces of old clothing, rusted wire cables,
broken plastic containers of motor oil and hair con-
ditioner, a torn foil pouch of fruit punch, a cold
drink cup from a 7-11 and dozens of other items of
debris lay among the weeds. In the air was the constant drum of departing jets rising from San Francisco Airport on the south side of the canal. An industrial saw buzzed from a complex to the north.

Above, a helicopter continued its repeated circling. Kowalski had moved swiftly in adding to the
search. If it there was one benefit a police officer
ever received from disregard for funding, it was the

search for his or her body when taken in the line of duty. It was a sad testament to their value: worth more dead than alive.

Looking up, he squinted as the sun, now at mid-morning high, assaulted his eyes and cast off an un-easy humid heat despite the stir of breeze in one of San Francisco Bay's coldest recesses. A whiff of lic-orice from the many anise plants dotting the area pierced his nostrils. He shrugged off his jacket, hooked is fingers inside the neck and slung it over his right shoulder. The tension and premature end of a night's sleep were really making themselves known. At least it had been a solid one. After a deep yawn, he shook his head briskly and walked a few more steps before the scent of licorice gave way to the aroma of eucalyptus from two small groves at the end of the canal approximately thirty feet inland.

Suddenly, Matt felt as if he'd been daydreaming for he'd not noticed the approaching San Mateo Sheriff's deputy until a voice called, "I'm sorry, sir. This is a police area."

Matt nodded as he produced his I.D. "Lieutenant Sloan, San Francisco."

"Sorry, sir," the deputy answered, his mind too ab-sorbed for him to be embarrassed. He also looked, Matt noticed, very tired. Another member of law en-forcement whose night had been disrupted. His doughy face was gaunt with fatigue. His gray eyes twitched nervously.

"Coming up with anything?"

The deputy removed his hat and wiped his brow on his sleeve. Perspiration beaded on a prematurely bald head. He was young, and he looked scared. "I'm hop-ing it's not me that does."

"I don't blame you."

"Rogers and I . . ." The deputy pointed toward the robust older deputy slowly rising from the clumps of weeds clustered around the base of one of the eucalyptus groves. "We've been here almost an hour. Combed every inch within a quarter mile. So far, it's been just a lot of junk. My guess . . ."

"Dave!"

Matt and the deputy spun around. In front of the copse of eucalyptus Rogers was frantically waving both arms, his face blanching.

Oh Shit! thought Matt as he bounded toward Rogers. When they hit the grass, still slick from morning dew, his feet threatened to slide out from under him. His heart was pounding by the time he reached the trembling deputy.

Coming to an abrupt stop, Matt turned and looked into the shadow of the trees where Rogers had been kneeling and knew he would never forget the sight.

Lindy Hansen lay on her right side, her right arm extended forward. Her left arm slumped from its shoulder with the back of her hand against the ground. Coated in a thick film of dirt and mud, she was concealed by the shade and the ground cover. Matt flung his jacket aside and pulled back the clump of weeds covering her face. Blood and mud caked in an open gash in the left side of her neck. Her face had no color, save for the tinge of blue around her lips open in a light part. Her eyes, those magnificent blue eyes he had found so hypnotic, were half open and stared emptily ahead.

Matt drew in a deep ragged breath, then swallowed the dry knot in his throat. His voice sounded miles away as he addressed the deputies standing behind him, "Got a radio?"

Both deputies stood back in mute horror and repulsion. Not until Matt shouted another request did Rogers snap out of his daze, unclip the radio from his belt and hand it forward.

Matt hit the button but found he couldn't say a word. He looked at the inert form and silently cursed fate once more. He hit the button again. "This is Sloan," he announced tightly.

The Chief's tense voice crackled instantly. "What is it?"

Matt's mouth opened to pass the along news everyone feared, then instantly went slack. His jaw hanging, he blinked and leaned closer.

"What is it, Sloan?" the Chief's voice boomed and quickly fade into the recesses of Matt's consciousness as he watched those half-parted eyes suddenly widen, then look up at him.

As she had mentioned, Lindy's brother, Larry, was a blond. With the same blue eyes and thick, glossy hair, he looked more Nordic than Native American. At the moment, he looked in shock as he entered the visitor's room of San Francisco General Hospital's Intensive Care Unit after several distressful moments at his sister's bedside. With him was his wife, Allison or Ally.

Ally was an escapee from the dense populations of the eastern coast. An accountant from New Jersey, she had moved to California eight years before and found her way to Humboldt County, California where she met and later married Larry. Ally was the obvious business brains behind his museum and her adjoining boutique, promoting works of the local artisans. She was also a ballsy, take charge kind of woman and perfect for what Larry needed at this moment. Also blonde, she wore a skirt and blouse of artistically mismatched denim and cotton print. Only when she opened her mouth did she resemble a product of the east. New Jersey flowed from her lips.

"He wasn't prepared to see her this way," Ally

quietly told Matt after seeing Larry settled on the couch.

Matt had met them when he arrived shortly before a nurse escorted them into the ICU. He'd dropped by to check on Lindy's progress and discovered the group assembled with the same purpose. Grim faced, Joe and Matheson had just left. Paya, Maria and her son, still dressed in the clothes they'd worn to the funeral of Chris Cortez, sat silently on another waiting room sofa. Their short acquaintance with Lindy had produced an obvious bond, and the boy's distraught face touched everyone.

Lindy's elder landlord and landlady, Gerald and Norah Endicott moved quickly, offering support to Larry. His eyes softened in gratitude.

Not a person to mince words, Ally said, "This is the absolute shits. Lindy is all that Larry has left of his immediate family. There were no other children. He lost his parents four years ago in a car wreck."

"How's Lindy doing?" Matt asked.

"She's not doing anything at all. They keep throwing around the term blood gases as if we know what the hell that means. They explained it was because she'd lost so much blood. They also said it's normal for her not to have responded by now. Shit! There's nothing about her that looks normal. Hooked to all those machines, she looks more like the Bride of Frankenstein."

"Lieutenant Sloan?"

Matt turned toward the woman calling his name. Moments before, he'd inquired if Delmer could be allowed at Lindy's bedside and explained why. Her name pin said JUDY DAVIS, RN. She appeared to be in her early twenties, but her expression revealed enough experience and compassion to allay any concerns that she might lack the professional knowledge to administer the care of the patients in the Intensive Care Unit. As she stood in the door of the waiting room, she directed her warm brown eyes to the teen-age boy seated between his mother and grandfather.

Delmer felt more helpless and guilty than when he'd first found out about Chris' death. If only he hadn't told Agent Kowalski about Colma, Lindy wouldn't have gone out there, and she wouldn't have those machines keeping her alive.

"Thanks," Matt told Judy Davis. Stepping back into the room, he addressed Delmer. "We can go in now, Delmer."

Delmer looked up and nodded silently, then rose. After quick glances at his mother and grandfather, he followed Matt into the hall. He had met the Lieutenant the day before at the hospital when his mother had brought him for his first visit. Then, it had been a mayhem of police and physicians absorbed in Lindy's fate. It was the Lieutenant who had noticed Delmer's dispirited face and had stepped aside to explain as much as he could. Delmer hadn't understood any of it outside the fact that Lindy had almost been killed . . . and might still die. He *did* understand the Lieutenant's concern for Lindy was very genuine, and he felt good to see that the Lieutenant was at the hospital again when he came back.

Before they entered through the wide doors to the Intensive Care Unit, Matt looked down and smiled lightly at Delmer. "I'm sure things are going to look worse than they actually are," he said as much for himself as the boy. "Are you ready for that?"

Delmer's lips tightened anxiously against his teeth as he nodded.

Lindy lay propped on her left side in full view of the nurses' station. Around her a monotonous chorus of bleeps and pulsating sounds came from the high tech state-of-the-art gadgetry mounted in the wall and on wheeled platforms. Through the bed rails, her left arm was visible laying alongside her. An aqua, plastic-covered board was bound to her arm with two Velcro straps holding it straight. Fluid from a clear plastic bag hanging from a pole at the head of the bed dripped into her vein. Her chest rose and fell in chorus with the hissing bellows of the machine connected by an accordion plastic tube to the hole in her trachea, barely visible amid the thick white bandages around her neck. From her right nostril, a clear plastic tube extended to a suction canister mounted on the wall. Her eyes were closed; her face was as white as the sheet drawn loosely against her chest.

Matt glanced down at Delmer. The boy's face remained passive. He appeared contented that she was alive, though no movements were of her own. Long moments passed while they stood in silence. Matt thought she actually looked worse than when he'd last seen her as she lay under the brush. Her eyes were open then. He knew that they weren't focusing, but somehow he couldn't shake the notion that she had been watching him until a mob of police and paramedics poured down the embankment in response to his radio message that she was alive. It would help, he thought, if her hair was washed, but that was the least of her problems, just one of those odd things pricking at one's conscious when feeling helpless.

A tug at Matt's sleeve snapped him from his thought. He looked down at Delmer clasping something in his right hand.

"Do you think they'd let me leave this with Lindy?" Delmer asked.

Matt shrugged. "I'm afraid we'll have to ask them." He turned and saw Judy Davis keeping an eye on them. Patting Delmer on the shoulder, he stepped over to the young nurse. "The boy has a question for you."

Judy Davis smiled. "What can I do for you?" she asked, arriving at Delmer's side.

"Can I leave this with Lindy?" he asked, opening his palm. In it lay a crude turquoise carving. "It's a bear. It's for good health." To Judy Davis' puzzled expression, he added, "Lindy's an Indian, too."

As Judy Davis looked at him, Matt nodded.

"My grandpa carried it in World War Two," Delmer explained. "It kept him alive. I was hoping it would do the same for Lindy."

Her eyes softened. "Of course. I'll clean it off with some alcohol . . . That's all right, isn't it?"

Delmer nodded and watched her open a canister on the bedside table. She lifted out several alcohol-soaked two-by-two sponges and wiped the surface of the carving. "Now," she asked, "where would be the best place to put the bear?"

"I'm not sure," answered Delmer.

She took a few seconds for assessment. "How about here?" She lifted Lindy's left arm. "What say I tape it to the arm board? There's no way for it to put pressure on her skin."

"Fine, I guess," Delmer returned.

She pulled a role of one inch transparent tape from her pocket, tore off several strips and adhered them to the bed rail. She lifted Lindy's arm again and one at a time applied the strips of tape over the carving until it was securely attached to the arm board. "That should do it."

Delmer looked back to Lindy's face. "I hope so. I just wish I had as much faith that she'll get well as she had in my grandpa and me when we met her."

The young nurse's eyes lifted and met with Matt's. He saw how moved she was by the boy and couldn't help wonder how Judy Davis and her kind held up with the endless flow of relatives and friends who watched and waited helplessly for a sign that might never come. Tapping Delmer's shoulder, he said lowly, "We need to be leaving now."

The look in the boy's eyes didn't help matters at all. Neither did the shakiness of his voice. "I thought that seeing her would make me feel better."

"Let's just keep thinking we're seeing her still alive," Matt answered in words that failed to convince even himself. Quickly, he added, "We'll come back tomorrow."

"You promise?"
"I promise."

In the waiting room Paya sat on the couch and rubbed his legs. They throbbed like bat's wings and ached like hell. His toes were numb. After a while, he rose and began another series of paces to stimulate the circulation. He grumbled. He scratched his head. His oath was more of a grunt.

"Sir?"

Paya turned to the middle-aged nurse standing at the door and smiling in gentle concern. "Yes , ma'am?"

"Are you all right?"

"Oh . . . oh yeah."

"Just checking."

She was half turned when he called, "Nurse?"

Turning back, she asked, "Yes, sir?"

"I have a question."

"What is it?"

His arm rose. His finger indicated the patient area. "Those people in there. Well, the doctors say I need a tube put in my belly so my legs will get better circulation. If I go ahead with it, will I look as bad as them?"

Her gentle smile remained. "If you don't go ahead with it, you'll end up looking worse."

His copper face tightened. "That's what the doctors keep telling me."

"Then if I were you, I would listen."

Paya grunted. "I was afraid you'd say that."

Standing at his desk, Joe was waiting when Matt returned to his office after a two hour stint spent with his captain concerning a series of bomb threats over a restaurant chain. Evidence pointed to a group of employees who had been fired for black marketing steaks to a competitor. It was a mess. Union involvement and all.

"How's Lindy?" Joe asked. "You took off so fast, I never got the chance to ask."

Matt shook his head. "No change."

Joe sighed and plopped back into his chair. "Connie is as upset over this as I am. The last time she saw Lindy was at a party this last Christmas. We thought she was going to move to Seattle with that professor from UCSF." He leaned back and rocked on the chair's back legs. "She started dating him when we were on patrol together. Now, I really wish she'd gone with him though I always thought of . . . Rick was his name . . . as a self-centered jerk. I guess she must have finally realized that, or else she'd be in Seattle."

Looking away, Matt silently chided himself for not even considering that Lindy might have a man in her life. He suddenly felt like a love-sick fool having fantasies over a woman about whom he really knew nothing.

"I believe I'll call it a day," announced Joe. "How about you?"

Matt shook his head. "I'm behind on some reports."

With a low groan Joe rose from his chair and reached for his jacket draped over the back. "Well," he said, shoving an arm through a sleeve, "don't work too late."

"Yeah," Matt returned, not really catching Joe's words as he entered his office. Closing the door, he hoped no one would intrude upon his solitude. He pulled off his jacket, hung it on the wooden rack and sat down at his desk. He actually did have reports to finish, but too many things were getting in the way. Turning his chair to stare through the window, he settled back to sort out his thoughts.

It had been five years since he and Susan had divorced. A career military officer, herself, and daughter of one, she had refused to follow him into the civilian world. She had married the military more than him. It had been a jolt to realize that their marriage lacked a bonding stronger than the Army.

Since then, he'd carefully guarded against allowing a woman to get too close. He'd had his relationships . . . the kind that weren't meant to be relationships at all. And he'd passed up some good women along the way. The last had been Deborah Cole, an assistant Medical Examiner. Their affair lasted long enough for him to decide if it was to continue or to stop. He chose to stop it. Amazingly, Deborah had taken it well. She wasn't the panicky type who felt all was lost when things didn't happen on her schedule. That was a definite mark in her favor, but he refused to kid her or himself. She hadn't been for him. None of that right woman, wrong time. So what was it with Hansen? Would he get the opportunity to know? Frowning, he muttered aloud, "What you need, Sloan, is a few days alone at sea on the *GDB*. The *God Damn Boat* was his thirty-two foot sailboat he'd spent so long restoring and was now his home in the Marina.

Matt shook his head to clear his mental fog. He checked the papers in the IN basket. Nothing to warrant immediate action. The OUT basket was fuller than he liked to see it, but at least it could be mind absorbing.

Half an hour later he was into his third report when the call button blinked on his line.

"Lieutenant Sloan."

"Lieutenant, this is Tom Kowalski. Is Sergeant Barnett still around?"

"No. He left . . ." Matt checked his watch. "I guess it was almost an hour ago."

"Shouldn't you be gone too?" Kowalski's voice had a definite lift.

"I probably should, but it seemed a good time to finish up some paper work." Matt leaned back in his chair and rubbed his eyes. "You want me to get hold of Barnett and have him call you?"

"Just give him a message."

"Sure thing."

"He asked if I would call if I had any news about

his former partner."

Bracing himself for the worst, Matt leaned forward, unaware of his white-knuckle grip on the telephone.

"You can tell him," Kowalski continued, "that I'm at the hospital right now. I stopped by to see how things were going. Twenty minutes ago, Inspector Hansen opened her eyes. And when I told her my name, she squeezed my hand and nodded. The docs said she's going to pull through and probably without any problems."

Matt leaned back in his chair and allowed welcomed relief to take over. "That's . . . that's great," he said after a few seconds to find his voice. "I only hope . . ." He began to chuckle. "I know Joe will really appreciate the good news. He and Matheson have been taking this pretty hard."

"From what little I got to know of her, I can understand."

"You guys got anymore clues?"

"Not a thing. Oh, I take that back. The check on Hansen's rig turned up two different hair samples. One matches the one from the Cortez site. The other is also from a woman. They've narrowed it down to a Mid-Eastern type. Next time we're going to be ready . . . really ready. From what Paya says, there's been no more than three nights pass between transmissions. Oh, I meant to tell you, it's between us, Okay?"

"Okay."

"Wilson said that during the call on Saturday morning, a transmission was identified as coming from Chicago. I just hope whoever's out there makes a mistake that will lead us to them before they do whatever they're planning."

"It would be nice."

Standing in the dark at her front window, Virginia parted the ruffled lace curtains and watched as Edna's two renters stepped onto the sidewalk and headed east. She strained to hear if they were saying anything, but as usual, they kept their voices low. Just like clockwork, she thought. Every night without fail the girls took off a few minutes before nine. Every morning they returned home just after sunrise. At least every morning until the previous Saturday. That day they had been late.

"Mark my word," she whispered as soon as they were out of sight, "those two are up to no good, and it scares the willies out of me." She cringed and backed into the room, the motion causing her to bump into something heavy. With a sharp gasp, she turned around and saw the pink Impatience trembling atop the antique marble-topped table.

"Virginia, you can't go on like this."

Shuddering, she walked through the dark room and into the kitchen. Reaching out her arms, she groped for the light, then squinted against its attack on her eyes when her fingers flipped the switch. She shuffled to the table, pulled back a chair and sank wearily into the seat. Propping her elbows on the table, she rested her head in her hands and mumbled miserably, "I know I won't sleep a wink tonight."

After a few moments, she raised her head and looked around. The kitchen, as the rest of the house, was spotless. Night after night, she applied her housekeeping chores savagely to keep her mind from its constant fear. Absolutely nothing remained to be cleaned.

"I should call the police. But if those two found out I did such a thing . . . Oh, dear God."

Kowalski was running on a good mood and an adrenalin high. It was seven minutes before eight, and he had the unshakable feeling that luck was on his side. His mood had been lifted by the response to his informing Paya and his grandson that Hansen was showing good and strong signs of recovery.

"It was the bear! Wasn't it Grandpa?" Delmer had asked.

Amused, Paya smiled at his grandson.

"I know it was!" Delmer exclaimed. "It got you through the war. It got Lindy out of her coma."

"Whoa. I'm sure that those paramedics and doctors had more to do with it than that old piece of stone."

"You'll never convince me that the bear didn't help."

Paya winked at Kowalski and patted Delmer's head. "Well, maybe it had a little something to do with it."

Kowalski chuckled at the boy's excitement. "We may all need a bear before this is over."

They were standing in the specially equipped

communications van Kowalski ordered parked in front of Maria's gallery. From there, Agent Ron Whitcomb had just made radio contact with the different teams of agents placed at the various sites offering optimal transmission and reception . . . the very same sites Delmer had determined the week before.

As the communications network was being established, Delmer had watched in awe the mass of electronics. Compact and extremely efficient, the array of radio and video equipment was a miniature Disneyland of high tech electronics.

"This is awesome!" he said. "I've never seen anything like it, even at the hamfests." He looked up to Kowalski. "I bet you can eavesdrop on just about everything."

Kowalski grinned. "Just about."

"Grandpa and I once heard Air Force One. That was when the President was on his way to Los Angeles in March."

"I don't doubt you did, son. I guess there's no need to tell you that hams pick up quite a lot if they listen enough." Kowalski looked over to Paya sitting at the controls of the van's transceiver.

Paya nodded. He was ready for a hunt. His prey, if it appeared tonight, would be somewhere between 7100 and 7150 kHz on the forty meter band.

"Care to place a bet where we'll find them?" Kowalski asked Delmer.

Wide-eyed, Delmer grinned and answered, "A dollar on the Presidio."

"I'm going for Harding Park Golf Course. But if you're right, I may have to hire you. Better yet, I should take you up to Reno. We'd clean house at the tables."

Delmer returned a flattered smile and turned to watch his grandfather's fingers press against the tuning knob and begin with the blue numbers: 7100.0. Through the atmospheric hiss came a rapid flow of *dits* and *dahs*. Paya looked up as Kowalski's eyes popped open. "That's code practice at twenty words a minute."

Kowalski grimaced. "I keep forgetting."

Paya's fingers moved again. 7100.4. A stronger flow came across.

"The same station but better tone," Delmer explained.

At 7102.8, nothing came but more more atmospheric hiss. 7108.0 delivered a distant and much slower flow of code. Paya leaned closer and listened, then shook his head. "Just a novice."

7108.8.

"Another novice."

7109.6. Louder and faster.

"Two guys, Mike from Bellingham, Washington and Bob from Fort Scott, Kansas."

Delmer leaned toward Kowalski and whispered, "It's raining in Bellingham, and there's a tornado alert in Fort Scott."

Kowalski looked genuinely amazed. "You're putting me on."

Snickering, Delmer turned his attention back to his grandfather.

7120.2.

"Tonawanda, New York," muttered Paya. "Eric just passed his test for General."

"Clinton, North Carolina. Moab, Utah."

7135.7.

Paya's eyes narrowed. He leaned closer. After a few seconds, he straightened and smiled. "Abbeville, Louisiana. Guy named Monroe is talking to Juan in Puerto Rico." He nodded. "Good contact. Juan is going to New Orleans next month. Wants them to meet."

7142.1.

"Stan in Bonneville, Indiana. Paul in Miami."

7145.5.

"Ted on an off-shore rig out of Pascagoula, Mississippi. He's giving directions to . . ."

Paya suddenly frowned but remained quiet for a few moments while he listened intently.

"A boat's making a delivery," Delmer explained to Kowalski, curiously observing Paya. "Says it's drilling bits."

"I doubt it," said Paya. "It's midnight down there. Probably a clandestine effort to help the oil profits."

"Meaning?" Kowalski asked.

"My guess it's drugs."

"Shit."

Paya looked up. "Aren't the DEA agents on top of them?"

Kowalski sighed. "There's only so many."

Paya hastily scribbled across the pad in front of him. Ripping off the top page, he handed it to Kowalski. "Here's their call signs."

"Thanks," said Kowalski, folding the page and slipping it into his pocket. "I'll pass it along."

7147.3.

"Minot, North Dakota. Airman talking to another airman in Lackland AFB out of San Antonio, Texas. . . Old friends from basic training. . . Two jet engine mechanics."

7149.2.

"Corbin, Kentucky. Corpus Christi, Texas. It's in Spanish. Pablo says Wally's Spanish is *muy mejor*." Seeing the furrow deepen in Kowalski's brow, he added, "Wally's Spanish is getting much better."

Kowalski nodded.

As the dial stopped at 7150.0, Kowalski released a long sigh of disappointment. Thirty-seven minutes later and two more rounds on forty meters, he began to pace in the small confines of the van as Paya patiently remained at the controls. The transmissions he wanted to come through had yet to appear, but he'd heard more than he cared to. Among the idle chatters in code he learned that the Neo-Nazis in the Idaho panhandle were planning another meet and had invited up a group out of Prescott, Arizona. Prescott had accepted. So had Broken Bow, Nebraska, Clinton, Oklahoma and only God knew who else before the night was over.

"A friggin' network?" he screeched.

"There's a few out there," Paya returned.

"How come so many get away with this?"

"Not too many take the trouble to use the code anymore. A lot lose their proficiency from lack of practice.

Kowalski continued to pace. He swore. He paced and paced and paced and swore and swore and swore.

"Come on, ladies."

He paced again. He swore again until, behind him, Paya's deep grunt made him look around.

With pencil in hand, Paya leaned closer to the radio and listened closely.

The blue numbers read out: 7138.4.

And sounds of the *dits* and *dahs* of International Code filled the van as everyone froze.

Slowly, Paya began to scribble across the notepad.

Kowalski leaned over Paya's shoulder and read: CQ CQ CQ DE WF6ANQ WF6ANQ WF6ANQ K. He watched Paya copy the message twice more. His heart began to pound in his ears as he prayed silently, this has got to be it.

The sound of the atmospheric hiss hung in the air for several long, eerie seconds until the *dits* and *dahs* started again. CQ CQ CQ DE WF6ANQ WF6ANQ WF6ANQ K came three more times. More long seconds of hiss. Again came CQ CQ CQ DE WF6ANQ WF6ANQ WF6ANQ K.

After a sixty second pause, the transceiver began to speak again, and Paya wrote down: WF6ANQ WF6ANQ DE WE3DNT TNX FER CALL. UR RST 579 579 K.

As another sixty seconds passed, Kowalski saw Paya's nod. "I think they're coming through," he said to Whitcomb.

Whitcomb transferred Kowalski's message into his communication network while Kowalski watched Paya continue scribbling the next flow.

WF6ANQ WF6ANQ DE KE1XTL TNX FER CALL. UR RST 579 579 K.

"There should be one more," Paya said as another sixty seconds lapsed.

The words were no sooner out of his mouth when the radio began to speak again.

WF6ANQ WF6ANQ DE KT2TNC TNX FER CALL. UR RST 579 579 K.

"They're all on channel," Paya announced.

Special Agent Dick Westbrook was in no mood to be crouching in the cold while the rolling fog wrapped its chilling fingers over the hills around the bay. Pulling the zipper of his black coveralls up to the neck, he ground his teeth in irritation. He had miscalculated the weather. The day before had broken a sixty year record for heat, so he'd left his thermal sweater in the van which had dropped each of the six agents at selected points in the upper elevations of the Presidio's dense eucalyptus groves. If any of them had to move, it would be downhill.

Absently, he wiggled the ear plug of his receiver and checked the luminous dials of his watch. It was nine fifty-seven. The last message from their control operator in the van had come one hour and twenty-eight minutes before, saying all six were in place. None had reported anything unusual as each had continued to scan his surroundings with infrared binoculars.

Westbrook swallowed the groan, threatening a haggard exit from his throat. He envisioned sitting and shivering throughout the entire night.

Laying his Uzi in the crook of his left arm, he inserted his thumbs into the armholes of his flak vest
and shifted again to prevent an accumulation of
sweat releasing valuable body heat. At least he was
prepared. Seaton might still be alive had *he* been.
Seaton had not been a friend but a fellow agent . . .
now a dead fellow agent, and Westbrook suddenly
felt his irritation at the cold give way to the gut fury
shared by all the agents as they had learned of
Seaton's death.

He lifted his binoculars for another scan. Nothing.
It was so damn dark and so damn cold. At moments
like this he actually missed Iowa. This time of year,
he would sit on the back porch of his parents' farm
and watch in fascination as fire flies danced their
aerial ballet above the lawn. It was always the fire
flies he missed the most about Iowa. Right now, he
could use some Iowa summer night heat. The distant
drone of fog horns made him miss the grunting of the
hogs. That was what Iowa summer nights had always
meant to him . . . hog grunts and fire flies. He never
thought he'd have seen the time he missed them. Then
another shiver raced through him just as his ear piece
buzzed, and Jordan's voice interrupted his fantasy.

"Kowalski just called. Our friends are transmitting from the rear of the Presidio. He says it's north-
east of the Arguello Gate. Westbrook?"

"Here."

"You're closest. Wait for Price and Hill to meet up
with you. Price? Hill? Do you read me?"

"Price, here. I read you."

"Hill, here. I read you."

"The three of you merge to the view point on
Arguello. Our friends appear to be on the second rise
to the east of there. Make contact with me when you
meet up."

"Will do," answered Westbrook.

"The rest of us are working our way over. Now
move."

Westbrook stood and quietly shook the stiffness from his knees. The point of contact was approximately fifty yards east. Swiftly and silently, he moved his thick soles over the ground as he kept a distance from the road. It wouldn't do for a passing car to come upon him with his blackened face and Uzi. He ducked twice at the headlights rounding the curve before he got to his destination. Panting, he stopped and crouched beneath a shrub and waited. In less than two minutes, he saw the black shadow of a man moving through the parking area. Whistling lowly through his teeth, he swung his arm in a high wave at the man turning toward his signal. He recognized Price from his tall stature. Crouched in the seclusion of the shrubs, neither spoke. In less than another minute Hill's shorter frame appeared in the parking area. Westbrook whistled again, and Hill quickly joined them.

"It's about damn time," Hill ground through his teeth. "I was about to freeze my ass off."

Westbrook had forgotten about the cold the second Jordan's voice began to rumble in his ear. "Okay. Now, we stay together. Be a little embarrassing for one of us to take a shot at the other. Ready?"

Hill's and Price's heads bobbed in unison.

Westbrook pulled the small radio from inside his coveralls and kept his voice low.

"Control, this is Westbrook. Price and Hill are with me, and we're ready."

"All agents," came Jordan's voice. "This is control. When you get our friends in sight, do not, I repeat, do not try to take them on until the signal comes from control. Begin moving."

"Let's go," Westbrook whispered.

With the same quiet precision that brought them together, the trio crouched and headed downhill. The grass was damp and slick from the fog. For the first time, Westbrook appreciated the change in the weather. Had the grass been dry, their movements would have been heard for a hundred yards. Slowly, they eased up to the first rise. Hill and Price kept down while Westbrook carefully stretched his neck to peer over the crest and scan with his binoculars. After a long moment, he looked down at his partners pressing their chests against the damp earth. He nodded. Keeping on their bellies, they pulled their Uzi's under their chests and moved on their elbows and knees over the crest. At the bottom of the second ravine, they paused for a last quick moment. From his position in the middle, Westbrook tapped Price and Hill on their shoulders. Silently, they crawled upward, again keeping low as Westbrook's head rose again.

Lifting his binoculars, he began at his left. Long trunks of the eucalyptus trees stood with their branches slowly swaying in the breeze. Twice, a nocturnal bird moved in low flight across the lenses. It was the same view as from the ridge behind them. Left to right . . . the same until his sights moved ten degrees to his right. Then instantly, he froze. A movement caught his eye. Protruding from a bulky shadow, a round nub slowly bobbed in the dark. Then the bulk shifted. An assortment of small differentiated lights came into view. Westbrook felt the surge of adrenalin as the shadow cleared into definition. It was human, and it was squatting beside a radio set on the ground.

Instantly, he retreated behind the ridge and tapped Price and Hill again. In the lowest whisper he could manage, he said, "I see one . . . on a radio. At least twenty yards. Ten degrees to the right."

He heard Price and Hill swallow their frustration. He tensed as he wondered, where was the second . . . or the third...or whatever? Each sensed the other's thoughts. Knowing an unseen party was close produced the tension of isolation.

Hill was the youngest. An agent for only three years, he was first to react. Pulling on Westbrook's sleeve, he leaned and whispered, "What if I drop back and call in that we've got one in sight?"

Westbrook's head shook vigorously. "Patience."

Hill drew in a long breath of frustration and felt the reassuring hand of Westbrook squeeze his arm. Clutching his weapon to his chest, he lowered his head and forced himself to gain control. Seaton's death, the first he'd experienced since becoming an agent, was still fresh in his mind and was doing a number on his resolve.

On Westbrook's other side, Price remained motionless. He'd been through enough incidents of creeping up on suspects to know how slowly time could pass. The worst had been a stretch of more than thirty-six long gut-eating hours while he waited for the assault on a house on a small island off Puget Sound. More than a hundred agents had been assembled to go after the leader of the Neo-Nazi gang of which a member had killed a Denver radio talk show host. They'd tried everything in the book to draw the man out: SWAT teams, dogs, tear gas, the works. In the end, a helicopter dropped white phosphorus illumination flares on the roof. The resulting flames reacted with the multitude of explosives and turned the fugitive into a crispy critter. It hadn't been the planned outcome, but Price couldn't have been more satisfied.

While Westbrook's attention was drawn to easing the anxiety of the young agent, Price kept his senses finely tuned to their surroundings. The fog horns continued their warnings. One at a time, the small birds fluttered overhead. Price felt so calm he actually yawned, making a dull popping sound from the crack of his jaw. He saw Westbrook's head snap around. He grinned as he heard Westbrook's uneasy sigh. They wouldn't be lonely for long. A matter of minutes and a net of agents and police would have the area tightly surrounded. Price rolled from his side, propped himself on his elbows and let his Uzi rest against his right thigh. He looked around. All was the same. The same darkness with a faint glow of civilization peering through the trees. The same quiet, save for the fog horns and an occasional fluttering of another bird and sound of another car coming down Arguello.

Price glanced over at Hill. The young agent was doing fine. Westbrook was taking another quick peek through his binoculars. Lowering them, he looked down at Hill and Price and nodded. The transmitter was still at work.

Any minute, Price was thinking as the sound of another bird sharply turned his head. And that old gut instinct made him reach instantly for his weapon as he recognized the bird's flight was unlike the uneasy nocturnal flutter that had been so commonplace that evening. It was an erratic, frenzied motion . . . like an escape.

Just as he pushed himself off his left elbow, both Westbrook and Hill looked around. None of the three recognized what came first . . . the muffled staccato sounds or the series of blue- orange flames coming at them.

They only knew it was death.

Twenty minutes later the car had yet to come to a complete stop when Kowalski pushed open the door and jumped out to face a stunned and shaken Jordan. Kowalski, himself, was stunned but from disbelief. His mind could only keep replaying his convictions that they had really been ready for this event. How in God's name could Jordan's frantic report actually be true? Even Jordan's face, pale and eyes glazed as the horror of reality gripped him, failed to register with Kowalski that the plan had was now a disaster.

"What happened?" Kowalski asked.

"We lost them," said Jordan. "And we lost three men."

"Dead?"

Jordan swallowed hard as he nodded.

Kowalski looked around and suddenly noticed the

scurrying of solemn agents. From the dark of the eucalyptus groves came low, angry shouting. The tally
of dead agents was now four. The grief and rage was
beyond measure.

"How the hell did it happen?"

Jordan shook his head. "They were ready for us."

"Any signs? Any clues?"

Jordan's arm lifted, pointing toward the angry
voices. "For now, only two. We've located the wire
they strung in a tree to transmit. And they left behind
their antenna tuner."

Suddenly, Kowalski felt an ice cold tremble as his
vision filled with the confident and eager faces of
agents during the afternoon's final briefing. They
had motivation, real motivation after Seaton's death.
They had training, the best available. They had equipment, the finest of communications and weapons.
And three of them were dead. And their killers had
slipped through the net, a tight net, a very tight net.

"Jesus, Bill," Kowalski said, shaking his head as he
felt the quiver of his voice. "Who are they? What are
they?"

"They're killing machines, Tom."

Oscar Munoz yawned as he stood at the deli's counter and waited for his order of bratwurst and sauerkraut. God, I'm tired, he thought. It had been a short night with his doubling back after an evening tour. The summer flu had knocked three patrolmen out of Mission Station. Five hours of sleep just didn't do the job. Eating a heavy lunch would be adding insult to injury, but Margaret's talents in the deli's kitchen couldn't be resisted. Munoz considered the establishment one of the big pluses in his patrol area. The other was the multitude of familiar faces he'd known since childhood.

"Long day?" Margaret asked, setting the steaming plate before him.

"Short night," he answered through a second yawn.

Her pale blue eyes sparkled in her smooth China white face. "This should perk you up."

Laughing, he shook his head. "More likely it'll help me die a happy man."

"I like my men smiling. But better, I like them alive and smiling. Care for a beer?"

"I'm afraid not, ma'am. Not if I plan to leave here

on both feet."

"Ah!" She giggled and flipped her hand in dismissal. "A good beer is an essential part of a German meal."

Munoz smiled. "Not while I'm working."

"Then you will have some apple strudel. I just took it out of the oven."

Moaning, Munoz rubbed the slight paunch of his belly. "I don't stand a chance with you, do I?" As she snickered her satisfaction, he carried his plate to the small square red and white checker covered table. The chair legs dragged noisily across the plank floor as he pulled it back and sat down. He smiled and looked over his shoulder. "Thank you."

Margaret smiled before greeting her next customer.

Munoz settled his chair closer to the table and began his ritual. First, he slit the two fat sausages lengthwise across the top. From three selections of condiments, he chose the brown German mustard and liberally spooned it into the links. The sharp aroma danced across his eyes and assaulted his nostrils. Absolute heaven!

Margaret, he said to himself, I hope you weren't into overkill with the caraway.

The first bite said she was. As she set the coffee beside his plate, he said as his eyes began to tear and his nasal membranes ignited. "I think I'll take some water, too."

"All right," she said, patting his shoulder, "but beer will work better."

"Yes, ma'am. I'll make sure that the next time I come here, I'll be off duty."

Her index finger waved as she turned. "Now, now."

Munoz took a big gulp of the strong black coffee as temporary relief. Picking up his knife and fork, he sliced off a bite of sausage and had it half way to his mouth when he paused at the sight of the elderly woman entering the front door. Above it, two small brass bells jingled from their red ribbons.

"Hello, Mrs. Pearson," he said. "Little early for your walk, isn't it?"

Virginia Pearson's afternoon walks was one of the first routines Munoz had noticed after he began patrol. Like so many local senior citizens, she found Margaret's mini loaves of sourdough rye made from an old family receipe appropriate for one living alone. She was visibly strained, he noticed. The tremor in her voice brought a deep wrinkle in his forehead. Quickly, he laid down the knife and fork, then pushed back his chair and began to rise.

"Don't get up," she said, shaking her head. "Do you mind if I join you for a few minutes? I don't want to interfere with your lunch."

"No problem," he answered and settled back in his chair as she took the chair across the table.

At a closer distance he saw the red rims of her eyes. This concerned him more. He knew her to be fiercely independent for eighty-one years. She had little use for others' opinions, including doctors. He surmised that she hadn't seen one outside of an optometrist for years. A widow for twenty-three years, she was childless. She survived by her grit and the high tolerance of the neighborhood. She was considered too nosy for most people but really did little to interfere with their lives. Munoz had always thought her amusing but not today.

"What's on your mind, Mrs. Pearson?"

"I'm worried sick," she answered tightly.

Munoz took a bite, silently prayed that Margaret's attention to spices weren't misinterpreted on his face and waited for Virginia to continue.

Virginia laced her fingers together and leaned forward. Hurriedly, she glanced around the room. An elderly couple stood at the counter and were ordering their lunch. Absorbed in the morning paper, Maynard Foley sat at a table in the far corner by the window. Foley wouldn't have been able to eavesdrop due to his poor hearing or his concentration on the crossword puzzle.

"It's about Edna," she continued, keeping her voice low. "You know how trusting she is?"

Munoz smiled around strings of sauerkraut. He considered Edna Wallace a saint as did half the block on which she lived.

"She's got these two renters . . . two women. It's been a little over a month. I'm convinced they're prostitutes or something worse. Every evening they go out for the entire night. God only knows what kind of people they're linked up with. What if it's a group of gangs or drug dealers or one of those cults that slice up people? And what if they start bringing them home? Edna keeps too much money laying around. More than one old lady's been knocked in the head for a few dollars."

Munoz slowly chewed on the bratwurst for a few seconds. "You've talked with Mrs. Wallace?"

Virginia's palm slapped the table furiously. "I can't talk a bit of sense into her." She sighed. "That's what I'm hoping you can do. Edna may not be concerned, but I'm scared spitless. It's to the point that I can't eat or sleep. Every night lately, I find myself sitting up and listening to see if she's in trouble."

Munoz wiped the bratwurst grease from his lips and nodded. "I'll check on her, Mrs. Pearson. Right after I finish lunch. Need a ride home?"

Slumping back in her chair, Virginia attempted to smile. "I believe I'll have a slice of Margaret's cheesecake, then finish my walk."

"Good idea."

Through her screen door Edna's cherubic smile greeted Munoz standing on her front porch.

"Well, good afternoon, Officer Munoz."

He smiled and nodded as he tipped his hat. Clearing his throat, he hoped his concern prompted by his discussion with Virginia remained checked. Feeling a little more than foolish, he said, "Good afternoon, Mrs.

Wallace. How are you this afternoon?"

Edna was as puzzled as delighted. "What brings you around?"

"I just thought I'd drop by and see how things are going."

"Then do come in," she invited, opening the door.

"Thank you," he said, removing his hat as he stepped inside.

Following Edna across the living room, Munoz' police eyes took a quick assessment for signs of disorder. The place was as immaculate as ever. The furnishings were old but the kind that were meant to last. Across a walnut coffee table a heavy green damask sofa faced two chairs, one matching the sofa, the other, a sturdy high-backed rocking chair. Beside the rocker sat a tapestry sewing bag opened on its frame. Four inches of white lace doily, its crochet hook still in the loop and threaded through a large spool set atop the basket. Suppressing a grin, Munoz wished he had a nickel for each piece Edna must have crocheted in her life. A light fresh breeze fluttered the lace curtains of the front window.

"Have a seat," she offered as they entered the kitchen. "I just brought in a jar of sun tea. I'll pour us some."

"Thank you, ma'am." With a quiet grunt over his full stomach, he sank into one of the kitchen's chairs and laid his hat on the table.

Removing two tall glass tumblers from the cupboard above the sink, Edna asked over her shoulder, "And how's your wife and the baby?"

"Fine, thank you."

"Goodness," she said, opening the freezer compartment of her refrigerator. "Pablo must be near walking by now. Ten months, isn't he?"

Munoz smiled. Edna never forgot a thing.

"I can remember," she said, beaming a bright smile. "My son and two of his children were born in August. I was married in August. A million years ago."

"Pablo manages about three steps on his own. He sure gets upset when his bottom hits the floor."

Edna winked. "Determination."

Munoz chuckled. "I hope that's what it is."

Edna banged the ice cubes loose and put them into tumblers, then poured in the tea while Munoz thought, *if she tries to feed me, I'll strangle her.*

"I baked a carrot cake yesterday."

Oh shit!

Munoz rubbed his tired eyes and waited until Edna had sliced off a piece of cake and was seated before him. He stared at the empty space in front of her. "Aren't you going to have some cake, Mrs. Wallace?"

She laughed. "Oh, my no. I had some with the young man who mowed my lawn before lunch."

Munoz took a heavy breath and pushed his fork through the cake.

"Mrs. Wallace," he said after a bite. "I came to talk to you about some concerns in the neighborhood. Have you been having problems with your renters?"

"Neighborhood, my foot!" Edna straightened in her chair, but Munoz saw she was obviously not really annoyed. "It's Virginia. Don't try to fool me. Did she call the police?"

"No, ma'am. I just ran into her at the Anhalt Deli. She's only worried about your safety."

Edna rolled her eyes and sighed. "Virginia's a born worry wart. She always *was* a busy body. But she really hasn't been the same since old Mr. Jackson passed away. He was one of my previous renters. That was two years ago. You didn't know about him, did you?"

Munoz shook his head. "That was before I began patrolling this area."

"He went peacefully. Died in his sleep at seventy-eight. Virginia discovered him. She caught the smell of his body while she was emptying her garbage. The poor old man had been dead for almost a week. Thankfully, I was visiting my son in Roseville.

Virginia hasn't been the same since."

"I can see what a shock that would be."

Edna nodded sympathetically. "I'm afraid it was just the shock Virginia needed to affect her mind. She's been afraid of her own shadow ever since."

"Then your renters are causing no trouble?"

"Heavens no! They don't have the time."

"In what way?"

"They work every night. Long hours too. Such lovely girls. Rosa and Luisa. They moved up from Tucson to help their aunt with a janitorial service. They sleep during the day. They're downstairs asleep right now. Quiet as two little mice. And so considerate. Every evening before they leave, they check to see if I need them to pick up anything."

Munoz nodded and finished chewing his cake. "I might as well go ahead and tell you Mrs. Pearson's other concern."

Edna rolled her eyes but grinned as she sat quietly.

"Do you keep much money in the house?"

"The girls pay their rent in cash. It's difficult for me to get to the bank since I gave up driving a few years ago."

"I can help you with that, ma'am."

"Oh, I'm quite all right."

"But *I'm* not." Munoz's brown eyes twinkled as he finished his last bite. "I don't want to take any chances with your carrot cake."

10

"So how's our girl?" Matheson asked the third year surgical resident with whom he, Paya and Matt had just exchanged introductions.

"Getting reacquainted with her voice," answered Dr. Shively.

Matheson shot back a stern *quit the bullshit, Doc* look. Matt and Paya weren't buying the glib answer either.

Shively sighed. He was tired. He'd spent most of the night observing an elderly man who, during surgery to remove his gallbladder, had developed a series of cardiac arrythmias, which had taken their own sweet time to settle into a nice and regular pattern. On top of that, he'd not even been on call. Tonight he was. and the emergency room was already beginning to generate into the usual Friday night free-for-all.

"Well, Inspector Matheson," said Shively, "physically, she's fine. She's a young and healthy woman with a strong will to recover. That always helps a great deal."

"And?"

"We plan to discharge her late Monday afternoon."

"Come on, Doc. What are you holding back?"

"Inspector Hansen is the victim of a brutal attack. Right now, she has a memory lapse about it. She's been having nightmares the last few nights. That's very common in such incidences. We in medicine call it post-traumatic stress. Until she can recall and confront what happened and return to a feeling of security, she's probably going to have some rough times."

"What about her going back to work?"

"In time. There's no reason to think she will be incapacitated in any way. But I want her to see a specialist in post-traumatic stress Monday morning."

"A shrink?"

"A nurse that's a clinical specialist in post-traumatic stress."

"A nurse shrink." Matheson grunted in disgust. "Now, listen to me. That's my partner in there, and she doesn't need anybody playing around with her mind. I was shot once myself in the line of duty. I was a little edgy for a while, but I snapped out of it."

"That must have been some time ago."

"Seventeen years."

"Well, we've come a long way since then. We don't just stitch somebody up and ship them out the door." Shively watched Matheson's scowl deepen and added, "Look, all the nurse is going to do is talk to Inspector Hansen and tell her what to expect for a while. She'll also give her some guidelines as to what she can do about it. It's basically a matter of education. There is absolutely nothing wrong with your partner. She's a normal woman who went through an abnormal experience. Being a policeman, certainly you know about victims' groups. Inspector Hansen has been a victim. The fact that she's also a police officer doesn't make her immune to a normal human reaction."

Matheson's head swung around to Paya. "Do you buy that?"

Much to Matheson's surprise, Paya nodded.

"When I came out of the war, the first thing my Navajo grandmother did was take me to a specially built hogan and put me through a purification ritual to cleanse me of the devils of war. Most of us who had the ritual did fine."

Matt noticed Shievely listening intently and had to check his grin. The young physician was in for it now.

Matheson was intrigued. "What was this ritual like?"

"My grandmother built a fire in the hogan to make me sweat. Then she made me drink a special brew. For three days I vomited and had the runs."

"You're shittin' me, Dan!"

Paya's eyes twinkled. "I did a lot of that."

As Shively's eyes rounded in astonishment, Matt turned his head and held his breath to hold a chuckle. During the recent days the three men had formed a unique friendship as they gathered to be briefed on Lindy's progress. Mostly, it had been one of Matt in a constant state of amusement while listening to Matheson and Paya. Matheson was a crusty older street wise cop with a crusty older street wise cop's answer for everything. To each of Matheson's answers, Paya added a bit of Navajo wisdom. At times the combination had a most entertaining result.

Recovering from his surprise, Shively grinned and added, "Perhaps I should just order Inspector Hansen sent to physical therapy for a session in the whirlpool."

Matheson was absolutely serious. "Good point."

Paya shrugged, and Matt held his breath again.

"And for *you*," Shively addressed Matheson, "I recommend some of Mr. Paya's grandmother's special brew."

"Good point," said Paya.

Matt held his breath one more time.

"Well, if you'll excuse me," said Shively, "I need to get to the emergency room. I hope the three of you keep your visit short this evening. After the FBI agents were done with their interview, she needs her rest."

Matheson and Paya nodded and began making their way down the hallway. Matt exchanged grins with Shively and followed.

Entering her room, they found Lindy looking as tired as she probably was. She was seated in a chair by the window and studying a piece of paper. To her side, a dinner tray sat on a low table and revealed that she'd made a respectable effort to consume her dinner. Realizing she had company, she looked up. The wound on the left side of her neck was an ugly dark pink against her pale skin. A small, square white dressing was taped over the incision which had closed her tracheotomy three days before. Dark circles crescented beneath her eyes, softening as she smiled at her guests. Laying the paper aside, she looked from one to the other.

"Hello," she greeted them in a voice, thick and raspy and not much more than a whisper.

Matheson moved quickly beside her and took her hand. "How are you doing?"

"I'm doing fine. Much better than I sound."

He smiled as he would to a daughter. "You sound like Lauren Bacall . . . with a big hickey."

She laughed.

Paya had no appreciation for Matheson's humor. He frowned as he leaned for a closer look at her neck. "They said they were going to fix your neck to keep it from having such a big scar."

Her smile faded. "They were. But I don't want anyone cutting on me again. And I'm tired of being in a fog from anesthetics. Three trips to surgery is more than enough."

Paya nodded.

"I don't blame you," said Matheson, giving her hand another squeeze. "Say, Doc Shively says you're

getting out of here on Monday. Betty wants you to
stay with us for a while. Jenny's room is just waiting
for someone to use it."

"Thanks, Jim," Lindy said. "I really appreciate that,
but the Endicotts beat you to the offer, and Larry and
Ally are coming down for a few days. They went
home to square away a few things with the shops."

"Too bad you're not going to spend the time up there.
Some time away might be the best thing."

She shrugged. "But I'm still part of an investigation.
Agent Kowalski thinks I'll come up with something
that will provide a clue."

Paya frowned his disapproval, then snorted something that sounded foreign.

Matheson glanced at Paya then back to Lindy.
"That's a Navajo swear word. You wouldn't believe
how my vocabulary has been increasing lately."

"I can just imagine," Lindy said, smiling at Paya.

"Dan's been using it a lot of Navajo swear words
with Kowalski. They're really having their differences."

Paya snorted again.

"What kind of differences?" she asked, frowning.

Paya looked at Matheson and shook his head.

"Tell me, Mr. Paya," Lindy insisted.

Paya looked at her sternly as if considering the present moment not the time to unload his frustrations.

"Come on," she pressed. "I don't want to be
coddled."

Matheson rallied quickly to Paya's defense. "The
Doc says you've had enough for today. We really have
to be leaving. Doctor's orders."

To one, then the other, Lindy gave that look a woman gives to a man when he realizes it's time to fold
his cards.

Matheson and Paya looked anxiously at each other,
each shifting his posture while waiting for the other to
begin.

Having no energy for patience, Lindy looked

between them directly at the man leaning against the wall. She recognized the man to whom she'd brought Paya. He'd believed Paya's tale and responded at once. His was one of the many whose faces had appeared in and out of her levels of consciousness. Standing quietly, he'd looked amused at Matheson's and Paya's hoverings over her but not at the moment.

"Lieutenant Sloan," she addressed him directly, "has the cat got your tongue, too."

She still had that spunk, he thought. A small smile of admiration spread across his lips.

"I believe I have a right to know," she insisted.

Unfolding his arms, Matt pushed away from the wall.

"Would you mind stepping outside?" he said to Matheson and Paya.

Both men grumbled, then nodded.

"See you tomorrow," Matheson said, squeezing her shoulder.

"Yes," Paya added.

Quickly, they stepped into the hall.

Matt waited until they were gone and walked across the room and stood by the window.

"I'd like to know," she repeated, "what's going on. As much time as Agent Kowalski has spent with me during the past few days, he's not really telling me anything."

"He's not telling me much either," said Matt. "I've concluded he really doesn't know much."

"But what does he know? And what's got Mr. Paya upset with him? From the look on his face, it's plain as day. I want to know," she said again. "Everything."

"All right, but I'm going to make it short."

She nodded.

"Two nights after the attack on you and Seaton, Dan picked up the transmissions again. The local was coming from the Presidio. Kowalski had a team of agents waiting. Apparently three of them spotted the transmitter and were waiting for the other agents to encircle the site. By the time all agents were in place, the transmissions stopped . . . abruptly. The agents moved in. The transmitters had slipped through their net. The first three agents were found in the bottom of a small ravine. Someone had emptied a full clip of 9mm's into them."

Like a stone, Lindy did not respond.

"It appears," Matt continued, "that the *ladies*, as they've been tagged, were prepared for visitors."

He related how a second hair sample had been recovered from her carryall along with another matching the one from the Cortez site. "Two is all we really know of, and that a transmission came out of the Chicago area and another out of Boston. That leaves two more. There have been no more transmissions since that night."

Her eyes lowered in thought. For long seconds she said nothing. "There must be more clues than that."

Matt nodded. "In their rush to get away from the Presidio, they left behind an antenna tuner. Every dealer within a hundred miles has been contacted to report purchase of theft of one. All personal thefts have been screened. We've gotten nowhere. The only other clues are the fingerprints left in your carryall. From two women, but they match nothing on record. Apparently, they're getting a perverted pleasure out of playing a game with us. They even left your carryall four blocks from the Hall of Justice."

"To taunt us."

"That's the way it looks."

She frowned. Her teeth bit into her lower lip. "They're very good. Whatever they're planning to do, they must have been planning it for a long time."

He nodded . . . as much to her astuteness as in agreement with her statement.

"What do you think they're up to, Lieutenant?"

"My name is Matt. And I think they're planning to set off a series of bombs . . . here, Chicago, Boston and two other cities. Question is, exactly where and when and why?"

Sighing, she slumped back in her chair.

"Monday, Kowalski's going to brief me on a report from the Behavioral Science Unit."

"So he said this afternoon." She winced. "I just wish I could remember something . . . anything after Seaton and I got to the cemetery. Tuesday, I'm going back there."

"I know. I'm taking Dan."

Her brow wrinkled in curiosity.

Matt smiled. "You really have a champion in that old man, and in his grandson."

Smiling lightly, she lowered her head for a second. "He's really something, isn't he?"

"He really is. He insisted he be there to keep Kowalski from being too hard on you. *I* have to keep Dan from being too hard on Kowalski."

"I can tell they're not getting along."

"Dan's upset with Kowalski for sending you and Seaton out alone. Kowalski needs him too much to argue, and Dan is not a person to be impressed with any threats to put him in jail for interfering with an investigation." He paused as she smiled and nodded. "Are you sure you're ready to go to the cemetery?"

"I'm ready," she answered seriously. "I'm ready to get out of these walls . . . to walk on the beach . . ." She glanced at the dinner tray and smiled feebly. "And after these hospital meals, I'm ready for a Szechuan dinner."

"You've got it."

His statement caught her by surprise. So did his soft smile and the light in his eyes. Then came the instant flooding back of the chemistry she'd recognized between them the day they'd first met. She remembered liking it. She liked it now. She had been unprepared both times.

She was still fumbling for a response when he said, "See you tomorrow, Lindy."

Atop the mound beyond the Sneath Lane entrance to Golden Gate National Cemetery, Old Glory softly snapped in the late morning breeze. To the east drummed the constant flow of traffic on El Camino Real. The foursome assembled at the base of the mound looked across the historic rolling verdant expanse with its neat rows of white military headstones. General and private lay side by side, some alone, some with their dependents, the only difference in headstones being their inscriptions. Most notable were Admirals Chester Nimitz and Raymond Spruance, those giants of World War II's Pacific Theater. Even in death they maintained their vigil over their country's western coast.

As she stood behind the low row of hedge encircling the base of the mound, Lindy was keenly aware of being the focus of attention. She was the reason they all were there. Returning to the site of the attack on her and Seaton might trigger her memory to offer a clue, which might lead to her assailants. She stopped and looked westward.

"It was here," she said. "We stopped here after de-

ciding the most unobstructed view was from here . . .
We'd left my carryall close to the entrance and
climbed through an opening in one of those concrete
sculptures in the fence. For a while, we just wandered
around, then decided to stop here. I carried the infrared binoculars. Gary had the short wave radio. As
soon as we stopped, he tuned it to forty meters." She
looked at the ground, then sank to her knees. "We hid
behind this hedge. We never expected to see anything.
I kept thinking that we were really doing this for
Delmer. About an hour later, I guess, Gary tapped my
shoulder."

She turned and lifted her arm to indicate the south-
east. "He pointed that way. I . . . I took the binoculars
and looked for several minutes before I caught a
movement. I wasn't familiar with viewing through infrared, so I gave the binoculars back to Gary. He
knew right away the movements were two humans."
Looking around, she paused, her forefinger indicating to her left. "He laid the radio down."

Kowalski nodded. "That's where it was found."

Climbing to her feet, she stepped to a small opening in the hedge to her right..

"We began to crawl," she said, pointing to the opening
in the hedge. "Through here." She stepped through.

Kowalski, Paya and Matt followed.

Good girl, Matt thought. It's coming back, and you're
doing fine.

She stepped onto the pavement and paused again.
After a few seconds, she nodded as if responding to
her own voice.

"As slowly and quietly as we could, we crawled
across the pavement." Reaching the corner, she
stepped onto the grass, then knelt down and
touched it. "The grass was wet and cold, but felt good
after the hardness of the pavement." She took several
steps along a row of headstones and stopped, looking
several directions to get her bearings. "No, this wasn't
the way. It was . . ."

Again, Kowalski tensed at her pause. And again, his eyes reflexively went to Paya. The old Navajo's face was screwed into a deep scow as he glared at him.

"Is there a problem, Mr. Paya? I hate to ask what probably is a dumb question, but does being in a cemetery bother you?"

Paya's glare grew harsher. "Being in a cemetery doesn't bother me. I spent three days in one on Iwo Jima before the landing. But I'd appreciate it if you wouldn't stand on the Admiral."

Kowalski's eyes flew to the headstone beside his feet. And as if Chester Nimitz's hand were reaching from the grave, Kowalski quickly stepped aside. Had they been there for any other reason, Matt would have burst out laughing.

Lindy turned and looked back to the hedge and pointed to the south. "It was this way," she said, moving forward. "Gary rose up from behind a headstone and looked through the binoculars. They were still there. He pulled my arm, and we began crawling again. We started downhill, between the headstones."

She continued southward and downhill till she stopped again. "I think it was around here we stopped and pulled out our guns." Her head began to nod. "Yes, it was. Just as I had my gun out of my holster, I heard the binoculars . . . Gary still had them hanging around his neck. They'd struck a headstone. It was so quiet that the sound seemed magnified. Then he swore. 'Shit,' I think he said. Then he rose up and looked. At first, I didn't see anything. Then he said angrily without bothering to keep his voice down, 'They heard it. Come on. Let's go.' We ran several yards this way."

She quickly retraced the path as it came to her until she stopped about twenty yards from the fence. Pointing to the concrete structure ornamenting the fence, she said, "I saw a form going through that opening in the fence. I . . . I said, 'I'll go after the one going through the fence.'"

She moved quickly until she stopped at the fence. Her hand trembled as it touched the base of the opening. A notable tremor rose in her voice as she pointed across the street.

"I saw someone run into those shrubs across the road. That's when I realized that I'd lost him . . . or her, I guess it was. I . . . I remember that I was so mad. I'd gotten so close. I remembered the Cortez kid's face and was so mad.

"I turned," she said, repeating the motion.

Her face was ghost-white. Matt recognized the mixture of rage and horror. Out of the corner of his eye, he saw Paya move. The old man sensed how close she was to breaking, but Matt put his arm out and shook his head. "We have to let her go on."

Paya snorted but held his position.

"I shouted out for Gary," she said. "He didn't answer. I assumed he'd taken off after the other one. I called again, and he still didn't answer."

Stepping away from the fence, she slowly moved past the three men.

Matt glanced at Kowalski and saw the man was reliving his own nightmare of guilt. He stood passively as she slowly sank to her knees.

Matt quickly stepped beside her and saw the raw terror in her eyes as she stared at the ground and struggled to speak. Easily, he knelt beside her.

A watery moan came from her throat. Sniffing back the emotion, she began to tremble. "I walked back to here. It happened so fast. It couldn't have been more than a minute." She wiped the back of her hand under her nose. "I ran into something. First I thought it was a headstone. That's all that's out here. But it was too soft. I . . . I knelt down. It was Gary. I felt the blood the minute I touched him. Then I started to get up. I was turning around this way." She turned to her left and froze. "I-I never heard a thing."

Matt knew this was the place to stop. Nothing more would she be able to recall. After she'd been discovered the following morning and taken away by the paramedics, he and the Chief went to the cemetery. A trail of blood, later identified as hers and Seaton's had extended from this exact spot to the fence where they'd been pulled through. Her Smith & Wesson had also been located here, propped against a headstone.

Then it all hit her and hit her hard. Wrapping an arm around her shoulder, he pulled her against his chest as she gave way to emotion.

"I . . . I'm sorry," she said through her sogs. "I can't remember anymore. Only that I kept thinking I was dying. Gary was dead, and I was going to die. I wish I could remember more, but I can't."

"You did fine," Matt said softly over her head. He looked around at Kowalski and felt sorry for the man obviously blaming himself. He looked at Paya, who paid no attention to Kowalski but watched Lindy crying on his chest. Matt wished he could read the old Navajo's mind. Something was definitely going through it. From the glint in those black eyes, he concluded it was as quiet and a chilling a rage as he'd ever seen.

By early evening the few visitors left on Baker Beach allowed the couple strolling along the shoreline a quiet end to a day which had held so much tension. Lindy's exhaustion was obvious, but she agreed the walk was a good idea.

They'd had the Szechuan dinner she had requested. The meal brought idle conversation with them exchanging bits and pieces of their lives, and Matt discovered himself more enchanted than ever.

"What are out thinking about, Lindy?" he asked. "You were so lively during dinner to be so quiet now."

Keeping her eyes to the sand, she shrugged and shoved her hands into the pockets of her windbreaker. "I suddenly thought of my great-grandmother. She was a Hupa sorceress . . . a self-appointed one. She was extremly sensitive and tended to take offense very easily. When she was upset with some-one, she found a way to retaliate. She lived until I was eight, and I was always careful not to displease her. In fact, I was scared to death of her.

"She had a series of chants she'd use against people. Usually, that was all it took. She'd begin one of her chants, and people rushed to hide in their houses for protection. But when she was really angry, she'd per-form one of her rituals.

"I remember one day, a tribal woman's husband brought her a gift. It was a new dress that he'd bought off the reservation. The woman bragged so much about her new dress that my great-grand-mother got very jealous. One day she followed the woman until she found one of her footprints in the earth. She picked up some dirt from the print and carried it into an area of the reservation where there was a rattlesnake den. Then she spread the dirt over the entrance and instructed the snakes to strike the woman's husband. The man worked as a logger with my father. The very next week he was bitten by a rattlesnake while working in the forest."

Seeing her smile, Matt chuckled. "I'd be scared of her, too."

"He didn't die, but he suffered for two days. My great-grandmother was delighted. After that, she was notorious."

Looking up to Matt, her smile deepened. "You can just imagine how careful people were about where they walked."

"I believe I can."

For several moments they strode quietly, and again, she looked at the sand. Her smile faded.

"Yesterday morning, I had a talk with a woman. Her name is Sandra. She works with people who've been victims of brutal attacks. She said one of the most difficult things for them to overcome is the fear of loss of control. We talked for a while about things I might begin to concentrate on doing right away. Like

getting back to my running. Working with other victims. And start making real plans about getting back
to work and exactly what I'll do until returned to full
status. Probably administrative duties for a while.
And it helped when Jim came by and said Lieutenant
Walker . . . he's our division head . . . asked if I'd be
interested attending a department computer class so I
can assist with the crime database. I can begin any
Monday I choose, two days a week.

"I actually had something to hang onto when I left
the hospital. I don't think I would have been in the
frame of mind to go to the cemetery if I hadn't. I was
really feeling pretty much in control. But when I got
to the actual site where . . ." Her words grew thick.
Her right hand, balled into a fist, came out of its
pocket. "I knew that's where the person who killed
Gary and attacked me stood. And this . . ." Her hand
opened palm upward revealing a tuft of grass and
dirt. "I didn't realize until later that I'd taken it."

Expressionless, he stared at her hand.

She began to laugh. It was the laughter of irony. "Do
you think my great-grandmother's spirit reached
through me and pulled it from the ground?"

He looked up and smiled. "I'm thinking that it's too
bad the aquarium is closed. We could pay a visit to the
reptile room and look up a rattlesnake."

It was dark by the time Matt walked Lindy up the
stairs to her apartment, the second floor conversion
of the Endicott's townhouse on Sixteenth Avenue.
The building stood out in the row of Painted Ladies,
the local name for San Francisco's often brightly
colored Victorian homes. This had been remodeled in
modern California . . . weathered shingles around
windowed walls.

The Endicotts were out for their weekly Bingo
game. Reluctant to leave her alone, Matt considered
asking Lindy to invite him in until the elder couple
returned. But, he concluded, she'd had a long and

tiring day and needed the rest more than company.

"Thanks," she said as they reached her door. "It helped a lot . . . your coming along today."

"Sure you'll be all right?"

"I'll be fine."

Their eyes met. Silent promises suspended both in a paralyzed moment as each realized, with the slightest hint from either, the night was going to last a long time.

Later, he ordered himself.

"Good night, Lindy."

"Good night," she answered and, using the doorjamb for support, watched him turn, offer one last glance and head down the stairs.

Not until he was out of sight did she unlock the door. Walking in, she noticed the living room light on. Puzzled at first, she recalled leaving it on during the night. She and Sandra had discussed how she might find herself doing different things for a while . . . things like sleeping with the lights on. I must have forgotten to turn off the light when I left this morning, she thought.

After locking the door, she tossed her shoulder bag on a chair, walked across the room to the window and watched as Matt was making his way across the street to his car.

"Thanks, again," she whispered.

Reaching his car, Matt pulled out his keys, then turned and look back across the street. He smiled at the sight of her standing at the window. And just as he lifted his hand for a final wave, it froze in mid-air when he suddenly saw a man's shadowed form move behind her and she spun around.

12

His hand had almost made contact with the door when it swung open, and Matt found himself staring into the blue eyes of Larry Hansen. Instantly, he realized how foolish he must look. Ragged of breath and his gun drawn, he stood suspended in the throes of alarm as Larry threw back his head and roared with laughter.

"Hey, Lindy," Larry said over his shoulder, "it's the cavalry."

As Matt released a long sigh and reholstered his weapon, Lindy came into his view, still looking somewhat rattled as Larry's sudden appearance behind her had given her a jolt. Her uneasy smile broadened when she saw Matt and realized he'd come rushing to what he thought was her rescue. Simultaneously, they began to laugh.

"Come on in," Larry invited, stepping aside.

His eyes still focused on Lindy, Matt accepted the invitation. "I thought you were coming tomorrow," he said to Larry.

Closing the door, Larry said, "We were, but we got

here about half an hour ago. After checking out the kitchen, Ally decided to pick up . . ." The flow of chemistry vibrating between his sister and the man from whom she couldn't seem to remove her eyes stopped Larry like a clap of thunder. Neither, he realized, had heard a word he'd said. "Excuse me," he said quickly. "I think I left something outside."

What Matt and Lindy *did* hear was the closing of the door as Larry made a sudden exit.

"Where did Larry go?" Matt asked.

"Where any good brother would go," she said, her eyes softening. "To get lost."

Matt's next words knotted tightly in his throat. Silently, he cursed himself. After more than two weeks of mental foreplay over this woman, she was standing there with absolutely no objection to his making a move while his damn shoes were nailed to the floor. He swallowed and watched her fold her arms beneath her breasts and slowly close the space between them.

Lowering her head for a few short seconds of thought, she then raised it and moved her eyes back and forth against his.

"You were there every day. While I was in the hospital," she said softly.

Awkwardly, he nodded.

She smiled that low shy smile he'd come to recognize as her way of saying, "I'm glad."

He expected to hear the words "thank you". Instead, he was stunned when she offered what he sensed was the most intimate gesture he'd ever received from a woman.

Taking two more steps, she uncrossed her arms, stretched on her tiptoes and softly brushed her lips against his cheek while allowing no other physical contact. Settling back on her feet, she lowered her head and said in a voice still raspy from its prior havoc, "I'm not certain of what this is, but it's pointless to pretend it isn't there."

Somehow, he managed to move. His curved finger slid under her chin and raised her face. She was trembling slightly, just as he was, but her eyes met his directly. They held strength and fear, recognizing the risk but showing the courage to face it.

Finding his voice at last, he said thickly, "It's definitely there. And if your brother weren't pacing outside the door, we'd begin right now on finding out what it is."

For a short second, her eyes narrowed. Then, moving aside, she stepped around him, reached and turned the deadbolt. She leaned back against the door. "As I said, Larry's getting lost."

He needed no more prompting. His arm swung around her waist and pulled her hard against him. The other arm found its way around her shoulders as both of hers wrapped around his waist. His head lowered in firm but gentle capture of lips parted to meet his. Their lips, their tongues moved against each other in determined exploration. His hands came to her head and laced their fingers through her hair. Pulling back her head, he continued his exploring kisses, covering her eyes, her nose, her ears, her throat. Lazy little circles of his tongue against her ear began drawing quick, shallow gasps from her throat.

Her senses reeling, she leaned further into him and felt his urgent, demanding arousal. Shuddering, she gasped again as his lips found hers. This was no meticulous exploration. This was a conquest, a profound maneuver to encounter and defeat any form of resistance.

She had none.

His arms thrust beneath her windbreaker and tightened around her in a crushing snare, as hers climbed the taut muscles of his back. Each pair of hands tightened and probed their way up the other's back. Their breaths escalated into mutual, low groans of spiraling arousal, each spinning toward its own fulfillment until suddenly their exploring hands made synchronous contact with the metal mass each had beneath their jackets. Abruptly, each recognized the other's holstered pistol.

"I think," Matt said, laughing as he raised his head, "I've found a woman who's armed and dangerous."

Lindy also leaned back and laughed while his hands slipped up her windbreaker and pushed it from her shoulders. The garment landed on the chair. Her holster and weapon followed.

Her eagerness matched his. In a flash, Matt's jacket and holstered weapon lay on top of hers. Her fingers worked loose the knot in his tie. While she drew it over his head, he began unbuttoning his shirt. Within seconds, it joined the pile; and with one swift motion, he pulled her turtleneck over her head. The garment joined the pile on the chair. Her bra quickly followed.

An arm reached around her waist and pulled her hard against him, pressing her breasts flat against his chest. His free hand slipped instantly around her hips and firmly clutched her left buttock, then moved between her legs and hard against her crotch as his lips again captured hers. He wanted to bury himself deeply inside of her but not until he drove her to an aching to match his. His probing tongue parted her lips and invaded her mouth just as his hand unsnapped her jeans. Releasing her zipper, he plunged his hand down the soft firm length of her belly and into the warm, moist recess swelling in its welcome of his sweet assault.

Groaning in slavish euphoria, she wrapped her arms around his shoulders and dug her fingers into the taut muscles.

The arm around her back slid under her buttocks and lifted her from the floor. Her inner thighs pressed against his hips as his fingers continued to stir an increasing frenzy.

She groaned again and tightened her arms.

His lips softened against hers. "I want you to come," he whispered into her mouth.

Her light protest to say she wanted to feel him in-side of her was buried beneath the hard pressure of his lips. Immersed in the rapture he was beckoning, she slumped against him and concentrated on obeying the command he issued again.

"Come for me, Lindy."

She was growing hotter and wetter as his fingers worked their spell. Her arms clung greedily around his neck. Her mind began retracing every memory of him.

His magnetic smile and the green flare in his eyes the first time she'd met him.

How those eyes had roamed over her and made her struggle with the warm rush he evoked.

His voice calling, "Hang on, Lindy. It's Matt. We've found you. You're going to be all right." Glimpses of his concerned face weaving in and out of her fog until the day her vision cleared to see him standing beside her bed.

Another warm rush when he had said, "You've got it, Lindy."

The solid strength of his arms around her earlier that day.

His smile when he said he'd return.

The promise in his eyes when he'd left her at her door only to rush back to her when he'd thought she needed him.

The fevered torment of desire drove a current pressing for release and flamed hotter with the hard insertion of his fingers inside of her. His finger tips pressed against the front wall of her vagina and massaged the inflamed channel until, suddenly, the flame ignited. The blazing torch tore through her senses. Gasping, her lips fell from his. Her head slumped onto his shoulder. Deep inside of her his fingers continued their assault against the series of constricting spasms of muscles until her long shud-dering sigh signaled this stage of passion was coming to an end.

His lips coursed their way along her forehead, down her cheek and to the left side her neck. Lightly, his tongue traced the angry red mark on the side of her neck, and he tought of how closely he'd come to not having this moment. He smiled to himself. But he *had* had this moment, and it was only the first.

Lifting his head, he looked around the room until he saw the short hallway. Gently, so as not to disrupt the afterglow of her passion, he turned and, with her still wrapped around him, carefully made his way into the bedroom.

Easing her down on the bed, he drew an arm around her shoulders and tenderly lay her back in his arms. His free hand caressed and fondled a passion-swollen breast. Soft, velvet kisses rained on her face. Her low moans were the music of wonder. Her fingers laced in his hair. Her mist of ardor sluggishly lifted, allowing the vivid blue of her eyes to roam over his face.

She smiled, warm and sated.

His eyes locking with hers, he returned the smile.

Her smile broadened. Her eyes glistened and continued their straying until without warning, they widened and froze, locked with his.

"What is it, Lindy?" he asked, a sudden alarm rising. She couldn't be having a change of heart! Not now!

"I . . . I . . . ," she stammered, then felt silent.

"What is it?" he pressed anxiously.

Biting her lip, she shyly glanced away. "I need a few minutes."

Then it hit him. How stupid of him not to think of it before. He nodded. "You don't have any protection?"

"I . . . do, but . . ."

"In the bathroom?" he asked raggedly.

She nodded and tried to rise.

"Don't move. Where? In the medicine cabinet?"

She tried to rise again. "It'll only take a moment."

"I'll take care of it," he said, getting to his feet.

"B-but . . ."

Playfully, he tweaked her nose. "Stay put."

Obediently, she relaxed against the bed, turned onto her side and drew her knees toward her stomach. Quietly giggling into the pillow, she felt her cheeks flooding while she listened to the noises coming from the bathroom.

The creaking of the medicine cabinet's door as it opened.

The fumbling among its contents.

The creaking of the door as it closed.

In a few seconds came the whine of his zipper, the jingle of his pocket change and the thud of his shoes hitting the floor.

Her giggles were swallowed by a heavy gulp as she felt the sagging of the mattress from his weight as he settled beside her. Warm lips moved against the back of her neck and along her shoulder as he gently pressed her on her back.

"I don't believe this," she said, laughing.

He was laughing also. "You will any minute."

Suspended in a trance, she watched him unlace her running shoes, slip them from her feet and toss them on the floor. Her socks followed. His hands slid up her ribs and cupped around her breasts where his thumbs began a slow massage of the peaks, raw from passion. Taking his own time, he took one crest then the other into his mouth. He sucked and nibbled as they rose pebble-hard to greet his tongue until another series of short, heavy pants rolled from her throat. Her entire body throbbed under his sweet assault, and another gasp came as his teeth lightly bit the skin between her breasts. There, he nibbled before making a path of tiny bites down over her abdomen until reaching her navel where his tongue made another series of lazy circles while his fingers snaked into her waistband. Pulling alternate sides, he worked the rest of her clothes downward; his mouth continuing the same direction.

When, at last, no barriers remained, he rose above her and smiled, startling her as one arm slipped under her back and the other beneath her knees. "I think," he continued, lifting her onto his lap, "it's time for some serious business."

Lindy wrapped an arm around his shoulder and kissed his ear, and in her moment of distraction missed his quiet actions. When she drew back and looked down, she gasped.

"What are you doing?" she asked, increduously staring at the object in his hand. It was her diaphragm, a layer of cream circling its lip.

His eyes lifted and bore into hers. Their green fire held her in a gripping spell.

"This is for both of us. I want to be a part of it. Now," he said thickly, "open for me."

She couldn't speak or move. Her eyes still locked with his, she could only think that this was a moment she'd never shared with anyone. It was so private. It was the last plane of womanhood, and he wanted domination. Instantly, she knew she wanted him to have it and was aware of nothing but the marvel reaching into the very depths of her soul. A gentle nudge of his hand against her inner thigh, and with her eyes still held captive by his, she followed his lead. Her eyes wilted under the sweet erotic fondling of his hand while it slowly worked deep inside until her protection was in place.

His eyes never leaving hers, Matt eased her back on the bed. His knee wedged between her legs, and his hands brushed the thick raven locks from her forehead. He shifted and made ready for entry. When his tip made its first contact with the passion swollen portal crying for entry, her gasp brought a instant he was tempted to prolong. But he'd waited long enough. His hand lowered to guide himself gently in. Once he'd filled her, he began a slow rhythm against muscles still raw from her climax. Her little gasps and cries escalated with his tempo. With her climax, his tempo accelerated to the feral pitch of a primitive animal until came the low grunt and shudder of his release.

Still looming above her, he could only continue gazing down into her eyes, clearing as the veil of passion slowly lifted but refusing to free him of their spell.

Munoz was scared out of his wits as he climbed over the fence. His radio had reported that a suspected burglary might be in progress, and the address was Edna Wallace's house on Twentieth Street. A neighbor reported that he'd seen what looked like someone with a flashlight behind Edna's house. It was three-thirty in the morning. What the hell was going on?

His pistol drawn, he sneaked his way through the small unlighted back yard adjoining Edna's. Beyond another fence, he saw the sudden swing of a flashlight beam. He crouched behind a rose bush and waited for a few seconds to decide if he was about to face a lone intruder and should call in for a backup and was about to turn to do just that when he heard the muffled scraping of galvanized steel and crunching of what sounded like ordinary trash breaking the quiet of the night. He stretched and peered over the fence. The beam continued to swing back and forth in a short path. He listened again before determining it was only one figure. Without making a sound, he reached both arms over the fence and pointed his gun.

"Freeze! This is the police!"

A loud gasp came before the intruder's exasperated response.

"Good heavens! You scared me to death."

He lowered his weapon and stared as he recognized the familiar voice. "Mrs. Pearson?"

"Officer Munoz," she said in relief and shone the beam into his face.

Squinting against the light, he stepped from behind the fence and pushed through the gate. "Mrs. Pearson, *what* are you doing?"

"Good Lord!" She sighed heavily.

"Mrs. Pearson, it's three-thirty in the morning. Just what are you doing up at this hour and going through Mrs. Wallace's garbage?"

"Keep your voice down," she whispered sternly and moved away from the garbage. "Come on into my house. I've got something to tell you."

Munoz was speechless.

Passing him, Virginia headed for her back steps. "Come on," she said impatiently. "I was planning to call you tomorrow anyway."

Munoz heaved a sigh of relief and confusion. Five times in the last two weeks, he'd listened to Virginia's insistence that she feared Edna was in trouble. He had talked to Edna, listened to Virginia, talked to Edna, eaten more cake, listened to Virginia, talked to Edna. The only thing he'd managed to accomplish was to gain four pounds. Virginia was still agitated. Edna still hadn't a care in the world.

"Mrs. Pearson," he said once they were in her kitchen, "will you please tell me what this is all about?"

She pointed to the kitchen table. "Have a seat."

Wearily, Munoz sat down.

Virginia laid the flashlight on the counter. "Care for some coffee?"

I could use a stiff drink, he thought.

"Thanks," he answered, realizing that he might be there for a while.

Virginia hastily filled two mugs and joined him at the table. "I couldn't sleep again."

Munoz looked at the coffee mug in front of her. "That's not going to help."

She flipped her hand. "I made this after I couldn't settle down. It's been this way for three weeks."

"So, what's on your mind tonight?" He took a sip from his mug.

She stiffened with indignance. "Need you ask?"

He rolled his eyes. "Mrs. Wallace's renters. Mrs. Pearson, I've talked with her several times. She's very contented with the situation."

She snorted. "Edna wouldn't know the difference. And since I can't get anyone to do anything, I decided to check things out myself."

Munoz shook his head. "Ma'am, you should leave the detective work to the police."

"Haven't I been trying to get them . . . get you . . . to get involved?"

"Ma'am, I've taken personal measures to see that Mrs. Wallace is not in trouble."

"Humph! Personal measures. Talking never got anything done."

"Mrs. Pearson, a person's privacy is something we all have to respect."

Virginia's finger wagged furiously in his face. "Now, you listen to me!"

Munoz wilted back into his seat. "Yes, ma'am."

Rising from her chair, she stepped to the pantry and opened the door. "These," she said over her shoulder as she removed a dented cardboard box, "I got from Edna's trash bin last night." She set the box on the table and began shifting through it. "You must realize that everyone's secrets end up in the garbage. I know those two women are up to something, and the clue is probably in here."

Munoz struggled to keep from revealing his frustration as he silently watched Virginia carefully remove the crumpled items from her collection, smothing out the wrinkles as she laid each on the table.

"Now," she said, "what do you see?"

He stared at the objects and frowned. "It's only packaging from batteries. D cells." He looked back up at Virginia. "So?"

Her hand spread through the air over the table. "Look at them! There's over a hundred. A hundred and thirty-six to be exact."

It *was* an unusually large amount, but Munoz

could only look up at her and shrug.

"I'm telling you," she said, "those two must be prostitutes. Why else would they need so many batteries?"

"I'm not sure I follow you," he said, lifting the mug to his lips.

Virginia's chest rose and fell under a heavy sigh. "For sexual aids!"

Munoz felt the instant burn of coffee spurting through his nose.

"You know," she continued, ignoring his efforts to recover, "like vibrators and clitoral stimulators . . ."

Munoz coughed.

". . . and those G Spot stimulators . . ."

And a list of things that would never convince his wife where he'd been at three-thirty in the morning if he tried to tell her.

13

The sound piercing Lindy's sleep seemed so distant. For a moment, she simply ignored it and settled deeper under the covers. Mentally, she replaced the buzzing sound with another . . . the gentle sound of his voice. The light had only been faint when he was telling her, "I've got to go to work, Lindy." She offered him breakfast, but he only chuckled and said as he planted a kiss on her forehead, "Larry never returned with the groceries, remember?" She had moaned and nodded as she reached out to feel him. His stroked her cheek. "I'll call you from work later."

The sound buzzed again.

Opening her eyes, she looked around. Only a small stream of sunlight pierced the room's darkness. She closed her eyes. The sound buzzed a third time. Abruptly, she pushed herself up and blinked as she recognized the sound was the doorbell.

"Larry!" she called, throwing back the covers. She sprang from the bed and raced to the bathroom. She unhooked her kimono from the back of the door and wrapped it around herself as she ran into the living room.

"Larry?" she called against the door.

"It is I," his amused voice announced from the other side.

Opening the door, she was greeted by the smiling faces of Larry and Ally. Ally held a sack of groceries. Larry held two.

"Believe it or not," Ally said cherrily, "the groceries did fine."

"Good morning, sis," Larry said as he entered. Leaning over the load in his arms, he kissed her cheek. "Sweet dreams?"

Shyly, Lindy ducked her head as Ally's elbow made sharp contact with Larry's rib.

"Ouch!" he said.

"Pay him no mind," said Ally as she sat the groceries on the snack bar. "You made his night. When I drove up, he came charging across the street blubbering his head off about us getting lost. We were two blocks down the street before I got any sense out of him." Grinning, she winked. "A good thing we brought the RV. A couple of hours later, we made supper from the groceries. For sure, *he* had sweet dreams."

Larry smirked and deposited his own two bags.

Lindy smiled, locked the door and was about to say something when she noticed the pile on the chair. Across her holster and pistol lay her turtleneck with her bra spread over it. Trying not to appear if she were doing what she was doing, she slipped quickly to the chair and hastily filled her arms.

"I hope you weren't inconvenienced," she said.

"Not at all," said Ally. "Things couldn't have worked out better. I've been trying to talk this big turd into starting a family for two years. We couldn't have exactly been working on it while camped out here in your apartment. Last night, I think I conceived."

Lindy rolled her eyes, recalling how close she'd come to getting carried away.

"Did I say something wrong?"

"Not really," Lindy answered lowly.

Ally smiled. "Good. Now," she said turning to Larry, "will you be a sweetheart and put away the groceries while Lindy and I have a chat?"

"Aren't I always a sweetheart?" Larry asked innocently.

"I hope not. I rather enjoy you being a naughty boy most of the time. Come on, Lindy," she said as she walked to the sofa and plopped down. "Tell me how you're doing." Glancing at the bundle in Lindy's arms, she added, "And I wasn't referring to that."

Lindy eased into the arm chair, "Fine, I guess. I'm really surprised at how much energy I have after two weeks and two days in the hospital."

"On the phone the other night you said something about getting back to work soon. You've got to be kidding."

"Only some light administrative work when I feel ready. It'll be another four weeks before the doctors said I should return to full duty."

"Good. Then you'll come back north with us."

Shaking her head, Lindy said, "Not until this mess is cleared up."

Ally looked again at the bundle in Lindy's arms and winked. "Are you sure *that's* the reason? I wouldn't blame you if it weren't. By the way, I approve."

"You've met Matt?"

Ally nodded. "He was there every day while we were here." Clicking her tongue, she added, "The guy's got it bad."

Lindy returned a wistful smile.

"When did all this begin?" Ally prodded.

Lindy shrugged. "I'm not sure."

Shifting to draw her sandaled feet under her, Ally said, "I want to know all about him."

"You always *were* nosy."

"How am I going to find out anything if I don't ask? I dare not leave it to you to tell me. Besides, I'm your big sister, remember?"

It was true. Ally was the closest thing to the sister Lindy ever had.

"Well," said Lindy, "he's thirty-seven. He's from Bodega where his parents are living their retirement on a small sheep ranch they sold to a corporation. He went to West Point and spent nine years in the Army, mostly in Europe, and he's been on the bomb squad here in the city for almost four years."

"Four years and he's the lieutenant?"

"They wanted his expertise and pulled some strings."

"Been married?"

"Once. It ended when he left the Army."

"Children?"

"No. His wife never wanted any."

"What about him?"

"Goodness, Ally! I never asked."

"Be sure to check that out. It's important, you know."

"Yes, ma'am."

Ally leaned around the sofa and saw Larry with his head in the refrigerator. "Hey Larry. How about putting on a pot of coffee. I could use a cup. I'm sure Lindy could."

"Yes, ma'am," he said, pulling his head into view.

"Now," Ally said only to be interrupted by the ring of the telephone.

"Want me to get it?" Larry called.

Lindy dropped her bundle and charged into the kitchen. Reaching for the telephone on the wall next to the refrigerator, she grinned. "Don't you dare."

"So what have you got?" asked Matt as he settled into the chair across from Kowalski's desk. He'd been in the middle of reporting off duty when the call came through that Kowalski wanted him to drop by his office. Kowalski hadn't said why. Matt didn't ask. "From the look on your face, it doesn't look good."

Kowalski leaned back in his chair, clasped his hands in his lap and tapped his thumbs. He looked tired. He also looked troubled. He sounded tired and troubled. "Yesterday afternoon when I got back to the office, the report finally came in from the Behavioral Science Unit. I have clearance to brief you."

Matt nodded.

"Before I begin," Kowalski inquired, "how's Inspector Hansen doing?"

"She's pulling it together."

"I'm sorry we had to push her so hard yesterday."

"She understands."

"Good. I just hope her day ended on a better note."

Matt's expression remained unchanged. "I hope so, too."

Reaching across his desk, Kowalski opened a Manila folder. "Here's the report. It's amazing what that group can come up with so little evidence." He lifted a sheet of paper. "You can read the details later, but first I want to point out the highlights to you.

"The first part relates to the evidence we sent in. Namely, the transmissions, their methods and contents, and the murders. The report reinforces our conclusion that the ladies are highly skilled. That means a great deal of training ... military fashion with a hierarchical command structure directing them. That they're able to remain covert indicates the command structure is from outside this country and has supplied them with sufficient funding to remain inconspicuous. All their needs are being paid for with cash. They're living a low profile to avoid gaining attention through large cash purchases. It's no secret that the government is keeping tabs on large cash transactions because of the drug trade. The ladies are definitely terrorists but have come up with some new tactics. Where terrorists have normally moved within the upper financial echelons, the unit suspects that the ladies are blending into the lower financial ethnic strata. It may or may not be Mid-Eastern as the hair samples indicate. That makes finding them even tougher. The lower financial ethnic population in this country is in the tens of millions with more being absorbed every day.

"They're unlikely to exhibit any overt sexual disturbances or sexual interest. In other words, no homosexuality and no overt interest in men. That might attract attention as individuals. They like drawing attention in a more dramatic fashion such as through theatrics. I'll say more about that in a minute.

"The Cortez boy's death was only a matter of his interrupting them and their not wanting to leave any witnesses. But all that changed with the attack on Hansen and Seaton. Their discovery in the cemetery alerted the ladies that we might be onto them. Two law officers show up the night after they'd killed someone. Obviously, one keeps watch as the other transmits. They had planned for one to distract. Probably as Hansen said when she saw one escaping through the fence. It was only a ploy, a planned maneuver, to draw her and Seaton in for the other to attack. It was good anticipation on their part. Then they discovered Hansen and Seaton were law officers . . . probably from their identification. It set the ladies into a brief period of frenzy. They must have grown very tired of waiting until something dramatic came of their efforts. That explains why they just didn't leave Hansen and Seaton in the cemetery. Dumping them into the canal and leaving Hansen's carryall so close to the Hall of Justice was a matter of innovative theatrics to rattle our chains. By reading the newspaper, they could have seen how it worked.

"Now, for the incident at the Presidio. We were set up. It was a high risk effort, but the ladies thrive on high risk, especially the kind that brings them such dramatic results. Another sign that they were growing impatient with waiting. They got a charge out of the immediate publicity. But whatever they're planning is to be more spectacular. They just enjoyed a shot in the arm.

"Last is they're women. The report speculates that all parties involved in the transmissions are female but not the powers directing them. It's not so unusual. Charles Manson used women. Lila Khaled was the queen of skyjackers in her day. Ulrike Meinhof and many in her gang. The SLA, the group that kidnapped Patty Hearst, was mostly women and so on. Women make good terrorists. Especially women who have a pent-up rage over a history of subjugation."

"Like Mid-Eastern women?" Matt asked, taking advantage of Kowalski's pause.

Kowalski nodded. "What better way for a woman to prove herself than through terrorist activities?"

Matt smiled, as much to himself as to Kowalski. "I can think of a few."

Kowalski laughed. "I stand corrected."

"Does that report have any suggestions where we begin looking for them?"

Kowalski shook his head. "The key is in their objective. Where do they want to set off a bomb if that's what they're up to? Any ideas?"

Matt frowned. "I shudder to think. It could be any number of places. If it's a foreign government behind this, this building might be one."

Kowalski rolled his eyes. "That was my first thought. And with the fragile situation in Southwest Asia, it's my second and my third. And I'll strike a wager that some very interesting cooperation between the top level departments is getting going. For us it's just a case of wait and see." Pushing himself away from his desk, he leaned over and handed Matt a copy of the report. He grinned. "If you come up with any more bright ideas, let me know."

Matt smiled as he folded the report and slipped it into his inside coat pocket. "I'll be sure to."

"Well, I think it's time to call it a day. At least try to. My twelve year-old has a little league game tonight. With a little luck, my beeper won't go off while I'm getting myself a change of scenery. I hate days spent in the office. As if the others lately have been a picnic."

"I know what you mean," Matt said as he rose. "Before I go, mind if I use your phone?"

"Help yourself. If anything comes to your mind before you leave, I'll be in the outer office. Got a couple of little things to attend to before I'm out of here."

"Thanks."

Kowalski closed the door behind him while Matt rang Lindy's number. After only one ring, a man's voice answered.

"Hello."

Matt frowned as he recognized Gerald Endicott's voice. Sensing a definite tension the other end of the line, he said, "This is Matt Sloan."

"Oh good," Endicott said hastily. "Could you come right over? We've got a little problem here."

14

A subdued Larry Hansen greeted Matt as he rushed into Lindy's apartment. Larry looked helpless. Pacing in the middle of the living room, Endicott didn't look much better.

"Where is she?" Matt asked.

Endicott's head tilted toward the rear of the apartment. "Out on the balcony. Ally, Norah and Dan are with her. I gave him a call when I couldn't do anything with her."

"Okay. Run it by me again. Exactly what happened?"

"You tell him," Endicott said to Larry.

Larry moaned and dropped into the chair. "It was around eleven. Ally and I had just arrived. She and Lindy were sitting here in the living room while I was in the kitchen. The phone rang. Lindy answered it. All I heard her say was 'yes' a couple of times. Then she hung up and said her carryall was being released as evidence and a couple of policemen would be bringing it by in half an hour. Neither Ally nor I noticed anything was wrong. But that's the way Lindy is. She's always kept her problems inside. She excused herself to take a shower and had just finished dressing when the two officers came, saying they'd left it on the street and gave her the keys. I should have never let her go out to look at it. I just wasn't thinking, I guess."

Matt and Endicott exchanged grim looks but said nothing.

Larry winced and continued. "I've never seen her that way. You know . . . how someone might look if they were cornered and about to be attacked by a wild dog? A kind of silent terror? Then it all came down on her. She just disintegrated right there on the sidewalk. Ally and I managed to get her back into the apartment. I kept thinking she'd settle down after a while. Finally, I called Jerry and Norah to see if they could do anything with her."

"I called Dan right after I got here," said Endicott. "She got quiet when she saw him. Then she went into a kind of stupor. Well not exactly, but she's not saying a word. Finally, Ally asked me to call your office, but you'd left and no one knew for where."

"I'm selling that damn thing tomorrow," said Larry. "In the meantime, I parked it around the block."

Matt pulled off his jacket and tossed it on top of the free chair. "I'll see what I can do."

Ally, Norah and Paya turned when Matt stepped onto the balcony. None said a word but looked relieved to see him.

Sitting on a wooden bench, Lindy rested against the shingled wall. Her arms were wrapped tightly under her breasts. The look in her eyes told the nightmare she was reliving.

Beside her, Matt lowered and spoke softly. "Lindy, it's Matt."

A few seconds passed before she responded. Then it was only her eyes moving and slowly meeting his. She looked so wounded and helpless, Matt almost gave into the urge to pull her into her arms, but he waited. Carefully, her arms unfolded. Her right hand, balled into a fist, opened. It held the piece of turf.

He looked up at her, smiled gently and stroked his knuckles across her cheek. "I understand," he said softly.

Turning to Paya, who was leaning to see what she had revealed, he explained, "It's a piece of the ground from the cemetery. It's where they stood."

Paya nodded as Matt repeated Lindy's tale of her great-grandmother's ritual to bring evil to an enemy. Quickly, he straightened and turned to Larry. "Light the fireplace. If we can't poison them, we'll burn them."

"I should have thought of that," Larry said, then disappeared through the door.

"I'll help you," said Endicott, rushing after him.

Lindy remained silent. Her hand tightening around Matt's was her only response. Her eyes stared at a haunting memory.

Matt looked at Paya for a sign of what else to do with her. The old Navajo stood without speaking as he kept watch over the tormented young woman. Then Matt realized that Paya was seeing into the recesses of a mind bonded to his by a common heritage. Lindy and Paya's visions were the same, only hers were seen with fear while his were seen with understanding. Matt looked at the wad of turf in Lindy's fist then up to Paya.

"Is this going to work, Dan?"

Paya nodded. "It will get her through the first step. There will be others."

"We've got the fire going," Endicott said a few minutes later, his head leaning through the door.

After gently coaxing Lindy to her feet, Matt guided her into the living room and before the fireplace.

"Lindy," he instructed quietly, "put it into the fire."

Without further prompting, she extended her

her hand toward the hearth and opened it. The turf hit the flames. Its moisture snapped in a series of tiny crackles. For a long moment she stared at the sizzling object before she turned and pressed her cheek against Matt's chest. Drawing his arm around her shoulder, he felt his own relief as she drew in and released a long breath.

"It's all right," he muttered over her heat. "It's going to be all right."

Silently, she nodded.

The Golden Retriever bounced and panted his way to the back door as Arnie Riley followed.

"Hold on, George," Arnie said, chuckling as he carefully stepped to avoid the excited animal.

At the door, the animal stopped and looked back while wagging its tail.

Arnie laughed at the nine month old puppy given to him by his son the previous Christmas. At sixty-seven, Arnie was past the age of enjoying his life long passion of pheasant hunting. Not so much his age, but the arthritis from his broken hip. The dog was a warm link to Arnie's love for his favorite sport and good companion after his wife's death the previous year. The emptiness without her had been pure torment. George with his exuberance had been determined to fill the great void in Arnie's life. He came very close.

Unlatching the screen door, Arnie laughed again. "There you go, boy."

George pressed his nose through the first crack in the door and forced it open before Arnie could perform the task.

Opening the screen further, Arnie said, "Now, make it a quick one. We're due to talk to Fred in ten minutes."

Acknowledging the order with a bark, George charged into early morning.

Grinning, Arnie shook his head as he closed the door. He checked the large digital numbers of his

wristwatch. *5:48 A.M.* He had twelve minutes. Enough
time for a bowl of cereal. Without Thelma around to
keep tabs on his eating habits, they had become sporadic. Often, he just waited until he was hungry and
grabbed something convenient. It was a lousy way to
nourish a body. He'd gained fifteen pounds the last
three months. His doctor kept lecturing him how bad
the surplus weight was for his hip, but he was getting
along. That was all that really mattered. His strong
years behind him, he was going to live his life the way
he wanted and to hell with everybody else.

Walking to the refrigerator, he reached and pulled
down the box of Shredded Wheat. From the drain-
board, he picked up the same cereal bowl and spoon
he used every morning, then retrieved a quart of milk
from the refrigerator. As he pinched open the lip of
the carton, he heard George's short whine at the door.

"That was a quick one," he said, setting aside the
milk. "But I guess I told you to make it one."

Arnie walked to the door and slid back the bolt. He
pulled open the door and gasped. "Oh, no," he groaned
through the instant rising of tears.

George lay slumped between the screen and door.
His head fell back as the door opened further. Blood
gushed from his neck. And before Arnie was aware
of anything else, he caught the glimpse of a silver
light reflecting from the glade arching down at him.

15

The look of disbelief on Lindy's face had Matt doubling over with laughter.

"You guys have lost your mind," she gasped.

"It was Dan's idea," Larry announced, nodding to Paya standing beside him. "He did the negotiation."

She looked at Matt. "Are they serious?"

"Looks like it to me."

Shaking her head, she walked toward the vehicle parked along the curb in front of her apartment. She still couldn't believe what she was seeing. It was a monster. It was unreal. But it was beautiful despite its need for some minor touching up. The baby blue and white two-door '57 Chevy Bel-Air was a dream.

"It's had only two owners," said Larry as she began circling the car. "And it's got new seat covers and a brand new transmission with only sixteen hundred miles. If you take it, they'll throw in a new set of white walls."

Lindy looked suspiciously at Paya, who kept nodding his approval. "Why this?"

"Why not?" Paya answered. "It'll last another thirty years, and you can still get all the parts."

"All the parts?"

Paya nodded. "If it breaks down . . . all cars do now and then . . . you can fix it."

Her jaw gaped. "*I* can fix it?"

"Jerry and I will show you how. It'll give you something to do while you're off work."

Lindy looked at Matt, who was still composing himself. He shrugged. "Why not?"

"Now don't jump to any decisions," said Larry as he saw her shake her head. "We can keep it overnight. Tomorrow, you can sign the papers, and it's yours. Or the salesman will pick it up, and we can start again."

Having made her way around the car, Lindy returned to the sidewalk. "What do you think?" she asked Matt.

Grinning broadly, he answered, "I think you should try it out."

"But I've never driven anything this big. How am I going to park the thing?"

"Angled or parallel," he said. "That's the usual way."

Lindy gave him a "wise guy" look, then laughed. "Well, why not? She looked at Paya, then to Endicott. "You're sure you know what to do with it?"

"Sure," they chimed.

"I've always had a car I could fix," said Endicott. "And I courted Norah in a car almost like this one. Worst mistake I ever made was to sell it five years later."

Feeling victorious, Larry held out his arm and dangled the keys. "Give it a try."

She groaned in defeat looked again at Matt. "Shall we?"

"I was afraid you wouldn't ask," he said, reaching and opening the door.

She sighed in surrender and slipped behind the wheel. From there, everything was an experiment. While Matt made his way around to the passenger door, Larry, Endicott and Paya stood enjoying every moment. She struggled to adjust the seat and the rear view mirror.

Climbing in, Matt asked, "How does it feel?"

"Big," she answered and, looking at the instrument panel, added, "but it looks simple enough." She inserted the key and started the engine. It turned over like a charm.

"Don Riley speaking."

"Don, this is Fred Thompkins."

"Well, hello, Fred. How are you doing?"

"I'm doing fine. How's your dad?"

"He's doing great. We had him over for dinner on Sunday like usual. Say, didn't you talk to him this morning?"

"That's why I'm calling. I couldn't raise him on the radio. The funniest thing is that I heard his call around eight-thirty. I answered it, but he didn't acknowledge. Just kept repeating the same message. Five, six times. Didn't make any sense at all."

"That's strange."

"Tell me about it. We haven't missed a call in six years. Not even when your mother passed away. Would you mind checking on him and let me know?"

"Sure thing. I'll give him a ring right now. I'm sure there's no problem."

"Thanks."

"You're welcome, Fred. I'll get back to you just as soon as I have an answer. Thank you for the call."

"Where do you think you're going?" Matt asked through a yawn.

With a smile and a grimace, Lindy said as she crawled over him, "I think I should give Larry and Ally a call." Planting her feet on the floor, she stretched and smiled as she noted Matt's green eyes roaming over her. "We were supposed to go out for a drive yesterday afternoon, not for an all night tryst on your sailboat."

Grinning wickedly, he reached out, gripped her wrist and playfully yanked her on top of him. "Little do you know," he cackled against her neck while she laughed, "Larry and I made a deal."

"Oh?"

"I have today and tomorrow off. Today and tonight I get you all to myself. Tomorrow I take Larry and the boat out fishing while you take Ally shopping. Larry thinks it's a fair trade."

"He does, does he?" Still laughing, she added, "He probably does. Ally must know every outlet within a hundred miles. Larry would agree to anything to keep from being dragged along as she hits every one. *You,*" she said, giving Matt's nose a gentle tweak, "have little cause to brag."

With a mischievous smile pulling at the corners of his mouth, his free hand began a slow exploration. "I disagree."

"Well, in that case," she returned through an impish smile of her own, "I think I should put together some breakfast. I have a feeling both of us are going to need our energy."

He climbed out of the berth behind her. "Good idea. There's enough in the galley to do the job. Here," he said, tossing her a shirt from the hook on the locker door. "Your robe."

"Thank you, captain," she said pulling the shirt around her shoulders. "Or do you prefer skipper?"

"I prefer you," he answered, swatting her behind as she turned.

Yelping meekly, she giggled and made her way through the salon and into the galley as Matt followed. Leaning against the chart table, he quietly watched her rumble through the cupboards and ice chest as she assessed their contents. Her movements captivated him. But, he confessed silently, he'd been captivated since the day he turned and saw her standing in the door of his office. So much had played through his mind since that morning. The startling awareness of the instant chemistry. The surprising despair of realizing he might not have the chance to explore it. The relief when hearing she was going to survive. The strange compulsion to drop by the hospital each day, even the days she was not conscious of his being there. The stunned look in her eyes when she realized that his visits were more than professional. His own need to give her the support she needed and still did. His discovery in her of a passion to match his own. He was even more captivated now.

"Here," she said, offering a mug of fresh coffee. Stretching, she kissed his cheek.

His free arm reached around her waist. "Careful," he said, lowering his lips to hers. "I'm already thinking of another way to enjoy breakfast."

Playfully, she swatted his shoulder, then laughed as she moved easily against him. Her lips parted and were pressing into his when a loud thump on the deck made her pull back her head. She cringed. "Visitors?"

"The morning paper."

She nodded and smiled as he reluctantly let her slide from his embrace.

He sighed in amused disappointment but decided to fetch the paper.

Lindy was just completing her assessment of what was on hand for breakfast when he returned from the deck. The paper was open in his hand. His look of disturbed distraction made her ask, "What is it?"

Matt lowered the newspaper and looked at her, his expression saying he really didn't want to answer.

She walked to him and looked at the bold headlines.

SLASHER STRIKES AGAIN!

16

Lindy's hands trembled as she took the paper, sank into the dinette seat and read:

"The body of Arnold Riley, 67, was discovered yesterday afternoon by his son, Don, at the deceased's Pacifica residence. Cause of death was hemorrhage from a deep laceration to the throat, severing vital arteries. The body was found on the kitchen floor along with that of his Golden Retriever, slain in the same fashion. Mr. Riley's son discovered his father's body in response to a telephone inquiry from the deceased's former neighbor, Mr. Fred Thompkins, currently a resident of Lake Havasu, Arizona. The two elderly men had lived next door to each other for twenty-eight years before Thompkins moved to Arizona after retiring from his Pacifica tire store. Long time amateur radio enthusiasts, the two men had maintained regular radio contact since Thompkins' move. Alarmed that Riley did not respond to their usual Thursday morning contact, Thompkins called Riley's son. Riley made news three months ago when neighbors began complaining about the seventy-five foot radio antenna on the roof of Riley's home. Riley was growing to be a local cult hero in his battle against his neighbor's complaints as his antenna had been erected long before most of his neighbors had taken up residence in the area. His son admitted that his father had been the object of minor harassments, but none had proved to be of a physical nature. The manner of his death strongly resembles those of Christopher Cortez and FBI Agent Gary Seaton earlier this month. Also a victim of the attack in which Seaton died was San Francisco Homicide Inspector, Linda Hansen. Hansen survived and was released from San Francisco General Hospital this last Monday. She could not be located for comment. The incidents earlier this month were explained by law enforcement authorities to be possibly drug related. When asked by this writer if the death of Mr. Riley was connected to those of Cortez and Seaton, authorities refused to comment at this time. Mr. Riley, a widower of fourteen months is survived by his son, Don, of San Mateo, daughters, Phyllis of Novato, Margaret of San Rafael and nine grandchildren. Funeral arrangements . . ."

Lindy lowered the paper and stared vacantly ahead as Matt read the article.

"What do you bet," she said after a long, heavy sigh, "the ladies found their antenna tuner?"

Matt lay the paper on the chart table and pulled her into his arms. Gently, he stroked her head, pressed against his chest. "We'll get them, Lindy," he promised. "We'll get them."

Ally answered the phone in Lindy's apartment when Lindy called.

"My God!" said Ally. "I'm glad you weren't here. The phone's been ringing off the hook. I got so damn mad, I called the Hall of Justice and reported that someone inside must have given your number to the

press. Have you ever given your number to a
reporter?"

"No," Lindy answered. "It's just part of the game of
being a policewoman. It happens."

"Game, my ass!" Ally shrieked. "I'm calling this
morning to get your number changed."

"That's probably a good idea."

"Are you still with Matt?"

Lindy looked at him sitting across the dinette table.
His expression was tight as if he were hearing Ally's
remark about the calls. "Yes."

"Good."

In the background, Larry's mumbling came
through the receiver.

"Oh," said Ally, "Larry wants to know what
you're going to do about the car."

"I guess I'll keep it."

"He'll be pleased to hear that. Now, stay put. We'll be
over in a while. You still have to sign the papers.
Want me to bring you some clothes for a few days?"

"I . . . I . . ."

"Oh hell! Let me speak to Matt."

Lindy lowered the phone and looked across the
table. Matt's eyes instantly flew to the telephone. His
hand shot out and grabbed it.

"Ally," he said.

Lindy slumped agaist the back of the seat while she
heard Matt exchange several comments with Ally until he gave directions to his berth in the Marina.
When he hung up the phone, she looked up.

"Well," he said, "that solves that."

"Solves what?"

"How I was going to find a way to keep you aboard
for a while."

She sighed raggedly and attempted to smile. "This
really isn't being fair to you. Taking up your time
this way."

His hand reached and took hold of hers. While hers
felt so limp, his was so strong. His thumb working

across her knuckles, he said, "I can't think of a better way to spend it."

She tried to smile again as the warm softness in his eyes washed through her. Instead, she suddenly burst into tears. Within seconds, she was wrapped in his arms and spilling large tears into the dark, silken hairs of his chest.

"Oh, God," she sobbed. "How long is this going to go on?"

"As long as it takes," he said over her head.

Her head turning into his neck, she began mumbling something he couldn't decipher.

"What was that?" he asked. "I didn't quite get it."

"I-I said," she sniffed, "I was going to fix your breakfast."

"Not to worry," he returned. "I'll take care of it." He expected his words to bring her some relief, but she only cried harder.

Lindy sat down her coffee cup and let out a long, shuddering sigh. They had just completed breakfast, and Matt was pleased to see that she had managed to eat most of hers. A good appetite was a good sign.

"Feeling better?"

She nodded. "But I feel so inadequate."

"You're pushing yourself too fast, Lindy. Don't expect so much so soon."

"I've had to push myself," she said. "I've worked really hard to make it where I am. If I lose confidence in myself, how am I going to expect Jim to have it?"

"I think you're not giving yourself or Jim much credit. He's been around long enough to understand that one simply doesn't bounce back from what you've been through."

"That's part of what frightens me."

"Care to explain that?"

She sighed again. Her voice was steady, but her eyes

held their tension as she began to speak.

"Matt, I'm a woman of an ethnic minority. Until I was eighteen, I lived totally with my own people. I never knew there was such a thing as prejudice. You can't imagine what a jolt it is to discover it at that stage of life. Every step I take is under its shadow. No matter how qualified I am for the job, I get affirmative action thrown in my face constantly. Every step I take up the professional ladder, I hear it over and over. My position in Homicide had to go to a female or to a minority. I filled the bill on both counts. I doubt anyone bothered to read beyond the blanks indicating sex and ethnic origin. I had better grades at the academy, better records on patrol and better shooting scores than any of the other applicants. Jim took me on as a challenge. For the first six months, he did everything he could to see if I could take it. And I did. I did because I knew that he was the best in Homicide. I also knew that he'd driven away more detectives than he'd kept. But I refused to allow him to defeat me.

"Finally came a day when I saw something in him I've rarely seen since I left the reservation. It was respect and pride. I don't want to lose that."

Recalling Matheson's reaction at the scene of her abandoned vehicle, Matt said, "I don't believe you have anything to worry about. You haven't lost it with Joe."

She smiled appreciatively. "Joe was like another brother. We got along from the beginning." Quickly, her smile faded. "It's one thing to spend a tour with only one person. But an entire squad is a different matter. There's only one other female in Homicide. Her name is Edie Cowles. She's older than I am and was a English Literature professor at Mills College before becoming a policewoman. She told me that it took her two years to get a compliment from our lieutenant. I have yet to see the man smile."

"From what I hear," Matt returned, "no one sees Wes

Walker smile." Reaching across the table, he took her hand. "I don't doubt that Jim is looking forward to your returning to work with him."

"You really believe that?"

"I really do."

She smiled. "Thank you. That means a lot."

"Here it is," said Ally, pointing to the two story building on Florida Street. The peeling blue paint and white trim seemed an unlikely site for a shopping spree.

The area was crowded with run down buildings and strewn with garbage. Many of its residents, uncomfortable in their own neighborhood, kept inside their homes. The only visible sign of the area being populated was a small gathering of teen-age boys, standing and talking idly against a battered fence several yards from where Ally pulled alongside the curb.

"Are you sure?" asked Lindy. "I don't see the numbers anywhere."

Ally turned off the ignition. "Trust me. I was here last year. This place has got to have the best prices in town for designer clothes. The worse the neighborhood, the better the prices in these outlets. Overhead, you know."

In the back seat, Larry groaned. "I wish Matt weren't back at work. I'd rather be fishing on his boat again."

"You boys had your fun yesterday. Today, it's we girls' turn."

"Yeah, I know. Shop till you drop."

"Wait till you hear the worst," Lindy said, laughing as she climbed out of the car. "Next stop is for you."

On the sidewalk, Larry eyed his wife coming around the car. "I don't need another goddamned suit."

"Oh, shut up," she said, snickering. "You only have one, and it's the one you wore at our wedding."

Larry groaned and rolled his eyes.

Lindy laughed again. "Larry, you know you don't stand a chance."

"Tell me about it," he returned as he glanced anxiously around. "Are you sure we're safe here? This area looks awfully mean."

"It is," cautioned Lindy. "When I was on patrol, I did a few relief stints in this district. That was three years ago. It's gotten worse since then with the growth of gang violence. This area is on the edge of the Mission District. Combined with the Potrero District a few blocks to the east, it's considered the worst in the city for patrol. It's boiling with racial and ethnic hatred. Even the barrio has barrios, so let's get inside instead of chatting on the sidewalk."

"Yeah," said Ally. "I'm ready to shop."

"Aren't you always," responded Larry as he pushed at the creaking wood gate.

Ally darted past him in a flash.

Lindy was in close step, still laughing at her brother's protests when suddenly, the mentioning of her name made her swing around.

"Well, if it isn't Officer Hansen," came the young man's heavily accented voice.

Amid Ally's scream and Larry's "Oh shit!" Lindy stared at the young man standing a few feet away.

"Get inside," she told them firmly as she continued to stare straight into the eyes of the young man in whose hand the blade of a knife flashed in the sunlight.

17

She recognized him instantly. His name was Armando Vasquez, also known as Mando. He must be close to twenty now. He'd been sixteen or seventeen when she first met him during one of those relief stints she had just mentioned to Ally and Larry. The anger he'd directed at her continued to smolder and now blazed in his black eyes flaring in his bronze face, smiling at his elation of discovering her alone on his own turf.

Alone because the young frightened couple were obviously not cops and could easily be disregarded.

Motionless, she waited. A quick glance to her right revealed the trio enjoying the meeting of their compadre and the young woman with whom Mando had repeatedly vowed to settle a score. Had he selected a time and place, this one couldn't have been more favorable.

His smiled broadened, revealing a crooked row of neglected teeth. "I read about you in the paper, Hansen. Read that someone cut you up pretty good." The knife rotated in his hand. His smile became satanic. "Too bad they didn't get your pretty face."

Expressionless, she looked at the glimmering blade then back to his eyes. "Don't be stupid, Mando." Her voice sounded amazingly calm despite the apprehension coiling in her chest.

"Stupid?" He laughed, his blade still rotating. "It wasn't me who wandered alone into these streets. You must have a short memory. Allow me to refresh it. I promised you the day would come when we would meet again. And it looks like the odds are in my favor this time."

"Lindy!" Larry called from inside the gate. "For God's sake, get in here!"

"Stay out of this, Larry," she said, keeping her eyes fixed on Mando and the pitch even in her voice. "Take Ally inside the building." When he didn't move, she said, "Now!"

Ally's muffled cry rose from behind the fence. Larry cursed.

"Now!" Lindy repeated. Looking her confronter straight in the eye, she said, "I can handle this."

Mando's face twisted in triumph as he snorted. "As I said, you're very stupid." His head cocked toward his friends slowly beginning to move. One leaned against the fence to her right. The second made his way to her left. The third positioned himself behind Mando. At her back stood the fence. "How do you expect to handle the four of us?" asked Mando.

Three more blades flashed in the sun.

Ally screamed over Larry's curse. "Please get in here," he yelled.

Lindy ignored them. The determination in her eyes clashed with the fury of the man leering at her. The coil in her chest slowly began to unwind as the instinct for survival raised its head. With no place to run, there was no reason to try.

"Mando, I have no beef with your friends. I have no beef with you."

Savagely, he spat at her feet. "My brother is dead because of you."

"Your brother is dead because he killed himself."

"It was *you* who put him in that hell!"

"He made his own hell. Just as you will do if you don't put away that knife."

His fiendish laugh pushed back his head. "Then I will take you with me." Solidly, he fixed his eyes on her breasts. "I could enjoy you by the fire. My friends also. You have such a nice body, Hansen. It would be a waste to cut it up more. I could get real pleasure from you. The kind of pleasure you promised my brother."

"Your brother's pleasure came from hurting women, especially little girls."

He spat again.

She kept her stance.

He sneered. "You tricked him!"

"I was a decoy. It could just as easily been your sisters I helped save when we stopped him. Think about that. If it had been another man doing what your brother was doing, you would have been grateful. Your brother was a sick man. You might even have stopped him. He could have gotten treatment for his sickness and been saved. Ever think of that?"

Through her tension, Lindy actually felt sorry for Mando. His brother had been a coward, directing the rage of his weakness against those who could not fight back. Neither Mando nor his brothers had done anything to stop Carlos, thus creating their own weakness and their own rage. It was an inbred, festering wound that never healed, only spread its poison until it consumed all reason.

Mando's black eyes began to flicker. In his hand, the knife trembled.

This is it, she thought. At her side, her right hand snaked toward the revolver holstered under her jacket while her eyes held his. If she had to, she could put him down. That wasn't what she wanted. Violence was too much a part of the poverty-wrecked lives of Mando and his kind. Violence bread violence. It tore at their souls, robbed them of their self-value.

"Go home, Mando," she said gently.

He continued to tremble. His eyes flashed in rage and confusion.

"Go home," she said again. "Your family needs you. They need you to be the man Carlos couldn't be. They need you to help ease the pain he put to them. They need you to be strong, not to give them the same heartbreak."

Mando's throat worked against the collision of his emotions. The woman facing him offered a challenge. Slowly, his raised arm lowered its weapon. The tension in his eyes gave way to a sudden and silent appreciation that she was showing she had confidence in him as a man. Vacantly, he gazed at her for a few moments, then looked around at his friends. Abruptly, he told them, "Come on."

She continued watching them move together and mumble quietly in Spanish. It was a departure, not a retreat, as they made their way toward the corner. Absorbed in their efforts to leave the site in a victory different from what they had planned, they jerked, startled at the loud screeching of a police cruiser breaking the silence.

Lindy looked to her right and saw the young Hispanic patrolman climbing from the cruiser.

"You all right, ma'am?" he asked, stepping onto the sidewalk. He eyed the foursome looking back nervously as they continued walking.

"Yes. Thank you," she answered.

"I saw them harassing you as I turned the corner."

"No problem." She turned and waved Mando and his friends away. The foursome strode cautiously out of sight.

Suspiciously, Munoz stared at the now vacant corner. "You sure?"

She produced her I.D. "Inspector Hansen."

"Oscar Munoz," he said, offering his hand. "Say, aren't you . . .?"

Lindy nodded.

"I thought you were still on sick leave."

"I am."

"Then what are you doing in this neighborhood?"

"Shopping."

Resting his hands on his hips, Munoz shook his head. His expression held comic disbelief. "Women!"

She laughed. It felt good. Better yet was that she had faced a challenge she feared would have her crumbling the day it came. Her work was filled with challenges of this nature. Her confidence had taken a severe beating. Miraculously, she felt some of it restored.

Munoz grunted helplessly. "I trust you didn't come down here alone."

"No. My brother and his wife are inside . . . I hope," she added, leaning to look around the gate.

The back door of the building suddenly creaked open, and Larry's face, still holding its alarm, jutted through. Seeing the uniformed officer standing with his sister, he heaved a sigh.

"Jesus," he said, joining his sister and Munoz. "Everything all right?"

"Everything's fine," answered Lindy. "How are you?"

"Scared shitless. Ally's inside. She raced upstairs and asked for the phone."

Just as he finished, the approaching wail of sirens filtered through the streets.

Larry cocked his head toward the building. "Ally called 911 and reported four guys with knives were about to attack you."

Lindy looked at Munoz and then toward the sound of the sirens. "Terrific."

18

Ally's frantic call had flared through the police air waves. Its message reached Matt's office within the hour. The later message that Lindy had suffered no injury did little to ease his anxiety. His efforts to contact her produced nothing. By the time his tour ended, he was near panic from the constant mental replay of her lying in those weeds and near death. From work he'd driven straight to Lindy's apartment only to discover no one there. His panic rose. Had they gone to his boat? No, he told himself. It was Ally's and Larry's last night in town before they returned home, and dinner had been scheduled at Lindy's apartment. At the top of the stairwell he paced. He cursed. Where the hell were they?

He paced and cursed and paced and cursed and paced and cursed; and when he finally heard the sound of Lindy's laughter coming through the opening door, his tension exploded without regard to its impact.

"Where the hell have you been?" he fired at the trio now at the bottom of the stairwell.

Ally and Larry gaped in stunned silence.

Her arms filled with shopping bags, Lindy paused. She looked up and stared curiously at the man she'd thought she had come to know in the last days. The man glaring down at her now was an absolute stranger.

"Matt?" she asked in wonder. "What's wrong?"

"What's wrong?" he thundered. "Over five hours ago I got the message that four guys were about to cut you up, and you vanished without a word."

Behind her, Larry giggled. "The tom-toms," he said in reference to the police air waves, "spread their messages far and wide."

Matt's icy glare sliced through him, Larry choked back another rising giggle.

"Stay out of it," Ally whispered to her husband. If no one else could, she certainly recognized a fight brewing between her sister-in-law and the man at the top of the stairs.

Still riding on the euphoria of her ability to handle the situation on Florida Street and the ensuing fun of the afternoon, Lindy laughed. "Oh, that?"

"Yes, damnit! That!" Matt returned furiously.

Her laugh wilted abruptly.

Ally nudged her husband. "We have an errand to run."

"Now wait a minute," Larry said, recognizing her effort to get him away. He looked up at Matt. "I don't want you talking to my sister that way."

"I can handle him," Lindy said, at last noting the strength of Matt's fury.

"But Lindy . . ."

"Larry," Ally cautioned through clenched teeth.

One look into his sister's eyes, and Larry realized that she could hold her own. After all, she'd confronted four angry young men with knives while he helplessly rushed his wife into that building. A tug on him arm and Larry back out the door.

Alone at the bottom of the stairs, Lindy calmly addressed the man whose scowl held pure rage.

"We've spent the day shopping," she said, beginning her journey upward.

"Jesus Christ!"

"You're overreacting, Matt," she returned, frowning as she reached the top of the stairs. "I'm sure it sounded worse than it was."

"Then tell me," he said through clenched teeth, "how was it?"

Digging her keys out of her canvas shoulder bag, she said, "We'll talk about it inside. Or do you want the neighbors involved?"

His temper rising, Matt stood in stone silence until Lindy led him into her living room. His slamming of the door behind him as she deposited her shopping bags on the chair startled her.

She swung around and stared at the man who suddenly seemed a stranger. "What's gotten into you?"

"The last five hours! Now, what happened?"

She could do nothing but to tell him. Somehow, she'd never considered how fast such news could travel.

"Have a seat," she said, hoping sitting down might relax him.

"I'll stand, thank you."

She shrugged. "Suit yourself. Can I fix you a drink?"

"Quit hedging on me, Lindy."

She sighed. "All right. After lunch we stopped at a clothing outlet in the Mission District. There was a young chicano . . . his name was Mando . . . on the street with some friends. I hadn't noticed him until he approached us."

As much compassion as repulsion reflected in her eyes. "Three years ago," she began, "I was a decoy to catch his brother. Carlos was a sickened soul defeated by the ravages of poverty and prejudice and turned into a sulking pervert. He'd raped and killed six young Hispanic women. Two were under fifteen. It was his demented way to vent his rage against the misery in his life . . . to gain some type of control. The decoy worked. We caught him one night in an alley. Despite all the psychiatric evaluation that he was mentally ill and belonged in an institution, he went to trial. His public defender was an out and out alcoholic, thankfully now out of the system. The deputy D.A. destroyed him in court. Carlos went to prison for life. He was there four months when a group of inmates decided to show him what rape felt like. That night, he hanged himself with his bed sheets.

"It really tore up his family. Mando swore he'd get even with me since I'd been the instrument in putting his brother away. He's been harboring a grudge for three years when, by chance, we met on the street this afternoon.

"But I handled it, Matt. I talked to him the way I've been trained to handle such situations. He and his friends walked away. I didn't realize that Ally was inside the outlet and making an emergency call."

Her account failed to impress him.

"Do you realize how easily the situation could have been the opposite way around?" he asked.

"I had my gun. I could have killed him if necessary. It wasn't."

"You were facing four of them. Could you have gotten them all before one or more of them got you?"

Lindy sighed again and eased against the padded arm of the chair. "Matt, I'm a police officer. We get people upset with us every day. It goes with the territory."

"Bullshit!"

"No, it's not. You just don't understand." Was he ever going to, she began to wonder. The confidence she thought would allow her to make him understand was fading to a small feeling of distress. How could he have been so understanding, so supporting when she needed it and not be so now?

"What I understand," he said through an anger that refused to ebb, "is that you came damn close to dying. And every time something reminds you of it, you fall to pieces. Now, you expect me to understand that suddenly you can take on four men with knives. That's bullshit!"

Her head shook from side to side. "No. It's probably just the thing I needed."

"Needed?" His hand raked savagely through his hair, then arched through the air. "For Christ's sake!"

"Yes," she insisted. "I had no choice but to stand on my own. Don't you see?" She was half pleading now.

He didn't see at all.

"Lindy, I've seen you with your throat slit open. I've seen you disintegrate as you relived the nightmare of that night in Colma. *That's* what I've seen."

Folding her arms across her lower ribs, she looked down. Then she looked up, her eyes studying him. "Matt, I think we have a problem."

"That's an interesting way to put it."

Long seconds passed before she said the words which she refused to allow to become tainted with emotion. "That's all you've really seen of me, isn't it?"

The crease between his brows deepened.

"Isn't it?" she asked again. "Is that what drew you to me?"

"I'm not sure I follow."

"You turned up in my life exactly at the time I needed to lean on someone. And I really did. And I'm especially glad it was you. I'm not sure you're ready for me to stand on my own two feet. I suddenly realized that you don't know what I'm like on my own two feet."

He said nothing, just kept staring.

Taking a hard swallow to keep her emotions down, she continued, "Maybe we just jumped too fast and too hard without really getting to know each other."

He stiffened, bristling at her statement.

Silently, she waited for a response.

It came after a long minute.

It was not what she was expecting.

"Maybe we did," he said icily. In seconds he was gone.

She flinched at the loud slam of the door. The sudden emptiness hit hard . . . like her entire world had been jerked out from beneath her.

"The big shit!" Ally said.

She and Larry had returned after an hour. Both had expected to discover Matt and Lindy recovered from a heated discussion. Instead, they discovered Lindy alone, offering little explanation. Only that Matt was gone.

"Let it go," said Lindy wearily. "If he *is* a big shit, it's best I learn it now."

"Then you're a *dumb* shit," Ally challenged. "You're crazy about that man, and you let him walk right out the door."

"He needs some time," was all Lindy could manage. "I think we both do."

"Easy," Larry said, putting a hand on Ally's shoulder before she could continue. "It's really their business."

Ally gave him a hard scowl.

Gathering his arms around shoulders of his wife and sister, Larry patted them both. "What say I take my two favorite women out to dinner?" Smiling, he looked from one to the other. "After all, it's our last night together for a while. If we try, we can make it a good one."

Smiling at him appreciatively, Lindy pressed her forehead against his cheek. "Of course we can."

Seated at her kitchen table as she had done for so many long nights, Virginia looked at her most recent addition to the collection she'd been compiling from the trash bins behind Edna's house. More packaging from batteries had turned up after her last talk with Officer Munoz. Now she had two hundred and seventy-two in the assorted items of refuse. In her pantry was the result of more than a week of nocturnal pilferings. Four brown grocery bags held every package label she had retrieved, each methodically categorized and diligently labeled with the date it had been recovered. Mostly, she had uncovered indications of every day living.

They don't cook much, she concluded. But then, they weren't the type of women who attracted men by their cooking. The number of soup labels testified to that. The only indications of their efforts at decent nutrition were the different fruit rinds and pits. She thought it strange that the amount of cosmetic wrappings were practically non-existent. Most whores painted themselves up like clowns. Some plastic shampoo bottles, wrappings from soap bars, sanitary napkins. Why no evidence of protection?

My God, she wondered, what were they bringing home? Didn't they believe in protecting themselves? Virginia shuddered. No telling what Edna will pick up from cleaning their toilets after they leave.

Almost gagging at her revelation, Virginia pressed her hand against her chest. A dull pressure had been nagging at her since afternoon. That her stomach churned from an indigestion-like burning, she failed to understand. She hadn't eaten since breakfast. She'd been too tense. She couldn't even finish her bowl of oatmeal. That puzzled her more. A bland breakfast shouldn't torment her insides this way. A tight cramp gripped her left arm. It had been progressively growing numb during the last hour.

She grunted against a building belch and pressed flat another crumpled wrapping. Her eyes strained to read the small lettering.

MODEL ROCKET MINI ENGINE WITH SOLAR IGNITERS.

They didn't make any more sense than the wrappings from digital timers that began turning up a few nights before.

Leaning back in her chair, she attempted to take a deep breath in hopes of easing the nagging pressure in her chest.

"I've got to get some sleep," she said aloud. She looked around at the clock on the oven. Her eyes refused to bring its face into focus. "It must be near dawn. The rest will just have to wait until morning."

Pressing her hands on top of the chair's arms, she began to push. At the effort, she groaned loudly. The lights of the room began suddenly spinning before her eyes. For a few seconds, they continued to dance. Like a galaxy in a motion picture, its planets and stars swirling on the fast forward dial of a projector, their speed increased.

She gasped.

The pressure in her chest throbbed, pressed harder, then exploded.

19

As they followed the specially designed Bomb Squad mobile, Joe grinned from the driver's seat at the man scowling on his right. Answering a woman's frantic call that a bomb had been planted in the kitchen of an insurance office near the Japanese Cultural and Trade Center, they turned left at Van Ness onto Geary and headed west.

Joe had no doubt of the reason behind Matt's irritable mood. An interdepartmental romance was difficult to hide. They'd had their first fight, Joe concluded. He knew both Matt and Lindy well enough to know that Matt's rigidity would eventually lead to a clash with her. He was impetuous. She was cautious. It always lead to conflict, though Joe hadn't expected it quite so soon. Since Matt had arrived at work, Joe had been biting his tongue to keep from razzing Matt over his bad mood. The tactic usually worked. Joe would deliver one barb after another until Matt was forced to admit how ridiculous he appeared. The look on Matt's face when he entered the squadroom that morning had said it all.

He was pissed.

Probably at himself, Joe thought. "Aren't you going to say 'Good morning?'"

"Huh?" Matt asked through his distraction.

Joe laughed. "All you've seemed to have on your mind this morning is to keep from tripping over your bottom lip while you stomped around the office."

Matt turned to Joe and frowned. "Good morning."

"Why, good morning to you," Joe returned. "Having a nice day?"

"Wonderful."

Joe laughed again. Matt's answer had been growled. "I'm so glad to hear it."

"I'm so glad you're so glad."

"I can tell. It's written all over your face."

Matt stared out the window. He could never fool Joe. "Good. I'd really start worrying if I thought you were psychic."

Joe cracked up as he leaned over the wheel. "This must really be love."

Matt's head swung back to Joe. His scowl was as deep as ever. He'd spent the entire previous evening trying to figure out what the hell it really was. After storming out of Lindy's apartment, he'd driven and driven and driven until he realized he was almost out of gas. Only when he'd pulled into the first available gas station was he aware that he subconsciously maneuvered himself toward Stinson Beach where he and Lindy had spent long hours walking along the shore.

More long hours, this time alone, he walked along the beach in another session of sorting out why this particular woman had disrupted his life. Disrupted. A poor word. She'd been an obsession since his first sight of her.

Sometime after midnight, he sat in the chilling breeze coming in from the ocean and concluded that she'd been right. They'd jumped too fast and too hard. They really knew little about each other; and what Matt had come to learn, he had come to like.

Like, hell! He adored her. She had turned out far better than anything he'd fantasized.

She was bright.

She was beautiful.

She was exciting.

She had needed him desperately.

And he was afraid of how it would be if she didn't.

And he'd made a total ass of himself in refusing to listen to her.

She obviously had been willing for both of them to take a hard look at the intense relationship that had engulfed them. That certainly hadn't sounded like sizzle and fizzle on her part. Now, he had his . . .

"Fences to mend?" Joe asked, breaking Matt's trance.

"You *are* a psychic."

Joe laughed again. "Who needs a psychic? You think you fooled any of us yesterday afternoon when that message got to the office? Come on, Matt. We know you too well. You're our resident bachelor." He snickered. "Yeah, I know it's a tough job. But, as they say, someone's got to do it. That puts you in the center ring of our circus. When you charged off duty, everyone of us knew you were headed for trouble."

Matt looked through the windshield at the heavy summer traffic on Geary Boulevard and sighed.

Joe was still grinning. "Want some advice on how to get out of it?"

"I have a feeling I'm going to get it whether I want it or not."

Taking those words as a "yes", Joe began. "First of all, I really don't think you're in trouble. Not with Lindy at any rate. I spent two years, eight hours a day, on patrol with her. You really get to know some-one well that way. She's not one to overreact to a single episode. She's not that shallow. She may be feeling a little disappointed at this moment, but she's not the type to let it get in the way."

"I see," Matt said, strangely feeling Joe's words

taking some of the edge off his mood. "It's nothing flowers and candy can't fix."

Joe's face abruptly went straight. No humor came with his next statement. "Don't try to buy her off. That won't wash with her. If you really want to find out if it can work between the two of you, tell her. If you don't, apologize for flying off the handle and stay out of her life. Hell man, you've been through the ropes before. What did you do then?"

Arching a brow, Matt glanced away. "We played Army."

"Night and day?"

"Night and day," Matt answered as Joe pulled alongside the curb in front of their objective.

Climbing from the car, both stepped into the late morning sun. It was turning into a hot Bay Area day. The detail wagon had arrived first and was parked just ahead. Its presence was beginning to draw a curious crowd. The sidewalk was slowly filling with the rubbernecks, as much a part of visible police investigations as anything.

And there was Paul Lewis with the bomb sniffing dog, Tobias, waiting patiently outside the detail wagon for Matt's direction.

What was *not* there was the lieutenant from Richmond Station, the precinct station charged with physical control of the crime scene. Its officers should have been the first to respond and begin evacuating the building.

"Looks as if we've got a little communication problem," said Joe.

At this, Matt was furious. Stomping up to Lewis, he demanded, "Anybody called Richmond, yet?"

"Hap's doing it right now," returned Lewis, not at all disturbed by his boss' foul humor.

Even Tobias seemed to think nothing amiss. His large black eyes simply looked up at Matt, then idly looked away.

Matt nodded. "Looks like it's up to us." We can get

started with evacuating the building."

Lewis waited until Matt spun around and headed for the building, then grinned as he looked at Joe. "Who peed in his Wheaties?"

"He did," Joe said, laughing as he followed Matt.

Among the businesses listed beside the front door was JOHN WOODS, INDEPENDENT INSURANCE ADJUSTMENT, the name mentioned by the anonymous caller.

Matt leading the way, Joe and two men from the wagon followed him into the building's entrance. Woods' office was the first door on the left. The two men behind Matt and Joe quickly attended to evacuating the other three offices.

A fortyish blonde receptionist sat at a desk directly across from the front door of Woods' office. Looking up, she smiled cheerily as Matt stepped into the office. "Can I help you?"

Matt produced his I.D. "I'm Lieutenant Sloan from the Police Bomb Squad."

She stared incredulously. "Bomb Squad?"

"Yes, ma'am. We just received a call that a bomb was placed in the kitchen area of this office."

"Oh, my God!" shrieked a skinny younger woman, standing in the door of an adjacent room. In her hand dangled an empty Melitta coffee carafe.

The lady at the desk jumped out of her chair. "Bomb Squad? A bomb in our kitchen? W-why I just don't understand how that can be. We've been all over this place since seven-thirty this morning."

"Oh, my God!" the woman at the door shrieked again.

"What is going on?"

Looking to his left, Matt saw a tall stout, balding man in his early fifties and wearing a dark gray pin-striped three piece suit of high quality and a most bewildered expression. "My name is John Woods. What's this about a bomb?"

Trying not to alarm them further, Matt asked,

"Mr. Woods, your office didn't call 911 and report a bomb in it's kitchen?"

"Hell no!"

"Well, sir, most of the time such calls are simply a hoax."

"As I'm sure this is," Woods said irritably but not directing it at Matt. "Though I fail to understand why."

Matt shrugged. "Unfortunately, some people just like to play crude pranks."

"I suppose you're right."

"Just the same, we need to check out the office. It means you and the ladies will have to step outside the building."

The women couldn't move quickly enough as they scurried through the door.

"But I've already made one pot of coffee this morning," groaned the one clutching the carafe.

The receptionist began to collect herself once in the hallway. "Really," she said over her shoulder, "we've been all over this place. Certainly, we'd have already set it off if there really was a bomb here."

Grumbling, Woods shuffled past Matt, Joe and the two men entering the office. "Make it quick, will you?" he said impatiently. "I have an appointment with a client in half an hour."

Once Woods was out of hearing range, Joe leaned toward Matt and whispered, "Another appreciative citizen."

Matt looked around the office and saw a nondescript business establishment. Pale gray carpet and matching walls. Dark veneer furniture covered in a cheap burgundy fabric. Budget decorator prints of irises and callas hung in slim silver-colored metal frames on the walls. The bleakness of the outer office was only broken by an assortment of green plants in ceramic planters along the floor and on top of the receptionist's desk.

"I take it we begin with the kitchen," said Joe.

Matt nodded.

"If you will step aside, Lieutenant," Joe said with pretentious formality, "we shall do our duty."

Ignoring Joe's humor, Matt ambled to his right as Paul Lewis and Tobias followed Joe into the reception area.

"Easy, boy," Lewis softly commanded at moments when Tobias began to appear over eager. Obediently, the animal slowed his actions and continued until Lewis was satisfied that nothing would be yielded from the reception area.

"Paul," said Joe, "try the kitchen."

Lewis nodded and guided Tobias to the small kitchen just off the reception area. The kitchen was inside the first door on the right. Down a short hallway from it were two doors, marked respectively, MEN and WOMEN. Lewis and Tobias went to work again.

Growing impatient after Tobias showed no signs of turning up any evidence of explosives, Matt ambled toward the kitchen and stopped just short of the door. "Anything?" he asked Lewis.

"It's clean in here," came Lewis' reply.

"Just as I figured," said Joe. "That Woods character seems like the type of guy someone would enjoy playing a prank on."

"I agree," said Matt. "Try Woods' private office next," he said, stepping aside for Lewis and Tobias to exit the kitchen.

Clearing the path for the dog and its handler, Joe did the same, moving back from the other side of the door. Crossing his arms over his chest, he leaned against the doorjamb and grinned while Matt shuffled impatiently in the hallway. "Remember," he teased at Matt's stern expression, "it's job security."

One eyebrow arched as Matt looked up and scowled. He was in no mood for this. Too much was weighing on his mind for him to spend his time being jockeyed around by some jerk with an ax to grind.

His eyes focusing behind Matt, Joe's grin widened. "Being in the shit house just seems to come to you naturally."

"Huh?" asked Matt, looking over his shoulder where his eyes were greeted with the white letters: MEN. He looked back to Joe. "You're going to play this for all it's worth, aren't you?"

Joe leaned back his head and laughed while Matt crossed his arms over his chest and absently leaned his shoulder against the door to the men's room.

Without warning, his entire world erupted in a deafening roar.

20

Joe was waiting for her when the elevator doors parted and Lindy, her face saying it all, rushed through. Behind her, Dan Paya calmly but seriously followed.

"Why did you wait so long to call me?" she asked in almost breathless fright.

Clasping his hands on her shoulders, Joe smiled gently and said, "All you could have done was worry."

"You think I'm not worried now?" she gasped.

"Just like I said on the phone, he's going to be fine."

Recognizing that her frenzied state was nothing to present to Matt's bedside, she stopped to steady her breathing. Thirty-five minutes before, Joe had caught up with her at Paya's where she was being tutored in how to change spark plugs in the classic car he'd selected for her. Having seen Ally and Larry off after breakfast, she decided spending the day occupying her mind with something constructive was the best thing. She called Paya, who was glad to hear that she was interested in his help. Afterwards, she drove to Haight Street. They and Delmer spent some time shopping for a small selection of automotive tools.

Then they picked up several cartons of take-out Chinese food and managed to coax Maria away from the shop long enough for lunch. They were good company, and she enjoyed them immensely . . . troubles or no troubles with Matt.

Drawing in a deep breath, she said, "Now, tell me what happened."

Joe took a few seconds to assess if she had calmed down. Her expression was tense but not abnormally so. A light grease smear smudged her right cheek along with the rest of her hands and the pale yellow cotton pullover with its turtleneck, which lately had characterized her wardrobe. Her faded jeans were for dirty work. After her phone was not answered, Joe called Matheson, who suggested the call to Paya. He briefly related the incident to the old Navajo and requested Paya drive Lindy to the hospital. And like the good friend he was, Paya did exactly that.

Seeing her anxiety continue to rise, Joe squeezed her shoulders reassuringly. "We were answering a bomb threat in an insurance office. Matt leaned against a door. There happened to be a bomb after all, and it was the pressure activated type. He was lucky. Only a few cuts. His clothes kept the blast from burning him. Right now, he just can't hear a fart in a jug. The doctors said his hearing should be restored in a few hours . . . tomorrow at the latest. He was only unconscious for a minute . . . more stunned than anything else. They were able to patch him up in the emergency room. As soon as he was settled on the ward, I started looking for you. You could have done nothing but have more time to worry. Remember, you're still recuperating yourself."

Lindy moaned and shook her head. "I suppose I should appreciate that." She sighed and let Joe wrap a brotherly arm around her shoulder. Fighting back the urge to break into tears of relief, she added, "But I feel like kicking your butt."

Laughing, he shook her shoulder. "I can recall a

couple of times in the past you thought of that. Just think of it this way: after yesterday, Matt probably had it coming."

The absurdity of Joe's remark made her laugh. "Is he always that way when he gets upset?"

"You think he was upset yesterday? You should have see him when we pulled that door off him. Yesterday, he was only worried. Today, he was fit to be tied. He didn't stop swearing until the sedative began taking effect. He's a pussy cat now."

Her relief taking hold, she felt the tension ebbing from her chest. "Can I see him?"

"Sure. But make it short."

She nodded. "Okay."

As Joe walked her down the hallway, Lindy kept thinking of the previous afternoon and compared her brief spell of anxiety to the hours Matt had spent before he'd seen her after hearing the radio message. She felt guilty for at least not calling his office and telling him personally about the incident. Her despair over his fury faded into a warm appreciation. Damn, she thought, I should have never opened my mouth about us not really knowing each other. And I should have made that damn call. It would have only taken a minute.

Arriving at the closed door to Matt's room, Joe gave her an *are you ready?* glance, and she nodded. Taking another deep breath, she pushed against the door and quietly entered.

As he and Joe waited, the old Navajo began to chuckle. "Those two are keeping this place in business."

"Yeah," Joe returned. "But I wish they'd quit meeting like this." He shook his head. "He was really lucky."

"How did it happen?"

"It was one of those detonators that's activated by a mercury switch. Apparently, his pressure on the door was just enough to alter the gravity that moved the mercury and activated the switch to the detonator. Whoever placed that bomb intended it to get only one person. Boy, that insurance adjuster was lucky that he'd arrived only about ten minutes before we did and didn't need to use the toilet. Had that thing gone off in his face when he pushed against the door, he'd probably have been blinded and needed his face reconstructed."

Matt was dozing quietly when Lindy approached his bed. She winced as she saw the stitches on his left cheek smeared with an ugly dark yellow ointment. His left shoulder was bandaged with a stained dressing, and part of his upper chest had been shaved to secure the tape. For a few moments she only stood beside the bed and watched, reassuring herself by the slow rise and fall of his chest that he was only sleeping under the effects of a sedative. Finally, his features twisted as his head turned toward her. For a few seconds, he began to grow restless. His head shifted again, and slowly his eyes opened. He stared at a blurred figure beside his bed. His eyes were a green mixture of relief and anxiety when he recognized his visitor.

Instantly, her hand reached for his and held it gently while his lips worked to speak.

"Lindy," he finally managed. "Sorry for being such an ass."

Knowing he couldn't hear her, she smiled and tightened her hand on his as she felt the tears build in her eyes.

He attempted to return the smile, but the movement of his facial muscles stirred the pain and he grimaced. "I really want . . ." He swallowed against the dryness of his throat. " . . . For us to try to work it out."

Gulping the emotion in her throat, she felt her eyes moisten. She reached her free hand into the pocket of her jeans and removed a small turquoise object she then placed into his hand. She watched his eyes strain to identify the small fetish given to her by Paya's grandson. When he finally smiled, she knew he'd recognized the turquoise bear. Closing her hand around his, she lifted it, kissed its back and held it against her wet cheek until he slept.

By the time she stepped back into the hallway, she was composed and smiled at Joe and Paya.

"Well?" asked Joe.

She shrugged. "He's on drugs. It wouldn't be fair of me to hold him to what he said." Seeing Joe's grin, she added with her smile broadening, "But I intend to."

Paya's copper face wrinkled in amusement. "He's in real trouble now."

"Poor bastard doesn't stand a chance," said Joe, beginning to lead them down the hallway. "That'll teach him to upset the great-granddaughter of a Hupa sorceress."

Reaching the elevator, they waited, chatting idly until the doors parted again, and a familiar figure stepped out.

Kowalski was having a rough day. That morning, a three year-old girl had been kidnaped from a shopping cart while her mother had stepped briefly into another aisle in a supermarket. It had been the second that week, the fourth that month. Evidence was pointing to a ring involved in the most hideous of the crimes his office investigated: child pornography. No witnesses, no clues in this particular case. Just another set of outraged and hysterical parents who stood a good chance of their lives being disrupted forever. New thefts of jet engine parts from Alameda Naval Air Station suggested a spin-off of the group, which they'd uncovered in February, continued their endeavors of selling stolen military technology and equipment to the Third World. He had two new agents to orient and still not enough to do the job. And there were no new signs of the local bombers. Hearing about the incident with Matt was another step downhill in a rotten day. He took advantage of the time between briefings and appointments to check on the man he'd grown to appreciate as a professional and as a friend.

"How's Matt doing?" he asked

"He's under sedation," Joe answered. "But he's going to be fine. He'll probably be discharged tomorrow or the day after."

Kowalski nodded in relief, then turned to Lindy and smiled. "Good to see you're looking well. Hate that we meet again in the hospital."

"Tell me about it," she returned.

Realizing that Matt's being asleep was an opportunity for him to take advantage of a moment of relief from the pressures of his day, Kowalski said, "Well, I'll come back when he's able to appreciate visitors. I think I'll grab a cup of coffee down in the vending area before I go back to the office."

He turned as the elevators parted again but was caught by Lindy's voice.

"Tom," she said, stepping away from Joe and Paya. "I want to ask you a question." She led him down the corridor and out of her companions' hearing range. "I want to know what's going on."

Kowalski frowned. "Lindy, we don't have much. And that's on a need to know basis."

Returning the frown, she put her fingers into the neck of her pullover and jerked it down and saw Kowalski cringe at the exposed scars which she would carry for the rest of her life. "Tell me," she all but ordered, "that I don't have a need to know."

He shook his head in defeat. "You can keep it to yourself?"

"Of course."

"All right," he said. Briefly, he gave a verbal sketch of the report he had given Matt the week before while she listened without expression.

When he finished, she asked, "That's all?"

"I'm afraid so."

She wasn't buying it.

"Okay," he conceded. "It should be on the national news this evening. A seven story apartment building in New York City blew up just before noon their time. Luckily, the press hasn't gotten wind that it was from an assortment of bombs that went off while being assembled. Just how many bombs were involved hasn't been determined, but it was enough to bring down most of the building and kill seventeen people we know of so far."

Receiving the news like a true professional, Lindy calmly asked, "What about the people assembling the the bombs?"

"Three women. They went with the explosion. At least that's one less group out of the five we're trying to locate. Plus New York we've got Chicago, Boston and San Francisco identified."

Slipping into a moment of silent thought, she leaned against the wall. "The man murdered in Pacifica last week?"

Kowalski nodded. "It was the ladies. Same fingerprints and hair samples. The only thing that turned up missing was his antenna tuner."

Another moment of silent thought passed before she said, "You know, somewhere they are leaving us clues. We're just not seeing them or recognizing them."

"That's the way it usually is."

Lindy stared out the window as Paya manipulated his pickup truck through the heavy traffic up Potrero Avenue. She kept thinking about her last words with Kowalski. Clues. Probably in plain sight. And no one recognizing them. Someone must have seen them, possibly be suspicious of them. She frowned at all of the secrecy. Protect the public. Protecting involved sparing them from mental anguish. If the public became aware that a plan was in the making to set off bombs in five major cities in this country, the panic would be monumental. Realizing that the law had had more than three weeks without being able to locate even one of the cities' groups, the public would be outraged. If the bombs were to go off as planned, it would be pandemonium. If the public were informed, there wouldn't be enough man hours to follow leads that went to nowhere.

The humid heat of late afternoon intensified the frustrations of those on the street. Horns blared. Tires screeched. Pedestrians raced down the sidewalks to retreat into air-conditioned buildings. Tension was contagious. Lindy felt its steel claws groping for her.

"What are you thinking about, Lindy?" Paya asked.

Startled, she looked around. They were at a red light. He looked half amused at her mental absorption. She realized that he must be thinking of her and Matt.

She smiled. "Did you ever go hunting?"

The question surprised him. "Me? Go hunting? A Navajo?" He chuckled.

"I'm serious."

His shoulders began to shake as his laughter rose.

"I realize it's a dumb question."

"Yes, I went hunting. Until I went into the Marines, I went hunting every day."

"Every day?"

The light changed to green. He nodded and eased the truck forward. "My grandmother and I were all that was left of her clan. She had a flock of sheep she tended for a living. It was my job to hunt down the predators . . . you know, coyotes and wolves . . . before they could get to the sheep. The rabbits and deer I shot fed us. I occasionally got a good coyote pelt in the winter. It brought in some extra money. I probably could have made a good living hunting if my grandmother hadn't insisted I go to school. But if I hadn't been able to read and write English, I would have never been selected for the Marines. What brought up that subject?"

"Just curious. Let me ask you this. What technique did you use?"

"The one that worked. At times, I found a trail and followed it. Other times, I waited along a trail for the animal to come that way again. Every living thing is a creature of habit . . . establishes patterns as it moves through life unless it's desperate or frightened. Same way with people. When the balance in one's life is broken, a person often becomes desperate or frightened. Then they can hurt each other . . . break laws. And then you, the police, become the hunters." Glancing at her, he grinned. "I guess you prefer the term investigators."

She shrugged. "I prefer stopping people from hurting others." Looking out the window, she stared blankly at the passing scenery. "Most of the time it seems to work. Other times, it seems hopeless. Like when trails turn cold or when it keeps on being the same crime but by a different person. Or when we keep passing back and forth over a trail and see nothing when all the time the clues have been right under our noses. Those are usually the hardest to see. Even with all the advancement in forensic science, there are times when there seem to be no clues at all."

"There are always clues, Lindy. You must learn to read them better. Science has no instincts, no gut feelings that something is there."

Looking back at Paya, she smiled. "Like how you picked up on those transmissions? Venison jerky in June. It only took those few words to raise your curiosity."

His eyes scintillated in sudden awareness. "So that's what's on your mind."

"It's hard lately to think about much else."

He grinned. "But what about Matt?"

"That's another matter entirely."

"He would be good for you."

"We'll see."

"I have seen it since the beginning. Since the day you took me to him. He wants you, Lindy. And you want him."

Looking down into her lap, she saw her hands gripping her thighs. "Yes, I do."

Paya laughed. "Then don't worry about it. Everything will be fine."

She looked up and smiled warmly. "You're very good at picking up clues."

"It's part of my heritage."

"It seems to give you an edge most of us lack."

"It's part of your heritage, too."

Frowning lightly, she asked, "How do you mean?'

"To understand the balance of life and recognize the smallest signs of change and to learn how to respond to them. Some changes are good . . . make life better. Some are bad. And sometimes, the smallest signs bring the biggest changes."

She gazed out the window for a few seconds. "Our only pattern has been the transmissions. Do you think they could still be sending them?"

"Could be," he answered. "Or could be that's what they want you to think. To tie up manpower that could be used better. I still listen. I haven't picked up anything. If they're still transmitting, they've established a new pattern that no one has figured out."

Continuing to watch the passing sights, Lindy muttered, "A new pattern and new clues. And no one is seeing them."

Sitting cross legged on her living room floor, Lindy stretched the stiff muscles in her back and looked again at the three by five inch note cards spread before her. She should be trying to get some sleep. It was almost eleven, and her body was telling her that it was still on the mend. Her mind paid no attention. It was absorbed in the thoughts stirred by her conversation with Paya.

Patterns.

Clues.

All telling only that a small group of women were highly trained and had a fanatical determination to render death and destruction.

The patterns had ceased. There must be new ones with a new set of clues.

Climbing to her feet, she shook her head to clear the mental numbness brought by uninterrupted hours of heavy thinking. After stretching her back again, she strode into the kitchen, filled a glass from the tap and took a long, cool drink. Refilling her glass, she returned to her notecards, knelt before then and, for another time, carefully read them over.

Subjects: Five parties. One known to be of Mideastern origin. Highly trained in terrorist activities. Fanatical.

Objective: Planting explosives.

Locations: SF, Chicago, Boston, NY City and one unidentified city in the eastern U.S.

Her note: *Common denominator?*

Transmissions: Coded. During ionispheric skip. After dark.

Nothing raised its head.

Beside her notes lay the front page article about the death of the man in Pacifica. Kowalski had confirmed the missing antenna tuner. The ladies needed it to transmit. They must still be doing it. But when? Paya had picked up nothing as he had continued to monitor.

"Something's there," she said aloud."I'm just not seeing it."

Settling on the floor, she carefully read and reread the notes and articles.

Think, she commanded herself. Something just slightly out of place.

Again, she read the notes and articles.

And she read them again and again until something slowly began to emerge from the depths of her conscious.

"Of course!"

Jumping to her feet, she raced back to the kitchen, grabbed the telephone and punched out Paya's number. He answered after three rings.

"Dan," she said impatiently, "I know it's late."

"That's okay," he returned warily. "What's the matter? It's almost midnight. You should be getting your rest."

"I just need to ask you a question. The skip? It's only at night?"

"On forty meters."

"And?"

"Hams can also operate on twenty meters during daylight hours."

"Then that's where they are! The ladies are still transmitting but during the day."

He chuckled. "Could be. I'll check the band in the morning."

"Thanks."

"Hello."

"Mr. Thompkins?"

"Speaking."

"Mr. Thompkins, this is Inspector Hansen of the San Francisco Police. I'm sorry to bother you so early in the morning."

"That's quite all right. I take it you're calling about Arnie? Have you caught the person who killed him?"

"I'm, afraid not yet, sir. But I need to ask you a few questions."

"Of course."

"Mr. Riley's son mentioned something about your picking up Mr. Riley's call letters after he failed to respond to your call. What can you tell me about it?"

"Well, I always talked to Arnie on Thursday mornings at six o'clock sharp. After he didn't respond to my signal, I was really worried. But you know how you keep telling yourself there's always a reason and don't panic?"

"I understand."

"So I fiddled around on the other bands for a while, thinking of trying to contact him again. After a couple of contacts with some other old radio pals. I was tuning through the twenty meter band. That's where I suddenly heard his call letters being transmitted. That was around eight-thirty. I tried for another response, but the message just kept being repeated. I thought maybe he didn't hear my call, but he was being answered by another. In fact, two or three more answers came to his call.

"Mr. Riley's son said you thought something was amiss in the message. Can you tell me what it was?"

"Sure. It was the RST signal report."

"RST?"

"Readability, strength and tone. You're not a ham operator, I take it."

"No, sir."

"Okay, I'll be as simple as I can. Readability, strength and tone. Each has a numerical designator.. A transmitting ham gives three numbers to tell the party on the other end how well the message is being received. The first time the numbers went out, I thought it was just a mistake. Someone getting sloppy or maybe just an operator who's rusty. But each time, the numbers were the same. Seven-three-seven."

"What about the numbers alerted you?"

"The first one. The one for readability. It only has a rating from one through five."

"Could you possibly remember the exact frequency?"

"You know, I just happened to have written it in my log. Can you hang on while I get it?"

"Yes, sir."

Crossing her fingers, Lindy waited the few but long moments until Thompkins was back on the line.

"You still there, Inspector Hansen?"

"Yes, sir."

"Do you have a paper and pencil just in case the numbers mean anything?"

"I do."

"OK, here it comes. The frequency on twenty

meters was 14.065 mHz. Got that?"

"14.065 on twenty meters. and the RST?"

"Seven-three-seven. If it turns out to be something, you will let me know?"

"You bet, Mr. Thompkins."

"Anything yet?" Lindy asked Paya an hour later.

Immediately after her call to Thompkins, she had called Paya and given him the frequency and RST before showering and grabbing a quick breakfast. When she arrived, he was still listening on twenty meters at 14.065 mHz. Behind him, Delmer made an antsy pace.

Paya shook his head and continued monitoring as Delmer asked anxiously, "Lindy, you're not going to try to go out to look for them again?"

She shook her head, but who was she fooling? Not Delmer from the look in his eyes. Finally, she smiled. "I won't make the same mistake again."

"Grandpa," he said, fretfully, "tell her not to."

"Shhh," she said, laying an arm around his shoulder. "Let your grandpa listen."

"How can you say that after what happened to Chris and you?"

Paya ignored him and continued to listen as Delmer moaned while Lindy continued her reassuring pat to his shoulder. But her efforts to ease his worries failed. He continued his distraught pleas.

This was always the hard part. The waiting, the anticipation. She was good at waiting. While some might succumb to rising tension, Lindy had learned to use such a time for mental preparation. Any second, she expected Paya to turn and announce that the ladies were on the air. What then? Inform Kowalski of her discovery immediately, of course. Then what? How many were going to die from repeated attempts to subdue the ladies? Too many lives had already been lost. Somewhere out there they were just as prepared and just as deadly as before.

Think, she ordered herself. What would she do if she found them again?

What did she do the first time?

What she did was let one distract her while the other was prepared to take advantage of the moment. It had been that way at the Presidio, too. Three agents had located the transmitter and were slain by the other, posted obscurely to observe for interference and be ready to strike if it came.

Another pattern.

That was probably how they moved. It was a pattern, which would distinguish them from any other pair of women moving along the street. As one's attention was absorbed, the other maintained a careful watch of their surroundings. It usually wasn't that way with women. They always seemed to have together, exchanging gossip, sharing their little secrets, mutually admiring or criticizing whatever or whomever intrigued them.

Yes, that was how women generally moved.

But not the ladies.

And where?

Golden Gate Park, Colma, the Presidio, and Pacifica. And something about them must add up to a pattern.

Now, for how.

How would I get around a city if I were not a native? she wondered. Not driving. Not two foreign wo-women. Too big a chance of being stopped or getting involved in a collision. Then there would be the problem of a driver's license. Too easy to draw attention. They had to be melting into the flow of the city's life.

"Delmer," she said hurriedly, "will you bring me a map of the city? The one you used with Chris."

He moaned again.

"Don't worry," she reassured him gently. "I'm not going anywhere. And bring your short-wave radio and your compass."

He sighed but offered no argument and left for

his bedroom

She looked at Paya. He was still listening. She looked at her watch. Seven minutes before nine.

"Here they are," Delmer announced a few minutes later as he rushed into the room.

"Okay," she said, taking the maps. "Delmer, I want you to tune into the same frequency as your grandfather. Using your compass, stay on the direction of the transmissions until he hears the one he's looking for."

His eyes widened in pure horror.

"I'm only going to locate them on the map. I'm looking for a pattern to the sites they select to transmit. That's all, I promise."

He looked pleadingly at Paya, too absorbed to pay him any attention. Finally, he held out the maps and began occupying himself with the shortwave radio.

Spreading the maps open side by side on the floor, Lindy knelt before them. From her purse, she grabbed a pencil; and while Paya listened and Delmer took his compass' readings, she marked the four sites on the relief and contour map. On the city map, only the park and the Presidio were included. Not exactly the substance to establish a pattern, but it was all that was available.

Carefully, she began to canvass every detail of each site, her mind methodically retracing the events at each. At the park, they had been disturbed by the ingenious curiosity of a teen-age boy. Next, they had selected a site distant from the previous one. Having been discovered the following night, they reacted boldly. That they had overcome two law enforcement officers had driven them into a frenzy. The night at the Presidio was a bolder still cat and mouse game as if they were daring to be discovered. Then came Pacifica. Arnie Riley had been in the newspaper over his battle with his neighbors. His notoriety, as much as his antenna tuner, had been part of their decision to

make him there next target. Again, their actions had
rallied the press. The ladies easily grew intoxicated
with power. Their confidence must grow with each
sip.

A grunt from Paya pierced her concentration.
Lindy looked up to see him motioning to Delmer.

"That it, Grandpa?"

Paya nodded and held up a piece of paper with
three numbers scribbled across: *7 3 7.*

Delmer scrambled to his knees beside Lindy. He
placed the compass on the street map atop the site at
which they presently were. Carefully but quickly, he
rotated the portable short-wave receiver back and
forth until the volume ebbed to its lowest. Turning
the compass, he put the needle on true north and
aligned it with the map's north. After correcting for
magnetic north, he jumped up, grabbed the nearest
straight edge he could lay his hands on . . . a
magazine . . . and took Lindy's pencil.

Within seconds, he leaned back and announced,
"It's coming either three hundred fifty-six to the north
of us or one hundred seventy-six south."

He and Lindy leaned over the map and looked at
the line.

"What do you think?" she asked.

"I think," he answered after a moment of thought,
"that the north is out. The only free space the line
crosses in that direction is the Presidio unless you
think they'd try there again."

Lindy shook her head. "I doubt it."

"Then south, we're looking at Twin Peaks, Glen
Canyon Park or Balboa Park. Those are the only
areas which wouldn't have much interference." Taking a moment to think, he said, "Personally, I'd rule
out Twin Peaks because of the transmitting towers.
They might interfere."

Lindy leaned over the map and closely studied
the other two parks and looked for something to connect them with Golden Gate Park and the Presidio.   It

didn't take long for the connection to jump right off the map.

"That's it," she said.

"Which one?" asked Delmer.

"Either one," she answered, looking again at the broken yellow lines running adjacent to each site. Smiling, she added, "We not only found them, Delmer. We just found what they're up to."

22

Standing in Kowalski's office, Lindy looked across his desk and waited for his response to her discovery that morning. His expression told her nothing. The detailed explanation of her conclusions had brought no response at all.

"Well?" she asked. "Doesn't it make sense?"

"It makes a great deal of sense," he answered, and she realized his lack of expression had been masking deep thought. Then she smiled.

"Have a seat, Lindy. You're supposed to be recuperating, not chasing terrorists. I can just imagine what you're like when you're running on a full tank. And I mean that as a compliment." His finger tapped the map. "This is good investigative thinking."

"Thank you."

He grinned, then his face went sober as he looked again at the map. "A series of bombs exploding in a major city is just the type of antics a terrorist group would employ. The right timing could turn into an economic disruption if our communiting work force was afraid to take the mass transits to their jobs. It would be especially bad in the eastern cities."

Her shoulders slumping heavily, Lindy said, "I'm not even certain those are the targets. What I *am* sure of is that's the way the ladies are getting around and that they're still transmitting. I only suggested the transit systems could be the targets. They're getting familiar enough with them."

"It's a good suggestion."

"What do you think the numbers seven-three-seven have to do with it?"

He paused to study the slip of paper from Paya. "I'm sending them forward. There's a whole fleet of cryptanalysts and decoders back east that will love to get their hands on this." Looking up, he smiled. "What does Mr. Paya think of it? Would it surprise you if I told you I heard he's becoming a small legend with that group?"

"That doesn't surprise me at all," she returned, smiling in her own amusement and appreciation that the Navajo's discovery had piqued such interest. "But he said nothing's ringing his bells right now. He's going to continue listening and will be sure to let you know if it does."

"Please tell him I appreciate that." He turned in his chair and paused again. His smile once more turned somber. "Now what are your theories on Pacifica and Colma? How and why?"

"I guess they'd just took a taxi on those two occasions. Colma, I think, was an effort to displace themselves from the attention drawn by the Cortez boy's death. Then Gary and I came along, and as your report suggested, they seized an opportunity to create a temporary furor. With his previous attention from the press, Riley's murder brought another opportunity." She shrugged. "It fits the profile, doesn't it?"

"Indeed, it does, as does selecting the transit systems as their objective, which must have been planned in the beginning . . . before they even entered the country."

"Why so sure they weren't here in the first place? There must be thousands of people residing in the country of Mid-Eastern origin."

Kowalski nodded. "There are over twenty-five thousand Shi'ite Moslems alone, many unfaltering in their dedication to the Islamic Fundamentalist movement." He paused to see her eyebrows rise. "This morning, I was in a conference call. The incident in New York has made this a bigger priority than ever. Yesterday afternoon, the Chairman of the National Security Council sat down with the heads of all of its subordinate groups around a table. Included was the Director of the CIA, who had some interesting information to share.

"It seems," he said, leaning wearily back in his chair, "that everything's pointing to an extremist faction in Teheran. The mullahs are having their differences of opinion on how to deal with us. The ones in control are more moderate than Khomeini. Their country's in the pits. But that's no secret. It makes them want to be very cooperative with the West. And with the Mid-East split over the events with Iraq, part of the Arab world is very ripe for someone to demonstrate he can become the power many had hoped Saddam Hussein was going to become. If that someone can strike this country in its own back yard, you can just imagine what fervor he could restore."

"And you buy that?"

He shrugged. "Who knows what to buy? Washington is only hoping that if our government doesn't overreact, the fanatics will eventually lose their hold as their country continues to slide. Despite what they call us, they have no objections to holding out their empty palms. Still, there are the old die-hards who insist that we are the Great Satan and must be destroyed." Knowing his next statements would bring a definite reaction from Lindy, he eyed her carefully.

"On the outskirts of Teheran is an immense park call Mazarieh Park. It's closed to the public, and surrounded by electrified barbed wire and guarded by armed guards of a group known as the Baseej. They're an offshoot of the Party of Allah. Their purpose is to train terrorists to spread their Holy War throughout the world. More than two million have received training at that site alone. Each one must be willing to die for their cause in order to be selected. One particular building, originally planned as a three hundred room residence for the future Empress of Farah University for Girls, houses the students. Some are women."

Her eyes bright with understanding, she waited motionlessly for him to continue.

"There's another camp more than twelve hundred miles northwest of Tehran. Beheshtieh. Women are trained there also. And not all are Irani or even Muslims. Some Irish . . . even some Americans if you can believe it . . . have received the same intense training. They've been nicknamed by our sources as the Brides of Death. From what's been demonstrated, it seems a good choice if they are, as is expected, our ladies. Personally, I prefer the term one of my agents came up with. Killing machines."

"I never did care for the term the ladies," Lindy said, after taking a moment to digest what she'd just heard. "Brides of Death, I'll buy."

"You won't get any argument from me on that one." His face split with a broad grin. "You'll never guess who came up with the term the ladies."

"Not in a million years," she said, returning the grin.

"Which reminds me, have you seen Matt today?"

"My next stop."

Kowalski chuckled. "I dropped by during lunch. He was sitting up in bed. His finger was massaging the ringing in his ears while he had the most bewildered expression I've seen in a long time as he stared at a little turquoise bear twisting in his free hand."

"Then, I think I'll get going," she said, rising. She

was instantly tired after all the chaos of recent weeks. The highs and lows had produced more strain than she recalled ever having had in her life. She was grateful that Kowalski was able to spare the time for her to share her discovery. It had brought a sense of accomplishment . . . another step in restoring her confidence. Each little victory helped.

"Where the hell have you been!"

Grinning, Lindy thrust her hands into her jeans pockets, strode into the room and stopped at Matt's bedside. He looked like the caged animal he was probably considering himself. "You still mad at me?"

He growled, then said, "Not about two nights ago. I apologize for that."

Still grinning, she said, "Your sincerity is overwhelming."

Matt shook his head irritably. "Just what in the hell are you doing taking off after those bombers? For Christ's sake, Lindy! You're still on sick leave."

Rocking on the balls of her feet, she answered, "I somehow have the impression that you had a visit late this morning by a couple of Navajos."

"They were worried about you. For some reason they thought I might be able to talk some sense into you."

"You?" She laughed. "All right. After I left Dan, I went to Kowalski's office and passed along what Dan heard this morning. Then I dropped by Lieutenant Walker's office and requested that after one more week I be returned to limited duty. I volunteered to help catch up on reports and whatever administrative matters need attention. He agreed. He actually smiled. And for the last fifteen minutes, I've been taking instructions on how to dress your shoulder and what other attention you require *if* you just happen to find a volunteer to take you home *if* your doctor agreed to discharge you this afternoon. He agreed. But I'm still thinking it over about volunteering. So, unless you can round up another volunteer or prefer to spend another night in this place, I suggest you at least give me a smile."

Matt snorted. "Threats! They usually work." Then he smiled a genuine smile, which was met with equal warmth. "Come here," he said, extending a hand quickly taken, then lifted his arm around her neck and pulled her into his uninjured shoulder. "I really am sorry for yelling at you," he whispered as she kissed his cheek.

She raised her head, her eyes seriously studying his. "I understand that you were scared," she said. "I won't exactly relish the idea of you going out on a bomb call, especially after yesterday. We're going to have to work on that."

Sighing, he nodded.

"There's no point in kidding ourselves," she answered and leaned back. The hand around her neck slid down her arm to take her hand. "There are a great many things about the work we do that can get in the way if we let them. It takes a great deal of effort on both sides to keep that from happening. If we're going to try to work things out, we have to agree on that. You think you'll be able to handle not knowing where I am twenty-four hours a day or my not being able to talk about things when my own superiors insist certain matters be kept within the squad?"

His frown deepened. "I'm not doing a very good job of it so far, am I?"

Her blue eyes softened but held their intent. "We have a whole week before either of us returns to work. By then we should have an idea of how we might go about working things out."

"Is that what you want to do?"

"That's why I came to take you home."

Paya chuckled as Delmer nodded while he listened on the telephone.

Lindy was reassuring Delmer that she now had Matt at her apartment and was about to feed him dinner. After that, she had to change his dressing and give him a dose each of Ampicillin and Darvon. By the time she finished her spiel, Delmer was solidly convinced that she had entirely too much on her hands to be running around hunting for terrorists.

"Oh, and Delmer," she added, "Matt wants to know if you, your grandfather and mother would like to go fishing two days after tomorrow. Since it happens to be the Fourth of July, you can stay at the Marina and have a great view of the fireworks from Crissy Field."

"Yeah!" exclaimed the teen-ager. "You think Matt'll be strong enough to take the boat out?"

Laughing, she answered, "Matt says he'll guide you through every step of sailing."

"Really? He really said that?" Delmer leaned back his head and howled as Paya motioned fo his grandson to give him the phone. "Hey Lindy, Grandpa wants to talk to you."

Paya was still chuckling when he told her, "I'm sending him to the movies with a friend in a few minutes. He's even going to spend the night at his friend's house. If I really had my choice, I'd probably send him to visit his cousins in Arizona for the rest of the summer."

She laughed. "I'll bet."

"So, you and Matt are okay?"

"That we are."

"Good. I'm tired of going the hospital."

Lindy's audible sigh of appreciation came through the telephone. "We really appreciate all you've done. You *are* going to join us on the Fourth of July?"

"We will be happy to."

"Good. We'll talk to you before then."

After the call, after Delmer had left and while Maria was organizing to close her shop, Paya leaned back in his favorite chair to enjoy a brief moment of solitude. The young were a joy to him. Their energy brightened his life. But sometimes their energy drained his. He yawned and rubbed his eyes. Tonight he would rest. No teen-ager in the house. No disruptions to prevent an early and solid night's sleep. Not even the radio, he attempted to convince himself as he glanced at the Collins receiver across the room. He shrugged.

Maybe for a few minutes before Maria closed the shop. Then he would help her with dinner.

Grunting as he pushed himself out of his chair, Paya stomped his aching feet against the floor and waddled to his radio bench. His stubby fingers brought power to the Collins. Still set on twenty meters, the Collins chatted in radio talk while the skip was available. Too tired to join in, he decided only to listen. Perhaps an old friend might come on the band. After adjusting the volume, he returned to his chair, leaned back and closed his eyes while his mind tuned to the electronic chorus.

That he had kept up with his radio was good, he had always thought. In these later years it made particularly good company. He could get involved as much as he desired. It kept alive his pride of those years so long ago. It was good to keep one's pride.

Leaning his head against the back of the chair, he yawned again while the electronic chorus slowly faded into a lullaby. He grunted and wiggled his hips deeper into the chair as his eyelids began to droop.

One after the other, the messages came. Short exchanges passed between friends and strangers around the country.

Until . . .

Instantly, Paya'a eyes opened and stared across the room. Grunting again, he pushed from his chair and trotted to the radio. It was still set on 14.065. Same as that morning. And, same as that morning and so many nights in recent weeks, a familiar exchange of transsions began coming across the band.

23

In his youth he often played a game with himself. Silently, he would step light-footed to see just how far and how long he could go before his presence disrupted the harmony along the mesas and amid the stone statuaries. The game slowly grew to a challenge. By his twelfth summer he could stand among a herd of deer, smell their strong musky scent, watch and listen to the flies buzz around their eyes while the animals acknowledge him with brief, curious stares, then returned to their browsing. He perfected this skill until the birds no longer flew nor the ground animals scurried across the sand and rocks. When he needed an animal to feed him and his grandmother or to remove a predator to her sheep, he used this skill to strike swiftly and silently.

In his nineteenth summer this skill saved his life. His radio useless in the tropical rains of the South Pacific, he carried his messages on foot, stealthily passing by Japanese patrols. They never noticed him.

No one noticed him now. He was only an old man shuffling through the park. The camera, hanging around his neck, and the bag, strapped around his shoulder, gave his presence credibility. Through the Exacta's telelens, he could keep watch without attracting attention.

Paya leaned against the tree and carefully looked across the park. He had not told Lindy how keenly he'd felt her mind working when she announced her suspicions of the targets for the bombs being the mass transits. He was content to have her carry that information to Kowalski, whose attention would sooth her energy. The restless spirits of those who had died by the hand which had attacked her drove her mind passed her physical strength. She was young and had yet to understand how to channel her bonding to those taken before their work was completed. That had been her torment while she knelt in the cemetery and when she looked into the back of her carryall. In those jungles and on those beaches long ago, he'd known the same torment. Not until he had returned and his grandmother had show him how to ease it.

Reaching into his jacket pocket, he felt his prayer stick, through which he had made a pact with his own restless spirits to continue the struggle for *hozhq*, a life governed by health, harmony and balance. He'd seen the commitment to that struggle in Lindy the day she'd arrived with news of the Cortez boy's death. In her blue yes flashed a rage against the disharmony, the *hochxq*, for all that was ugly in the world. *Hochxq* flourished in the absence of that rage, and Paya knew that was what had brought him to this place.

It must be here, he thought. The best place to hide in a city was amid the crowds. Balboa Park was the most active of the three parks in line. Adjacent to the City College of San Francisco, the park was alive with those enjoying the warmth of summer and reprieves from classes. The transmissions the night before came from the same direction as those yesterday morning and again this morning. With their accelerated frequency, he knew they would come again this afternoon. It was a new pattern, and its frequency told him that they were prepared to strike soon.

It was nearing three in the afternoon. He would know within the next two hours.

"Am I right, Doc?" Matheson asked the Medical Examiner.

The bushy white head responded with a nod.

The woman's body on the autopsy table had been discovered on the hill above Baker Beach by a young couple seeking privacy shortly before midnight. Her head lay grotesquely lolled to the side with her neck without support from the wide gash in her throat.

"Just as I thought," Matheson said as he inserted his unlighted cigar between his teeth. "Little Peggy, here, got messed up with a married man according to the people she worked with and was putting the pressure on him to leave his wife. My guess is he tried what he hoped would be a simple solution. I figured it to be a copy cat all along. Now it's just a matter of waiting for the forensic report on the tire tracks. Someone pulled off the road quarter mile from where she was found. The killer erased his footprints, but I'll bet by dinner, I'll be reading . . ." He paused to draw a crumpled yellow sheet from his side pocket. "Mr. Halstead his rights. He's under interrogation right now." He groaned. "Christ, I hope the bastard does us a favor and realizes he doesn't have what it takes to fool us old homicide dicks. They never learn."

The M.E. chuckled. "Were all your cases so simple."

Matheson cackled. "Three out of four of them are." Turning, he yawned. "See ya around, Doc. I think I'll go have some coffee while I wait for news on the tire tracks. On second thought, I probably should give my partner a call just in case she's heard about the latest slashing. Can't say I'd blame her for thinking the ones that attacked her did this. The news of that guy in Pacifica hit her pretty hard."

The M.E. peeled off his latex gloves and nodded to his assistant that he was done. The morgue attendant quickly covered the body and turned off the overhead lights.

"How's she doing?" asked the M.E. as he moved to the sink and began washing his hands.

"She'll be okay," Matheson answered. "You know how the young bounce back. Knowing her, my guess is that she's more upset about not being able to get her hands on this case than anything."

Matheson yawned again as he shuffled toward the telephone and grumbled about his wife allowing him to sleep past noon. After the girls were grown and had moved out on their own, Betty was concerned that he get plenty of rest, especially when he was on an off tour. Trouble was, he was getting used to it. He'd been on the job forty-five minutes and still wasn't feeling awake.

"Good," he mumbled when Lindy's answering mahine told him she was not home. Then he grinned as he realized who was absorbing her thoughts now. Yawning again, he shook his head and was reaching for the door when it abruptly swung his way. "Whoa," he said as the young Hispanic uniormed officer charged through the door.

Matheson recognized him instantly. "How's it going, Munoz?"

"Inspector Matheson," greeted Munoz as he removed his patrol cap and shook his head. "Pardon me. I dropped by to check on a friend."

"Oh, I'm sorry."

Shaking his head, Munoz said, "It's not what it sounds. An older lady from the Mission District. The lady next door, another older woman, found Mrs. Pearson dead yesterday afternoon. Sitting at her kitchen table. Been dead a couple of days from the looks of things."

"Something amiss?"

"No. Looks like natural causes. She was in her

eighties and hasn't been to a doctor in years. Just a
routine coroner's case. But I wanted to make sure." He
shook his head again. "Poor Mrs. Wallace, the neighbor.
She's taking it real hard. They'd been living next door
to each other for forty-seven years. Both had been
widows for a long time and were very close. We had to
call Mrs. Wallace's son who lives over near Sacra-
mento and get him to take her home with him. After
this, I doubt she'll ever live in her house again."

Sensing the distant sadness in Munoz's brown
eyes, Matheson returned, "The two must have meant a
lot to you."

Munoz smiled sadly. "Nice old ladies. It won't be the
same without them." He paused briefly, then laughed
shortly. "I'm really going to miss Edna and her carrot
cake and Virginia and her dildoes."

"Dildoes?" Matheson gaped before dissolving into a
ribald snicker. "Good God!"

Munoz' laughter loosened. "Virginia was a real character. She was convinced that Edna's renters were
prostitutes because the two girls went out every night,
and she dug a bunch of battery packages out of
Edna's garbage. Insisted they were for sexual aids.
Edna declared that Virginia was the neighborhood
busy body. No telling what Virginia thought of the toy
rocket boosters. She had the packages of those spread
out on the table when she was found." He shrugged.
"For radio controlled airplanes, most likely."

Matheson whistled. "Rocket boosters! I wouldn't
mind meeting those two, myself. This old dog just
loves learning new tricks. Rocket boosters? Are you
sure?"

Munoz nodded. "Edna has several great grand-
sons. Probably for gifts."

Matheson snickered. "And those boys must be dyin'
to meet her renters."

"I'm sure they would be, if Virginia's suspicions
were true," Munoz responded. "But Edna inisted that
they're just two young Mexican girls, moved up from

Tucson to work in their aunt's janitorial business. Each night when they go to work, Virginia thought they were going out on the prowl."

"With that imagination of hers, it sounds like Virginia's the one who should've been prowling," Matheson returned with a chuckle, then bent over a deep belly laugh. "Dildoes. That beats all I've heard in quite a spell. I see why you're going to miss them."

Munoz grinned. "I better get going, Inspector. My wife and I are having company for dinner. I have to stop on the way home and and pick up some fresh limes for the margaritas."

"Have a good one," Matheson said, still chuckling over Munoz's account as he left the morgue.

Lowering the telelens, Paya smiled. They were very good, he thought. No one would suspect that the woman, seated on the bench and idly looking through a fashion magazine while she ate an apple, was sentry to the woman who'd quietly slipped behind the bush. Just two young women, dressed in pastel sweat pants and matching jackets over white T-shirts and carrying duffel bags and tennis rackets, as much a natural part of the surroundings as any others. The transmissions began on the twenty meter band of his portable radio receiver shortly after the second woman's head had disappeared behind the bush.

Paya turned off his short-wave radio, inserted it into his bag and very casually strode toward the Balboa Station. He would be ahead of them to avoid their perception that he was following. In the station he purchased a round trip ticket from the machine. Sometime, he would need to return for his truck in the college parking area. Inserting his ticket into the fare gate's slot, he passed through, then retrieved his marked ticket and headed toward the escalator. In the tunnel a crowd was slowly building in wait for the trains, but he spotted an empty bench against the wall where he decided a short rest would be a good idea.

Damn, he thought as he rubbed his thighs. He'd been standing still too long. His legs were beginning to grow numb. Lifting his feet, he worked them back and forth to stimulate the circulation. The movements brought only slight relief. Rising, he began a slow, ambling pace while his eyes assessed the waiting passengers as the crowd steadily grew thicker, obstructing his view of the DOWN escalator. Carefully, he wove through the tight web of waiting passengers until he reached the wall bordering the escalator. Leaning his shoulder against it, he waited.

The arriving train slowed to its approach, drawing the crowd tighter only to press themselves and form channels for the departing passengers. This train was marked, CONCORD/ DALY CITY, the line's last stop. The exchange of passengers took but a few minutes, and the train rolled away. For the first time that afternoon, Paya felt the rising pace of his heartbeat in anticipation. Too many years had passed since he'd stalked a prey, a skill never lost but not kept honed. The tunnel began swelling again with waiting passengers, stretching their necks to peer down the tunnel as if the action would speed the arrival of the next train.

On the bench, where he'd been sitting, two young Hispanic mothers endeavored to quiet three small children, fussing and brooding from the exhaustion of a long summer day. One child, whining and teary-eyed, lay her head in her mother's lap. Another, her delicate face twisted in a pout, slumped against the wall while the third refused to comply with her mother's repeated demands to remain still.

Amid the crowd, a blonde woman spat a string of soft curses as her shopping, stressed from its load and the shoving of the people around her, split and dumped its contents on the tunnel floor. The instant whiff of a woman's floral cologne floated through the tunnel air.

"Oh, no," cried the blonde.

"Giorgio?" a second woman asked.

"It *was*," growled the blonde.

"My favorite."

"Mine, too," the blonde said disappointedly.

Quickly, Paya looked away, smiling at how easy it still was to become distracted by pretty women and their antics. His forefinger slowly tatooed the top of his camera case as he continued to wait.

Another train, its next stop, Glen Park, arrived, exchanged passengers, then left.

Within ten minutes a third train, FREEMONT/ DALY CITY rolled to a stop.

The cycle continued.

Paya waited.

Then he saw them.

Turning to the right as they stepped from the escalator, the two young women with their tote bags and tennis rackets emerged into his view and stopped less than ten feet away. Capturing every possible detail, he slowly moved his eyes past them. Mid-twenties, he estimated them to be with long black hair as so many young ethnic women preferred. They chatted quietly in Spanish with their eyes diverted to their surroundings. But they were not Hispanic. To the casual passer-by, they could easily be taken as such with their dark features and smooth olive complexions. Paya's alert eyes noted the thick, straight brows above their eyes, their noses, straight and regal. Their black eyes held not the shyness characteristic of young Hispanic women.

The eyes were cold.

They moved in deliberate assessment of those around them.

They were *hochxq*.

The crowed stretched and pressed together again as another rumble of noise preceded an approaching train.

Paya slowly drifted away from his objectives.

Increased space decreased awareness of his presence.

RICHMOND/DALY CITY rolled to its stop.

The crowd pressed together to offer tunnels for the departing passengers.

The two women entered the train and settled into adjacent seats, facing forward and easily visible from the adjoining train where Paya entered. He took one of the longer seats parallel to the side and kept the women in his vision.

The train began to roll.

The ride to Glen Park took three minutes.

The women remained in their seats as the pasengers departed and others entered.

The ride to Twenty-Fourth and Mission lasted six minutes.

More passengers left, others began to enter.

The two women climbed from their seats.

Paya pushed to his feet. The entering passengers pressed against him as he made his way from the train. Once in the tunnel, he was closer to the ascending escalator. Flowing with the crowd, he made his way up and into the station. The women no longer in his sight, he felt his heartbeat quicken. He could not lose them now, but if he turned, the possibility of alerting them was vivid. Calmly, he passed through the gate and headed toward the station's doors and up to the sidewalk.

Pausing briefly, he quickly looked around and spotted a newsstand. He dug into his pocket for change as he approached the metal structure. The action of purchasing a newspaper gave him the opportunity to turn.

The women had been behind him. Now moving swiftly but easily, they climbed the steps from the station and headed north on Mission and through the teeming barrio.

24

A thick haze of fog had replaced twilight as they arrived at the Marina. Lindy had driven in silent regard for Matt's injured shoulder, which had aggravated him less and less as the day had passed. Climbing from her car, neither spoke until they had stepped onto the sailboat's deck. There, she looked around and inhaled a deep breath.

"Something about the sea always smells so clean," she said, looking out into the density of the fog. "It must be the breeze. One always seems to be coming in from the ocean." An amused smile spread across her features as she turned to face him. "No wonder it's important to have it so much in your life. Like a cleanser for all the contamination you see so much of every day."

"That's a good way to describe it," he said, stepping beside her, and both stared into the floating mist. "A very good way though I really never thought of it quite like that."

"So, how have you thought of it?"

He shrugged. "Just as a change, I guess. Another rat race to replace the one at work."

"Rat race?" she asked, laughing. "This? It's so quiet."

"Not always. You haven't heard one group or another throwing a bash on one of these boats. Especially on weekends. And especially when I'm trying to get some sleep. They'll really start rolling around tomorrow evening. Individual parties grow into one large party as people hop from boat to boat."

"Oh, that's right," she said, suddenly aware. "The day after that's the Fourth of July. The days have really been running into each other lately." With a quiescent laugh she shook her head. "This day has really been something. I can't remember sleeping so long without an interruption. And with so much rest, I seem to have so little motivation. I've rather enjoyed spending a day doing nothing."

"Nothing? Every time I've opened my eyes during the past twenty-four hours, you've been changing my dressing, popping a couple of pills down my throat or encouraging me to eat and drink. I haven't had a woman pay me so much attention since I had the chickenpox in the first grade. I don't call that nothing."

"What *do* you call it?" she asked, turning her face up to his. All the lights in the Marina had found a stage to dance in her eyes.

He smiled. "Nice."

She looked back across the bay, and he saw her also smile.

"Good," she said. "It was nice for me."

Now, he really felt as if they were starting. His hand reached out and softly gathered hers, then held it between them. In serene acceptance of his overture, her thumb slid along his knuckles.

"Lindy," he whispered, "I want you."

Her hand gently squeezed his. Her head bowed, and he heard her thick swallow.

"And I want you," she whispered back, allowing him to pull her softly into the hollow of his uninjured shoulder.

His hand moved up her spine to cradle her head and felt the cool mist settling in her hair. Resting his cheek against the top of her head, he smiled as her arms slipped under his jacket and slowly encircled his waist.

"You sure?" he asked.

Against his shoulder, her head nodded. Her arms tightened. Her hands crept up his back.

"I'm sure," she said against his neck. "And this time, it's for no other reason than simply that I want you."

All the tension, which had plagued him since the argument, which now seemed so senseless, evaporated under her words. She wanted him, and was not afraid to say or live it.

A rush of capricious elation flooded through him, and he felt her arms tightening as he relaxed. As his hand lowered for his arm to envelop her shoulder, she lifted her head. Her lips were lightly parted as they met his in a fusion that was as slow and lingering as the drifting fog. Nothing, not the sounds of the Marina with the distant, chattering occupants from its many berths and the noises of land and water traffic or the signals directing it, could ebb the rising tide of passion pressing them together. They were oblivious to anything but their mutual desires. Embraces tightened. Cravings mounted unchecked until her hands crept upward and made contact with his maligned left shoulder. Instantly, he winced against her lips.

"Sorry," she said. Pulling back, she appraised the regret in his eyes of their broken spell. Her forehead leaned into the hollow of his throat. "I believe," she said, slightly giggling at the idea, "that you're going to have to leave this to me."

Easing from his embrace, she took his right hand and led him below deck.

Unable to remove his eyes from hers, Matt sat on the edge of the bed and surrendered control of the moment. She stood before him and smiled for quiet seconds, then crossed her arms and pulled her sweater over her head and tossed it aside. With a shy smile of anticipation, his eyes combed every inch of skin as it was revealed. Next, her fingers freed the small hooked front closure of her beige transparent brassiere, exposing her full firm breasts as the undergarment parted and slid from her shoulders. The snap of her jeans released loudly as did the zipper, and one graceful movement swept away her remaining clothing. Kicking aside her sandals, she stepped between his parted thighs, wrapped her hands around the sides of his head and pulled his face against her breasts. Hungrily, he savored the offered morsels of flesh, suckled and teased the crests into twin pink pebbles. His right hand eased up a velvet expanse of hip, then down the taut plane of her abdomen.

Above his head, she closed her eyes and spread her fingers through his hair while relishing the feel of his fingers moving between her legs and probing an entry, then slipping easily inside her moistening warmth.

"You're supposed to be leaving this to me," she said, laughing tightly as she sensed she was near to losing control.

"How can I?" he asked hoarsely. "My shoulder may be incapacitated at the moment, but another part of me is about to explode."

She giggled impishly and gently pushed him away. He moaned but compelled himself to retreat while her fingers nimbly worked free his shirt buttons. The first sleeve came off readily as she worked it over his right shoulder. The left she tugged gently over the bulky dressing. Her eyes softened with tenderness as it came into view. Leaning over, she brushed her lips against the bandage as she freed his arm from its sleeve.

Without a word, she pressed her palm against his

breastbone and pressed him slowly back onto the sheets. Her lips found the hollow of his throat and nibbled it in languid distraction from the work of her hands, unthreading his belt buckle. As her hands progressed, so did her lips, working, nibbling their way downward until they were greeted by the now freed, swollen length of heated male flesh, rising from its confinement. She bent and laid her lips over the tip. It twitched slightly, then she teased it with the circling of her tongue.

From above, he stared, mesmerized, holding his breath, holding the moments, while she continued her adoration. Her hands slowly completed undressing him. Her lips, her cheeks brushed softly, nurturing, cherishing the entire surface of his length until her hands were completed with their task and were freed for another. Then, one hand slid under his soft pouch and fondled it while the other curled around his hardness and guided it between her lips. Her head began to move back and forth, taking more and more of him until his low grunts signaled the nearing of his climax.

Subtly, she rose and stretched over him. Her knees beside his hips, she reached down and wrapped her fingers around his tormented, waiting muscle and lowered herself onto it, her eyes flaring with languorous rapture as he filled her.

"Have I ever told you," she asked huskily as she leaned over and propped her elbows beside his head, "how wonderful it feels to have you inside of me?"

"It's wonderful being there," he managed to say as his need to release continued to swell.

Her head bent down to flick her tongue against his ear, and her hips began a slow gyration. Until this second, he'd never realized that their unions before had been so much a mutual devouring of each other. Flesh slamming against flesh. Two people desperately driving to rid themselves of their separate torments instead of two people making love.

And that was what they were doing now.

Loving, sharing, giving.

She continued moving over him, around him. Raining light tender kisses over his face, his neck, she was giving him more pleasure than he'd ever imagined could be experienced. Never had such tenderness been brought to him. It was strange and delightful. So sweet, it was frightening, but only from the notion that refused to leave the back of his mind. He'd almost lost her twice. Once had been from his own stupidity. He'd never, never make that kind of mistake again. But before that it had been from her work. That would be his greatest challenge . . . knowing that every day she would leave him to face another chance of being taken away from him. With that, he reached and pulled her hard against him just as his release exploded. He clung tightly, carrying her along the drifting tide and listening to her low squeals of delight telling him her pleasure was coming from giving pleasure to him.

For long moments, they lay there. Limbs entwined. Passion-moist bodies welded together. Stroking each other. Moaning low sighs of satisfaction. Hanging on for as long as possible to the sensation that nothing else in the world existed.

Her palm opened against his chest, her fingers laced in the crisp dark hairs, she felt the thundering of his heart slowly fade to a normal rhythm. Suddenly, she snickered.

"Something funny?" he asked.

She nodded. "Your expression just before you came. Your eyes get glassy, your face turns purple, the veins stand out in your neck until you look as if you're about to have a heart attack. And you expect me to believe you live and breathe for such a moment."

"But I do," he returned, chuckling. "Believe me, it doesn't look that way from my side."

"That's a relief," she said, her laughter rising. "I'd

hate to think I bumped you off."

His finger slid under her chin and lifted her face. His eyes lit with amusement. "I'd die a happy man."

Gently, she tugged the hairs on his breastbone. "Don't you dare. I'm far from through with you."

Smiling, he returned, "You'd better believe it. Now," he said, shifting her position, "speaking of not through, it's your turn."

"How nice of you to think of it, kind sir," she said, setting herself upright. Grinning, she added, "I shall gladly return the reins to you."

"Come here," he said, pulling her back over him. He nuzzled one breast, then the other as they loomed over his face.

As his lips captured a pink tip, his hand slipped down to their adjoined nests where his fingers discovered her still hot and moist. She moaned deeply as he went to work, moving his finger tips across the hot satin surrounding the small tumescence from which her pleasure would ignite. Stroking her into the inarticulate lament of increasing hunger for all he could give, he was conscious of only her muffled sighs of building delight until he sensed her abrupt stiffening. Only then, was he aware of the ringing telephone followed by the garbled words being picked up by the recorder.

"Forget it," he ordered, seeing the misty cloud of his labors lift from her eyes.

She tried but could not. Little words in the message were piercing her sweet nirvana of joy. Looking down into his eyes, she saw that Matt's spell was also falling to the message being recorded.

It was Joe's voice, hurried and intense.

". . . Maria Sawyer called . . . Please call her as soon as possible . . . Dan Paya . . . not come home . . ."

"Oh no," Lindy said, lifting herself free. "Please, Matt."

He didn't argue. Stiffly, he climbed from the bed, reached for the phone, and anxiously punched the number to the squadroom.

Unable to take her eyes from Matt's face as he listened, Lindy rose from the bed and stood beside him. For a few short, tense minutes, the conversation was one-sided with Matt nodding and grunting to the information coming from the telephone. The minutes were agonizing. His mounting concern over the message he was receiving deepened the lines in his face and added to her building alarm.

Finally, she could stand there no more and snatched her clothes. By the time she had donned her jeans and sandals and was pulling her brassiere into place, she heard Matt's angry curse as he was returning the telephone to its cradle.

"What is it?" she asked, pulling her sweater over her head.

Wasting not a second, he drew his shirt over his damaged shoulder.

"Dan's daughter called the squadroom for them to call me. He left home to do some errands early this afternoon. He hasn't returned home. Maria thought he might have dropped by your place or mine for a visit."

"I got that," she said impatiently. "What else? Has Dan been in an accident? His health? He's been ignoring the doctors' advice about having surgery."

Leaving the shirt buttons, he pulled on his shorts. His expression grew darker as he continued. "Joe said the squad and every bomb squad in the area has been called in." He looked up, indicating irritation over what he had just been told. "The messages you found out about yesterday? The seven-three-seven?"

She realized that he was agitated that she had not mentioned it, but the subject had not risen. Why should it have? She had put everything aside for the sake of the man now struggling with his trousers.

"Sorry," she said meekly.

"Well, it seems that the cryptanalysts in Langley have decided that the three numbers refer to a day and time. July third. Seven o'clock. And they went along with your theory that the targets are the transit systems." Picking up his watch, he looked at the time. His scowl deepened. "It's nine thirty-four. Shit!" He pulled the time piece over his left wrist. "That leaves nine hours to search seventy-one miles of the BART's tunnels."

"But Matt, you're in no shape to be going out with the squad."

"I'm not going out with the squad," he said, reaching for his shoes. "We're going to look for Dan."

The realization hit her like a bolt of lightning.

"You don't think . . . ?"

"I *do* think. He's a crafty old devil. I have no doubt that he could have figured out the significance of those numbers just as well as anyone else. After all, he's the one who first stumbled onto this."

"But what if he finds those two?" She couldn't bring herself to say the ladies. "What do you think he would do?"

On his feet, he shrugged. "Let's just hope he doesn't." Stepping to the closet, Matt pulled his revolver from the cross holster hanging on the inside of the door. Unable to pull the holster over his injured shoulder, he stuffed the pistol into his waistband. "Got your gun?"

She nodded.

"Good. You drive. Now, do you have any idea as to just where we begin?"

Wearily, she nodded.

25

On her twelfth birthday two monumental events had taken place and had sealed her destiny. The first had come when she awoke that morning and discovered the sign that she had become a woman. It had bothered her greatly that her sister, a year younger, had entered womanhood four months earlier and was elated over the energetic planning by their mother to arrange a proper union which would make her among the blessed in the Faith. Nothing could make a woman more blessed than to assume the role of wife and mother.

"Don't worry, Kara," her mother had promised to ease a daughter's torment. "Greater plans have been made for you. Wait and see."

"But I am worthless," the young girl wailed.

"No. No," her mother reassured, taking the crying girl in her arms and wiping her tears. "Have faith, child." Smiling, she stroked Kara's dark, glossy hair and hugged her distressed child tighter. "Just remember," she said sweetly, "this is a very special day for us all. He is returning. Through him we will receive the supreme guidance to purify the Faith to which the infidels have brought so much contamination. That you have become a woman on so special a day must be a symbol of something divine."

Cradle against her mother, Kara sniffed back her tears and looked up hopefully.

"But how will I know?" she asked. "How will I know if there is a greater plan for me?"

"You will," said the mother gently. "When the time comes, you will know. Remember, you must have faith."

And on that February afternoon when her mother held her hand and pushed their way through the black-clad throng chanting in welcome adoration, Kara stretched to catch a view of the man whose teachings had inflamed millions.

Moving through a path cleared by heavy guards, he raised his hand in greeting of the faithful. Looking to one side then the other, he nodded in satisfied acknowledgment of their desire to restore the fundamentalist beliefs. That they had no concern for each other did not trouble him. Nor was he distressed that some were being injured, even trampled, in their frenzied desire to welcome him. He was most pleased that they were demonstrating the fervor to revitalize the Faith and spread it throughout the world.

Drawn into the mounting hysteria, Kara began to chant and wail, to lift her arms in salute. Her young voice rose in a shrilly cry along with the multitude. And when his eyes drifted among the faithful, she knew they paused to settle on her. His faint smile seemed to widen as his eyes met hers. And again, the tears stained her cheeks. But these tears were of joy. Her heart began a heavy hammering beneath unblossomed breasts. She cried harder; and as his eyes moved on, she heard her own scream before she collapsed.

Not until four months later had she come to know just what her blessing would be.

"You have been chosen," the old mullah said to her after her father had sent for her to be presented, "for a role for which most of our young women could never aspire." Gently, he took her hand in his and revealed a most magnificent tale.

"When the Great Prophet left us to go on his *me'eraj*, he entrusted the Faith to the care of his son-in-law, Ali. In turn, the Faith was passed to his son, Husayn ibin' Ali, whom the unfaithful slaughtered at Karbala. Avenging his death became the role of the most pure, the young virgins who from then on became daughters of this Prince of Martyrs. A special place in Paradise awaits them, and they will spend eternity married to the most perfect of young men.

"Our Faith has suffered much. Many of the Faithful are still being slaughtered by the infidels. Their souls cry for vengeance. My child, would you be willing to venture forth on this hallowed road to ease their cries?"

"Oh yes!" she gasped. "I would be so honored."

"Good," he said, his eyes shining in triumph. "It will take much dedication on your part. You must spend years in preparation before you are ready to begin training for your *me'eraj*."

"But I am ready now!"

He laughed. "Patience, my child. The time will come."

Now, Kara sat in the small apartment of the house on Twentieth Street and was breathless in her excitement. The time is now, she thought as she admired the photograph of another who had been blessed. That one had begun her *me'eraj* the day she drove a truck load of dynamite into an Israeli post in the south of Lebanon and killed twelve of their soldiers. The Great Redeemer, himself, had blessed her family in person.

Kara had been eighteen when she learned of the event. The joy of those, who'd spent years in train-

ing for such a moment, was immeasurable. It was the
same year that she had met Almira, another of the
blessed, who now sat on the other bed and was also
loading 9mm rounds into another Uzi's clip.

Five years before, part of the plan which would give
them eternity had been revealed to them. On that day
thirty-four of the blessed had been summoned into a
classroom at Manzarieh and informed that their role
in spreading the revolution had been decided. More
years would pass before they were ready. Each would
become proficient in Spanish, learn the cultures of
Puerto Rico or of the Hispanics of the Great Satan's
Southwest and learn flawless English. They would
master the forms of hand to hand fighting and explosives. They would learn to communicate through
the radio waves. Kara and Almira had the supreme
honor of directing the plan since the atmosphere permitted that only from the west could one transmission
be received by all at the same time. When they were
ready, they would live for a while in Puerto Rico or
the Southwest to further their studies of the cultures.
Then they would travel to their assigned cities. For
five long years, they prepared and of the thirty-four,
sixteen were selected. Only then were they informed
of the part they would play in bringing the Great
Satan to its knees.

For Kara the new training had been a delightful
change from the years spent in daily classroom lec-
tures where they had received instruction in the Faith
and in the decadence of those who sought to contam-
inate it. Years of isolation kept their minds pure as
they studied and transformed themselves into the
elite. When they finally left the beautiful world of
Manzarieh, their eyes opened to a world as decadent
as they had been taught it would be.

In the last seven months, Kara had been appalled by
the evil in the everyday lives of those who accepted
and lived the way of the Great Satan. Years of intense
indoctrination taught her to see how readily they

agreed to follow the paths of violence and destruction. Where she believed killing to be for holy purification, these infidels killed for no other reasons than selfish greed. Their women exposed themselves like whores. Both sexes flagrantly flaunted themselves at each other. They filled their bodies with the poisons of drug and drink. They spurned holiness. They deserved to be purged from the earth.

And, she now thought as she smiled pensively, she was playing an important role in the purification.

"Almira," she said as she reached for another empty clip and began loading it, "before we go, do you have any regrets?"

Almira frowned. "What do you mean?" Unlike Kara, who received her energy and purpose through her totally idealistic view of life, Almira was driven by rage, by the need for power and had seen being one of the blessed as the means of fulfillment.

"I have but two regrets. One is for our sisters who failed," Kara said, referring to their accident as they had been assembling the explosives in New York. "The other is that our Great Redeemer is no longer in this world to give his blessing to my family."

Almira's head snapped up, her black eyes flashing.

"Remember the comfort he brought you after your family was killed when the infidels shot down that plane?" Kara asked.

"I remember," came the icy reply. "He said I would be blessed with the opportunity to avenge them. "And," she said, lifting the Uzi and shaking it triumphantly, "I shall soon be. My only regret is that the infidel whore still lives."

Their final clips filled, both rose from their beds and spread open the mouths to the black canvas tote bags. Silently, they each inserted one dozen of the filled clips. Last went a loaded Uzi, its silencer attached to the end.

Around them, the air grew tense as each mentally replayed the plan.

For the last two weeks, they had carefully planted the explosives, each timed for the specified hour, the hour they had sent through the air waves each morning and afternoon since ending the nightly transmissions. Tonight, they would be there in the tunnels to guard against interference with their plan.

As she pulled on her beige summer coat and looked around the room, Kara wondered if this would be the last she would see of it. If they failed and survived, they must return and collect what was required to move to another location and eventually work their way home to begin another plan. Their skills were too valuable to waste.

But if they succeeded, it would be no waste at all.

"Well, Luisa," Kara said, smiling. "Are you ready?"

"I am ready, Rosa," Almira said, also smiling.

They clasped hands, then left their stronghold of the last three months and stepped onto the sidewalk leading to their *me'eraj*. As they moved, they continued their subdued scrutiny of their surroundings. Carefully, they watched as they advanced through the night's floating vapor. Crossing Dolores Street, they emerged from the quiet of the residential area into the parlayed commotion, rising from the Mission District and its barrio. The sidewalk began to fill with boisterous clamor. The music of Latino mingled with rock. Language consolidated in a vibrating staccato, assaulting the ears of those scurrying to seek secure havens.

Heads subdued but eyes ever watching, they crossed Guerrero Street where the ambling crowd grew thicker. They watched but failed to notice the staggering old man holding a brown paper bag and stumbling toward them.

As they passed, Almira glanced for a second to her side, then uttered a whisper to Kara.

"Infidels," she hissed. "They're forever poisoning themselves."

And they continued toward Mission Street.

And the old man continued in the opposite direction until he crossed the street and turned for a last look.

"*Hochxq,*" he muttered, then his stumbling gave way to a determined step as he headed up Twentieth Street.

26

Before she and Matt had left his sailboat, Lindy called Matheson, who luckily was at his desk.

"Jesus Christ!" Matheson snorted after hearing her tale. "How could he be so stupid?"

"He's not stupid," she answered. "Jim, he's probably got more smarts and more experience than any one working on this. Now, can you do me a favor?"

"Name it."

Relieved, she said, "Matt and I are going out to look for Dan. I really doubt it, but there's the possibility he might be sick and have been taken to one of the hospitals. We'll check with them if you can pull whatever strings it takes to get an APB out on his truck. If you turn up anything, you can get us the message through the radio in Matt's car."

Matheson's grumbled curse preceded his response. "All right. But don't you think you're over-reacting?"

"I wish. But what I really think is that Dan's lost his patience over the ladies not being found. And," she added, her heart quickening, "I think he was afraid that I'd go out and get hurt again. That old man's become like a second father to me. It wouldn't surprise me at all if he felt some sort of responsibility for my safety."

"Yeah, I noticed," Matheson returned, sighing. "And his opinion of Kowalski's ability to handle matters is poor to say the least. I'll get on the APB, and both of you be careful. If you do anything to keep your butt from getting back in this squadroom on schedule, I am personally going to kick it all the way to sundown."

"Why Jim, you sound as if you miss me."

"Damn right, I do.

In less than an hour Lindy stood beside Matt in the student parking area of the City College of San Francisco and stared at Paya's pickup truck. Painfully, she felt her heart sink.

Matt withdrew his hand from the under the hood. "The engine's cold. It's been sitting here for several hours."

The guard, a retired patrolman named Albertson, shook his head. "I didn't notice it until about an hour ago when the lot was emptied after evening classes were over. What's with the owner?"

"A friend of ours," Matt answered quickly, then offered Paya's health as the excuse for his and Lindy's concern.

"Was he a student in one of the evening classes?" asked Albertson. "I'd be glad to check inside the buildings. Maybe he had to use the toilet and got sick in there."

"We'd appreciate it."

Albertson nodded. "You two going to wait around while I check?"

"If we're not here and you find anything, call 911."

Leaning against the truck, Lindy suddenly moaned.

"What is it?" asked Matt.

"He's found them."

"What?"

"The ladies. Dan found them."

"Lindy . . . ," he started but stopped when the sudden infallibility in her voice hit him. Studying her closer, he saw the intent focus in her eyes as they were fixed beyond the campus until she abruptly spun around and slammed the side of her balled fist against the the truck's fender.

"He knew right where they'd be and what to keep his eyes peeled for," she said, angry with herself and with a certain old Navajo who'd grown to be very precious to her. "All he had to do was to sit and wait, then follow. And he's had more than six hours. I should have picked up on it when he took my conclusions about the transit system so casually."

"Certainly, he would have notified someone if he'd come across them."

As Lindy's eyes narrowed, Matt said, "I suppose not."

Carol Burleigh's mouth opened in a wide yawn. She glanced to her side and saw Monica Grant doing the same. Both laughed automatically.

"Goodness," Carol groaned through the end of her yawn, "Being here is a killer."

"Tell me about it," returned her partner in the BART Security System.

Carol shook her head to rid the fuzziness of interrupted sleep. "I just wish," she said, slumping against the rail post of the steps descending into the station at Twenty-fourth and Mission Streets, "that they'd at least explained why they hauled us in tonight. This 'need to know shit' is for the birds. *I* need to know what's so important that I had my sleep interrupted."

"You were already in bed?" asked Monica. "I got called during dinner. That was just after seven."

Carol yawned again and nodded as her fingers massaged her forehead. "I got less than three hours sleep last night. My future sister-in-law, Jenny's bachelorette party was last night. It was quite a shindig. God, I never drank so much wine in my life. By eleven, I threw up the first round, then gulped two cups of coffee and was three sheets to the wind in another two hours." She barked a short laugh and shook her head. "But it was worth every bit," she continued with a smirk. "You should have seen the commotion when Bob and the members of *his* bachelor party crashed the party of his bride-to-be. That was almost two o'clock."

Monica snickered. "That must have been a thrill."

"It was," Carol said. "Especially for Bob. When he and the guys arrived, our star of the evening, our gorgeous hunk of male stripper, was down to about four square inches covering his personality. The first thing Bob saw was Jenny down on her hands and knees with one finger hooked in the top of those four square inches as our star was gyrating practically in her face. She wanted to see if all of him could fit behind that little fragment. You should have seen the expression on Bob's face."

Monica tossed back her head and laughed. "I bet he almost shit."

"He did! I don't know if he was madder at Jenny or his buddies who were howling. At any rate, twenty-three people saw Bob and Jenny have their first fight."

Still laughing, Monica said, "Jeeze, what a way to start a life together."

Carol's laughter faded as she was overtaken by another yawn. Again, she shook her head. She looked around behind her at the closed station's doors.

"Damn," she said, "I wish I knew what was going on in there."

"Not much we can do about it."

"I'm afraid you're right," Monica said, bored.

A tired quiet descended upon them. Both looked up at the street to see the passing of occasional nocturnal pedestrians. Twice, they had to turn back would-be travelers with the explanation that the BART was closed for a few hours due to electrical repairs as they had been instructed as the reason for the lack of available transit. Diplomatically, they handed over schedules of alternate means of transit, which the customers accepted with only little frustration. Things were always going wrong in a city. It was a way of life. Frustrating but understood.

"Here comes another one," Carol said, seeing a figure descending the steps. She took a step forward. "Ma'am, I'm afraid the station is temporarily closed for emergency repairs."

It was a woman. Young with shoulder length dark hair, she was dressed in slacks and shirt covered by a loosely hanging, long summer coat. Her face was tight with what appeared to be a problem.

"Can you help me?" she asked, reaching Monica first. "My friend turned her ankle. I'm afraid that it might be broken. I'd like to call a taxi and take her to the hospital. May I come in and use the telephone?"

"I'm afraid not, ma'am. There's a phone up on the street several yards that way," Monica answered, pointing in the direction of the pay telephones.

"All right," said the woman, looking in the direction Monica was pointing. "Would you mind watching my friend while I call? I hate to leave her alone. She's just around the corner from the top of the steps."

"Of course," Monica returned with the courtesy instilled in all who protect the public from harm. She nodded to Carol, who nodded back, and followed the woman up the steps.

Leaning against the rail, Carol continued struggling with her fatigue and concentrated on anything that would keep her awake.

From the street above, a horn blared and was followed in a few seconds by the loud young masculine oaths.

A pigeon pecked a path across the sidewalk at the top of the steps.

The sounds of a ghetto blaster suddenly blasted Stevie Ray Vaughan's *Love Struck Baby* into the air. Carol's toes began tapping without instruction. *Love Struck Baby* gave way to *Texas Flood*, and she stretched and yawned again.

Another hopeful BART passenger, a middle-aged man carried one of the folded bicycles permitted as an extension of commuting down the steps. He grumbled and ascended the steps after she delivered another diplomatic recitation that the system was temporarily closed.

She yawned once more.

"Monica," she muttered moments later, "where the hell are you?"

Shaking her head, she climbed up the steps in search of her partner. At the top, she stopped and looked around.

No Monica.

No concerned young woman.

Stretching over the stairway wall, she looked toward the telephones.

Still no Monica.

She was puzzled but only for a second . . . the last second of her life ending abruptly as a thin wire descended over her head and was pulled around her neck. The last thing she felt was the choking bite of the wire as it broke through the skin of her neck and released a warm ooze down her throat.

Within minutes, two other young women, dressed in the uniforms of the BART Security System, slipped through the door of the Twenty-fourth and Mission Street Station. Each toted a dark canvas case and passed without notice through one of the gates toward the escalator descending into the tunnel.

The last explosive assembled was as unobtrusive as any assembled so far.

The most difficult step, and the one taking the longest time, had been the hollowing of the two volumes of Yellow Pages Directories. The directories were stacked one on top of the other with the first half inch of the top and the last half inch of the bottom left intact as had been all edges. A block from the last of the explosive material was slipped into the cavity and pressed snugly against the directories' spines. From the detonator, two eighteen gauge copper wires were connected. One stretched from a metal contact point fashioned from the rounded tip of a fingernail file. A second stretched from the detonator to the flash light modified into a battery holder, holding two D cell batteries. A third wire stretched from the battery holder to a second identical contact point. One half of a disassembled wooden clothes pin was wedged between the contact points. In the wide end of the piece of wood, one end of a thirty pound monofilament fishing line was tied to a small drilled hole. With a long length of the fishing line, the directories were bound firmly together. The line from the wood was pulled tightly but not so tightly as to exert pressure on the wood. Four inches above the floor, the line was anchored at the other end around metal post four feet away. Now, only the slightest increase in tension on the line would pull the wooden wedge from between the contact points and complete the electrical circuit.

Simple.

Cheap.

And deadly.

27

"Any news?" Sergeant Fritz Irving asked the man approaching.

Lieutenant Eugene Kincaid, head of the detail working the Twenty-fourth and Mission Station, shook his head and expended a frazzled sigh. He'd just come from giving an hourly report to the communications van parked a block up the street from the station entrance.

"Same as last hour," he answered. "We got nothing, they got nothing."

"And it's still nothing," said Irving. He shook his head angrily. "Christ, it's been over three hours since we began in this section of the tunnel. We've checked everything. The railway. The escalators. Trash cans. You name it."

Kincaid rolled his neck to relieve the stiffness. Then he rolled it again and suddenly stopped. His face tilted upward, his bleary eyes focused.

"What about the ceiling?" he asked. "The dogs'll never catch anything up there."

Irving's eyes looked upward. "Only place I can

think of would be in the lights," he said, pointing to the long narrow fluorescent structures mounted overhead. "But certainly we could see something if it's up there. It'd make some sort of shadow."

"Well," said Kincaid, "it seems to be the only stone left unturned."

"And nothing to do but give it a try."

Turning, Irving called out to two of the detail and motioned for them to come his way. "Get up the street," he instructed as they reached him, "and get a ladder."

Emmerson, the shorter of the two, looked to the ceiling, then down to Irving. His eyes rounded in disbelief. "How could two women get up there? In a busy place like this."

"Where there's a will, there's a way," answered Irving. "Besides, this place isn't always that busy. Like after midnight . . . like it is now."

Emmerson looked at the man standing beside him. Both shook their heads and moved toward the escalator and began their ascent to the street. Emmerson was cracking a muffled joke and slapping his partner on the back while they disappeared upward. Neither noticed the two women, dressed in the uniforms of the BART Security System and carrying black canvas shoulder bags, stepping from the descending escalator.

But Irving and Kincaid did.

Both men smiled amiably and were about to introduce themselves as the women in simultaneous motion pulled from behind them their instruments of death. Only the muffled echoes of silenced automatic fire could be heard as the bodies of four men and a bomb sniffing dog jerkily danced their way to death on the tunnel floor.

28

Matheson stared from one to the other as Matt and Lindy approached his car parked at the meeting of Fifth and Market Streets. Just as his tour had been nearing the end, news came that everyone would remain on duty and be posted as observers along the BART route. He'd volunteered for this particular site for no other reason than it was the closest to the Hall of Justice, and being the oldest present, he felt less need to travel. At eleven minutes after one in the morning, everyone was growing tired of a very long and tedious night.

"Did you find Paya?" he asked around his stubby cigar.

"We found where he was," Lindy answered disconcertedly.

"That was his truck at the campus?"

She nodded. "We think he's decided to find those two on his own."

Matheson shook his head. "Shit, shit, double shit. How in the hell does he think he's going to do that?"

"He found them before, didn't he?" returned Matt.

Pulling the cigar from his mouth, Matheson shook his head again.

Looking around, Matt noticed Market Street was deserted save for the few ambling homeless and nocturnal strollers. A few cars were parked along the curbsides of Fifth Street. Most were empty, and none were officially marked.

"They're really keeping this quiet," he said.

"Kowalski's orders," said Matheson. "We're even under radio silence to keep it off the scanners." His head nodded toward the street. "About half those folks you see out there are ours. It's the same around every BART station."

"Any news coming out of the tunnels?"

"Not so far. They're sending up a report each hour on the hour. Thirty-four stations and nothing. By the way, your squad's got the Powell Station."

Matt looked across the street. The Powell Station appeared absolutely abandoned. "I'm tempted to pay them a visit and see how they're doing."

"You'll have to clear it with Kowalski first. He's in the command center. It's in a van parked just out of sight on Eddy."

"Dare we tell him about Dan?" Lindy asked anxiously.

"I'm not sure that would be such a great idea," answered Matt. "Kowalski's got enough on his mind. Besides, there's just as good a chance that we're wrong in our appraisal of the reason Dan's missing."

He looked at the despair on her face and slipped his good arm around her shoulder. "I know how you feel. But if our suspicions are true, there's not much we can do."

"If Dan's looking for the ladies," Matheson added, "he's not going to find them in the tunnels. The guards are turning back anyone attempting to enter. Chances are Dan will just give up and go home."

"I don't buy that," said Lindy. "Not for a single minute."

Neither did Matt or Matheson, but neither commented.

"Come on," said Matt, tugging her shoulder. "Let's pay Kowalski a visit."

Her eyes softened at the man making an effort to ease her disconcern. Her apprehension over the old Navajo was not eased in the least, but Matt's effort was not entirely futile. That he was making an effort at all brought its own solace. Quietly, she nodded and permitted him to lead her across the street.

Shivering, Mendel Webb clutched his thick, torn coat against the night's chill as he stumbled forward.

"I've seen warmer nights in the winter," he muttered through alcoholic fumes.

He'd managed to panhandle enough loose change during the day from the passers-by to afford a half pint of Old Crow. The whiskey went down quickly, easing his stomach from the pangs of hunger. But it only exchanged one torment for the other. Now his gastric linings were on fire, ignited by the harshness from the bottle.

Reaching out a hand, he pulled himself along the cold brick wall and deeper into the alley and muttered again, "I should have gone south with Earl." He shook his head. "Cold . . . too cold."

His bleary vision was filled with watery dancing lights from the other end of the alley. His hand groped again, and he moved forward, stumbling and weaving. Then, without warning, he heard the grating scrape of metal.

"What the hell . . . ?"

His other hand released the coat's front. He reached for the obstruction in his path. "I'll be damned," he croaked in his thrill of discovering the garbage can. Straightening his bent frame, he grinned as he teetered and snickered appreciation of his discovery.

His hands, numbed from the chill and drink, felt the rounded edges of the metal structure. He pushed.

It moved little.

He belched. His hand felt across the top and located the handle. The lid pulled off easily, noisily.

"Still alone," he whispered in delight and shoved his hand into the can.

In the blackness, he blinked his eyes repeatedly to identify the object under his groping hand. Strange, he thought. It was both soft and firm. It was smooth and still fairly warm. And it was wet . . . wet with a warm stickiness. After wiping his hand against the front of his jacket, he reached into the garbage again and made contact with the same wet sticky warmth.

Jerking his hand up, he strained his eyes to see just what it was that might or might not be part of his only meal in two days. His eyes blinked twice as his hand suddenly reflected a light in in the darkness.

"What are you up to, old fellow?" came a man's sympathic question behind him.

Turning, Mendel found himself spotlighted at the end of a long beam of light from the entrance to the alley.

"I . . . I . . . was . . .," he was attempting to say when the voice at the other end of the beam rose in a high pitch.

"Jesus Christ! You're covered with blood!"

The beam wobbled in the air as the man rushed forward.

"Holy shit!" yelled Mendel's sudden companion. "It's a woman!"

Mendel staggered back, colliding with a second garbage can. The structure fell along with him as he lost his balance, and both suddenly lay along the alley. The second lid bounced from the can and rolled on its edge and down the alley. The light's beam swung to the second can. Its owner shrilled again.

Dazed, Mendel sat propped against the brick wall and listened in a fuzzy stupor as the man interrupting his dinner began an excited report on his hand-held radio.

"This is Donovan! I've got two bodies . . . both women . . . stuffed in garbage cans over here in the alley. From the looks of things, they were killed within the last hour. Their throats slashed."

Kowalski looked up and smiled as Matt's and Lindy's faces appeared at the door of his command center. He stepped onto the street. "I'm not surprised at all. Okay. What's on your minds?"

Matt's lips spread in a lop-sided grin. "Oh, we were just out for a stroll on a summer night and thought we'd drop by for a chat."

"Like hell."

Matt's humor gave way to a hard frown. "I got word about the date and time."

Kowalski knew it was useless to evade the issue. "All right, here's the scoop. Short and simple. Every subway system in the country is shut down for the night and being combed by bomb details for explosives. So far, we've come up with nothing." In the dim light from the van his head could be seen moving from side to side. His words came heavily. "If things are to pop loose at seven in the morning, the folks back east have less than three hours to prevent it. And somehow, the idea that we have an extra three is not much of a comfort."

"Not much at all," Matt agreed.

"Could be that Dan Paya was right all along. Maybe we *are* headed for a big squaw dance." He noticed Lindy's expression suddenly tighten. "I didn't mean that as an affront. I just recalled Paya's mentioning it as the term for bombing area."

"I know you didn't," she returned, "but . . . "

Matt's arm reached around her, hers snaked around his waist.

"All right," said Kowalski, his investigative instincts rising, "fess up and tell me the truth. What's with Mr. Paya?"

Lindy leaned into Matt's shoulder as he related

Paya's disappearance and their suspicions behind it.

"Damn," said Kowalski. "I knew the old guy's not my best fan, but I never thought he was short on good sense. What the hell does he think he can do about it?"

"I'm sure he's got something in mind," answered Matt.

"Well, he'd be turned back if he tried to get through a tunnel entrance."

Looking up, Lindy wanted to ask if there was any chance that the guards at the entrances could be contacted and asked if a man of Paya's description had attempted to enter the system.

"I know what you're thinking," he said, reading her expression. "I'm afraid that I have to think of priorities. I like the old man. I really wish there was something I could do."

"I know," she said, meaning it.

"Hey, Tom!"

The trio turned to see Whitcomb's tense face at the van's door.

"What is it?" Kowalski asked.

"Call came in from Twenty-fourth and Mission," Whitcomb said. "The two guards stationed at the entrance. Their bodies were just discovered in a nearby alley. Both were strangled and stripped of their uniforms."

Kowalski bounced into the van. "Contact the units at all stations south of here," he all but shouted. "Tell them to check on the details working their stations, and tell them to take everything they've got with them and why."

Whitcomb nodded and turned back to his radio. Reaching for the microphone, he saw the blinking light, signaling an incoming call.

"I'll take care of it," said Kowalski. "You just get out that message."

Matt and Lindy moved to the door and watched as Kowalski donned a headpiece and announced he would reeceive the incoming messages. Silently, their tension mounting, they watched as Kowalski's face twisted into a fury while he barked several short commands before he wrenched the headpiece free.

"Twenty-fourth and Mission Station," he said, his voice tight with forced control. "The entire detail has been wiped out."

"Shit!" Matt snapped.

Kowalski nodded. "Just minutes ago. Two of its members had gone up to get a ladder. Seems they were thinking about checking out the ceiling lights. They returned to find the rest dead. Looked like automatic fire. The ceiling lights!" he announced as the light dawned. "Whitcomb, pass it along to the rest."

Whitcomb's head jerked in a nod as he added to the message he was transmitting.

"Those are my men down in the Powell Station," Matt said tightly. "I'm going to them."

Having no time to argue, Kowalski nodded.

Spinning around, Matt saw Lindy moving behind him.

"Stay here," he ordered as he began to run.

"No way," she returned and took off after him.

29

What began as two people racing from Eddy Street toward the Powell Street Station quickly grew to a small funnel of police and federal officers. Orders were rapidly and quietly issued as the group moved forward with Matt filling in the macabre news of the Twenty-fourth and Mission Street Station. He paused at his squad's mobile unit, parked around the corner from Kowalski's command post and instructed the squad's remaining officer, Gil Newton, to follow with a ladder. Newton nodded, snatched the folding aluminum apparatus and was running behind the group within seconds. As they moved into Matheson's view, Lindy arched her arm in a wide wave, signaling him to join them.

"What's going on?" Matheson asked, panting from his short run as he reached them.

"They're in the tunnels," Lindy answered over her shoulder as she regained her stride. "They wiped out the detail at Twenty-fourth and Mission."

Matheson muttered something indecipherable and fell into a sporadic step.

The two BART security guards stepped quickly aside and held open the station's doors as a series of I.D.'s were flashed. The officers poured into the lobby and through the gates to the escalators.

By the time they were making their descent, Matt and Lindy were panting.

She gasped, gripping the rail. "I've got to get back to running. I haven't felt so weak since I left the hospital."

Matt nodded, feeling the jarring of his mad dash pounding in his injured shoulder. He grimaced. "I know what you mean. Neither one of us has exactly been chasing the bad ones lately."

"Promise me one thing?" she asked.

"What?"

"Don't try to be a hero."

He said nothing.

"Matt?"

"What?"

"Have you ever been shot at?"

He turned and stared at her. "No."

"Then please stay out of the way."

"Jesus Christ! What am I supposed to do? Hide behind your skirt?"

"I've been through this before."

"My time was bound to come."

"Not tonight. Keep your head and your butt down."

"As I recall," he countered, "I outrank you."

She looked around and delivered a tense smile. "But we're not officially on duty. Remember, you're supposed to leave this night to me. And it's not over."

He hadn't genuinely smiled in hours and suddenly felt himself grinning broadly as they stepped off the escalator. "How could I have forgotten so quickly?"

"Well, don't the two of you look happy?" Joe said to the two advancing figures. Donned in his protective Kevlar unisuit, the hood pushed back, he had been observing the unfruitful work of his peers. By now, he was as bored as he was frustrated. Then seeing the group emerging from the escalator behind Matt and Lindy, his grin fell flat. "Why do I get the feeling this is more than a social call?"

"The lights," Matt said, pointing upward. "Have you checked them?"

"Not yet." Joe raised his eyes toward the ceiling. "You really think two women could have climbed up there?" He looked at Lindy. "At your height, how would you manage such a thing?"

"I'd find a way."

Looking up to assess the most likely spot to reach the ceiling, she scanned the visible length of the tunnel. All along it was a monotonous length of shades of ochre and blue-gray, broken only by the framed posters promoting a hodgepodge of commerce and art on the opposite side of the railway.

Still searching the ceiling, she asked, "But wouldn't the lights be too hot to place an explosive around?"

"Not necessarily," answered Matt. "Fluorescent only burns around one hundred ten, one hundred fifteen degrees."

"Their electronics wouldn't interfere with the mechanisms to set off the explosives?"

"Not unless the explosives are radio controlled."

"This is getting simpler all along," she returned sardonically. "It's just . . ." Her visual browsing came to an immediate halt. "Up there," she said, pointing upward to a spot adjacent to the escalator's exterior wall. "I'd have to stand on someone's shoulders and probably need the support of the wall if I were to work with the lights."

"A woman's logic," Joe responded, smiling while Newton rushed to open the ladder under the light. "Okay," he said, stepping to the ladder. "Everybody step back."

As the group obeyed, Joe pulled his hood over his face and quickly pulled himself up the ladder.

* * *

Kowalski pressed the headpiece against his left ear to receive the in-coming message. "This is control," he answered. "What have you got?"

The message had to be repeated twice before he could understand the panicked words coming from the other end. At last, the caller managed to speak through loud, hasty gulps.

"This is Sixteenth and Mission! We've . . . got a . . . a massacre down in the tunnel!"

With the determined control of a man experienced in being in charge of chaos, Kowalski steadily issued his instructions. "Get all of your people down there with everything they've got. Clear?"

The answer came back in a shrilly falsetto. "Clear, sir."

"Civic Center?" Kowalski said into the mouthpiece.

"Here, sir."

"What have you got?"

"No answer, sir. Agent Fullbright just sent down some of our team."

"Keep them down there."

"Yes, sir."

Looking around at the agent standing in wait of instructions, Kowalski ordered, "Get down in the station. Sixteenth and Mission's out. Probably the Civic Center detail, too. The ladies are less than two blocks away and coming through the tunnel on foot."

Without a word, Agent Curran took off on a dead run.

Into his mouthpiece Kowalski delivered the same instructions to the team posted at the Montgomery Street Station while praying another detail would not fall to the ladies.

Whitcomb continued his contacts and paid no attention as Kowalski muttered, "We've got them trapped. And pray God this works."

Bingo!" Joe announced as he peered through the

light's drooping cover.

His proclamation drew the curious crowd in a circle around the ladder.

"What is it?" asked Matt, straining for a view.

Lowering himself a few steps on the ladder, Joe lifted his hood and answered, "A battery operated timer planted against the end. There's a coil of what I guess to be around a pound and a half to two pounds of plastique around the edge."

A splatter of curses rose from the observers.

Joe smiled down from his lofty position as he pulled his wire cutters from the suit's pocket.

"If the rest of you will kindly step out of the tunnel, I'll disengage this little baby."

"Don't have to tell me twice," said a relieved Matheson.

The group began to drift up the tunnel toward the ascending escalator when suddenly, the heard Curran's voice shouting above escalator. "They're coming this way!"

"Who?" asked one of the men.

Curran appeared, stepping hurriedly down the descending steps and shouting repeatedly. "The ladies!" His audience, momentarily caught in the perplexity of his message, stared at one another as Curran kept barking his delivery.

"Everybody hang tight," Curran instructed. "We think we've got them trapped." He was gulping hard swallows as he reached the bottom of the escalator. "Two stations to the south are down, probably a third."

Instinctively, hands reached for their weapons as Joe drew down his hood and stepped back up the ladder and abruptly slipped his wire cutters around the copper wires connecting the explosive to its control.

Heads swiveled around in search of the deadly intruders until Matheson's eyes, sharpened from years of experience, caught a movement in the dark of the tunnel.

"Everybody down!" he yelled, crouching and lifting his service revolver in both hands. Diving to the floor, he grunted on impact and fired at what he now could identify as two figures. Around him, the group quickly scattered to avoid hitting one another with their own fire.

The tunnel erupted in a fusillade of spasmodic exchange of gunfire.

In his peripheral vision, Matt saw two bodies spin and fall just before he felt a heavy thud and sharp sting in his shoulder drive him to the floor. I'm hit, he thought until he saw Lindy's anxious face over him and realized that she'd thrown herself against him, slamming her body into his injured shoulder and bringing him down just as the wall above his head exploded in a line of small holes.

Her own revolver, now in both hands, barked near his ear. It barked again, and one of the figures jerked and half spun, an automatic weapon dangling from a limp arm.

The ladies' welcoming committee continued their firing, its sounds echoing against the tunnel walls. Within seconds came the satisfaction of the two intruders beginning a retreating dash for the ascending escalator and disappearing from sight of their surprising hosts.

Matt heard someone shout a curse. All he could see was Joe still on the ladder and comically rubbing his posterior where the discharge of bullets had failed to penetrate his protective suit. Then he felt Lindy's weight shift and lift from him.

"Lindy!" he yelled through horrid awareness that she was running toward the escalator. Cursing at the added damage to his shoulder, he pushed himself to sit. His weapon lay where it had fallen when he'd been knocked off balance. Clumsily, he retrieved the revolver and climbed to his feet. He looked around. Two men were down, probably dead from their positions and the pools of blood swelling beneath

their bodies. Newton was propped against the wall
and holding a hand to his side as red streams oozed
through his fingers.

"You all right?" Matt asked.

"Newton nodded, his face tight with pain. "Just a
flesh wound."

"Joe?" Matt asked, looking up.

"I'm fine," returned Joe, patting his behind for
another time. "Thanks to modern technology."

Then all three jerked up their heads as the distant
sound of exploding rounds came from above.

His shoulder pain gave way to the tightening of
dread gripping his chest, and he moved heavily to the
rising steps. Clinging to the rail, Matt let the escalator
deliver him to the station's lobby. Another distant
round of gunfire exploded beyond the door. The first
thing he saw as he stepped from the steps was the
bright splotches of blood making a path to the exit. He
stumbled through the mess, then through the doors.

The thick, cold night air was ominously quiet.
He looked around to see nothing as he climbed the
steps to the street's level. He saw and heard nothing.
A whiff of damp breeze teased his nostrils as he
stepped onto the sidewalk. Still, there was nothing.
Looking behind him toward the street, he froze.

Four men were collected around a body lying
prone in the street.

It was a small woman.

30

His expression must have told his panic, for Matheson looked up from the huddle around the slain woman, then rose and stepped to block Matt's path.

"Take it easy, Matt" Matheson said, taking hold of Matt's arms. "It's not Lindy. It's the woman who had the misfortune to be driving her car down the street when the ladies stopped it, pulled her out and put a round in her head."

"Where *is* Lindy?"

"Calm down," Matheson instructed. "She went to tell Kowalski where the explosive was planted. The second we got out of the tunnel, I told her to get to him." He smiled proudly. "My little partner performs very well under stress."

Matt felt himself gulping heavy sighs of relief. "Glad she listens to *some*one," he delivered sternly. He gulped for a few more breaths and quickly looked up and down Market Street, seeing and hearing only an angry collection of officers voicing and exhibiting their frustration. "I suppose the ladies are gone."

Matheson snorted. "Just as we got to the sidewalk, a car was coming around the corner. Apparently the driver had her door unlocked." He shook his head in disgust. "Driving through city streets during the night with the car doors unlocked. Christ! Woman must have never watched the news or read a paper. Or else, she floated through life in total oblivion. Anyway, she showed up at the exact second for the ladies to stop the car and put an abrupt end to her journey in the wee hours of the morning. God, it happened fast. Like a bolt of lighning, the ladies had her on the street and were off into the night. The car never stopped rolling."

"Anyone manage to get a license number?" Matt asked, feeling only half interested. Somehow, the fact that he had yet to see Lindy refused the knot from unwinding in his stomach.

Matheson nodded. "Curran. He's calling it in for all the damn good it'll do. The ladies will dump that car as quickly as they can, hit the streets on foot and disappear into the city. They were out of sight before any of our vehicles could get an ignition fired."

Matt rubbed his throbbing shoulder. "You're probably right."

"At least," Matheson said with a shrug, "we put a stop to their plan for the subways."

"Thank God for little successes," came Matt's dry reply.

Matheson was finally able to chuckle. "I know what you mean." He crooked his arm and jabbed his thumb toward Kowalski's van. "Speaking of successes, get your ass out of here and try enjoying the one you've got."

Managing a week smile, Matt nodded and turned.

"And do me a favor," Matheson called after him.

Matt turned again. "What?"

With the devil's own grin spread across his face, Matheson said, "Don't knock up my partner. I'm just getting her trained. She's turning into a hell of a homicide inspector."

"I prefer to think of her as a hell of a woman," Matt

said and headed away with renewed energy.

Matheson watched the departing man and began to chuckle. "I guess only a fool would argue with that one," he muttered. Then with nothing else to do, he followed.

Within twenty minutes after Lindy had delivered her message, Kowalski heard three locations across the country responding with their own discoveries of explosives planted in the same fashion as the one in the Powell Street Station. He immediately transferred the information up the line. In the following hour, the group in and around his command center began receiving the encouraging news that like discoveries were being uncovered in Boston and Washington, D.C.

The only thing dimming their light in those wee hours of the morning was that only in San Francisco had there been the chance of apprehending any of the ladies, and it had been lost. Thirty-five minutes after their bloody departure from Market Street, the ladies' stolen car, a late model gray Honda, had been discovered abandoned just off Van Ness on Grove Street, a half block from City Hall and a last thumbing of their noses. Blood stains soaked the back of the passenger seat, but the amount had been minimal. No blood at all had been found outside the car, indicating that it had been brought under control.

"They'll be back another day," was Kowalski's disgruntled prophesy. "And with another plan."

"Who knows?" responded Matt. "Experience has taught me that our higher-ups might use this for some arm twisting with the new powers in Teheran. With any luck at all, it might be a problem they will settle internally if they really want to improve things in their country."

"It'd be nice," said Kowalski. "Right now, my biggest concern is that the press will stumble onto the fact that the country's major transit systems were shut down at the same time and put two and two together."

Wincing, he added, "My God, if the public ever finds out how close things got."

"I doubt they really want to know, said Matt. "They enjoying living with a sense of security."

"And it's a joy assisting them," Matheson said, lifting his Styrofoam cup in a toast.

A round of laughter spread through the van as more cups were raised to victorious shouts.

Only one of the van's occupants failed to participate in celebration of the night's success. Sitting cross-legged on the floor with her back propped against the bench where Matt and Matheson sat, Lindy unsuccessfully attempted to smile. When she felt Matt's hand softly cuddle her head, she turned and looked up.

Matt looked at the anguish in her face. "You're still worried about Dan?"

She nodded.

"I tell you what," said Matheson as he pushed himself to stand. "Why don't the three of us take a walk to my car? I'll radio in and request the hospitals be called again and ask if anyone resembling him has turned up."

Lindy's eyes softened appreciatively. Quickly, she climbed to her feet.

Behind her, Matt rose. "If you'll excuse us," he addressed Kowalski.

"Sure thing," returned Kowalski. "And good luck. I hope nothing's amiss with the old boy."

As the trio strode toward Matheson's car, they kept exchanging suggestions for formulating a better plan for locating the old Navajo. Nothing seemed better than the original: keep checking the hospitals and incoming reports. Matheson had been released from his over-time duty and was now on his day off. Lindy and Matt hadn't been on duty at all. They now had the time to put their minds, haggard as they were from the night, to finding Paya. The prospects offered little hope.

"Try to think of the bright side," Matheson said as they arrived at his car. "Maybe old Dan just got lucky and doesn't want his daughter to know." His shoulders began to shake with his laughter at the idea suddenly coming into his mind.

Matt and Lindy only stared at him.

"And," he continued, still laughing at his thoughts, "maybe he found a hot one. Two hot ones. Like old Virginia's neighbors. I'd sure like to know what they were doing with those rocket boosters."

Matt frowned. "Rocket boosters?"

"Yeah," Matheson returned and then related the tale he'd heard from Munoz in the morgue. "Old gal was convinced those two were prostitutes and using sexual aids. The batteries, I can understand. But the rocket boosters? Wow!"

Matt's eyebrows rose another notch.

Now, it was Matheson's turn to stare. His laughter stopped abruptly. His hand flew up to bounce his palm off his forehead. "Jesus Christ! It can't be!"

"Can't be what?" Lindy asked, looking from one to the other. The exchange between the two men meant nothing to her.

"You got that woman's address?" asked Matt.

"I can get it from the morgue attendant." Matheson answered promptly.

"Use the pay phone. Jesus, if this is what I think it is, we don't need it going over the radio."

"What are you two talking about?" asked Lindy impatiently.

Matt took her hand and began leading her as they followed Matheson, who was now racing across the street. "We're talking about things that just might be used for electrical circuits and detonators. And for some wild reason, I want to check out that address and hope that Dan hasn't found it first."

As they stepped up their pace, she groaned.

31

Sunrise was just over an hour away as the two cars parked three blocks east of the address given by the morgue's attendant on the night shift. Luckily, he had been absorbed with a crossword puzzle when Matheson called and was not in the least bit curious as to why a homicide inspector wanted an address for Virginia Pearson.

As the trio merged onto the dark sidewalk, Matheson asked, "What the hell do we do now? Walk up, knock on the door and announce that we're the police. And if they're the ones who planted the bombs in the BART, they'd better come out with their arms above their heads?"

"First, we take a look," said Matt. "From the outside."

After almost fifteen cautious minutes of moving quietly and slowly, they saw the small Victorian townhouse belonging to Edna Wallace. At street level was a door to what could be, they surmised, a converted apartment. The entire block was dark. Not a single sign of activity exhibited itself in the quiet residential neighborhood.

Matt checked the numbers again. They matched.

He looked around for a moment of thought, then said, pointing across the street at another row of town-houses. A row of shrubbery ran across the front of each. "Let's hide in those shrubs across the street and watch for a while. If we put in a call, Kowalski will want to evacuate the neighborhood before going in. And people getting out of bed and leaving their homes this time of the morning will look suspicious. As soon as the morning's activities begin, we'll put in a call."

"Sounds logical to me," returned Matheson.

Then they made a quiet slow journey across the street and eased themselves to the ground amid the shrubs.

Matheson grunted as his posterior made contact with the shrub bed. "I'll freeze my ass off on this wet dirt."

Ignoring him, Matt and Lindy leaned against each other for warmth.

"I just hope," she whispered, "that none of the neighbors caught sight of us climbing into the bushes. We'd have some tall explaining to do."

Even in the dark she could see his teeth flash through his grin.

"In that case, I'll explain we're having a tryst in the bushes."

"Oh," she said through a snicker, "and how will you explain Jim?"

"That he gets his rocks off by watching."

Grimacing, she bit her lower lip. "I bet he would."

The minutes passed. The cold began piercing their jackets. Matheson issued quiet snorts. Lindy pressed tighter against Matt and savored his warmth and strength as all three kept their eyes focused across the street. Feeling her next to him, he thought of how she'd pushed him to the floor of the tunnel. Good thing she did. He'd just pulled his weapon from his waistband and wouldn't have been able to pull the trigger by the time the bullets zinged by his head . . . possibly into his skull. But the fact that she'd taken such a chance and be taking them again when the situation presented itself made him shudder deep inside. What was it going to be like between them? Would he feel his heart skip a beat each time the phone rang and she was not at his side? Probably. No, definitely. And how long was he going to be able to deal with it? The road ahead was going to be rough.

He hadn't realized how deeply his thoughts were absorbing him until he felt her stiffen and press her hand on his arm. He looked around to see her pointing down the street.

Two figures were moving from across Sanchez Street. They were moving cautiously and slowly. One appeared to be keeping vigil as the second pressed uneasily forward and seemed to be supporting its right arm with the left. A few yards closer, and the dim glow of the street light revealed the figures to be two women, both with dark hair. Neither spoke as they moved closer to the Edna Wallace's Victorian.

The trio concealed by the shrubbery looked silently at one other, their bodies tensing with awareness.

More long seconds passed as the two approached even closer to the house across the street.

There, they stopped. One fumbled a hand into her pocket. In the quiet of the night came the tiny jingle of keys clinking together. Then came a low moan followed by a hushed voice, its words indecipherable from across the street.

"Patience," Almira instructed in a whisper. "Inside I've got something to stop the pain in your arm. You can sleep the rest of the day."

"I could sleep the rest of the week," Kara returned, grimacing from the pain.

Almira inserted the key into the lock and twisted. The door opened easily. Standing aside, she gently pushed Kara into the darkness, then followed and closed the door behind her.

* * *

Lindy began a hasty scramble to her feet. "I'll run back to your car and call in," she whispered to Matheson.

Matheson nodded.

On her feet, she moved from the concealment of the shrub and had taken only a few steps when, suddenly from behind, a hand grasped her shoulder. Abruptly, she swung around and stared into a familiar, lined copper face, its hue instantly deepening in the reflection of a strange glow just as she heard the deadly roar from across the street. Beneath her feet the ground vibrated but failed to pierce her astonishment as her dazed conscious momentarily delayed identifying exactly what had happened. Only when she turned and looked across the street, did it all come together.

Their jaws hanging in in surprise, Matt and Matheson rose and joined Lindy and Paya The four of them stood in silence and watched Edna Wallace's Victorian townhouse slowly crumble into a heap of belching smoke.

Along the street, residential lights began flicking on. Shouts and gasps started coming from doors and windows. In short moments came the distant wail of approaching sirens. In their night clothes, the residents poured onto the sidewalks and observed in stunned whispers the thick ribbons and clouds of smoke drifting into the street. And none noticed the quartet slowly joining them.

"I'll be damned," Matheson said, at last finding his voice.

Lindy could only look in pained disbelief from Matt to the old Navajo whose expression was deadly solemn.

"Oh, Matt," she whispered. "What will they do to him?"

"Why should anyone do anything?" he said, smiling down at her troubled expression. "You know what

what they say about people who build bombs?"

"What?"

"They eventually blow themselves up."

Matheson began to chuckle. "I think we'd all better get out of here. Dan," he said to Paya, who had kept his silence, "may I have the honor of seeing you home? If nothing else, I'd better be on hand when Maria gets a hold of you. I have a feeling you're in big trouble with her."

Paya grunted in understanding and nodded. He looked at the young couple and saw Lindy's eyes warm with appreciation of the man draping his arm around her shoulder. With a quick nod, he said, "It's over now." Then he turned and began walking away with Matheson, who was still chuckling as they began moving down the street.

As they crossed Sanchez, Matt and Lindy heard Matheson saying, "Well my friend, have you thought of any excuses to explain your absence?" When he got only a crooked grin for an answer, he added, "Let's tell her we went out drinking. That's an old excuse, but it still works. Care for a beer on the way home? My treat." He looked over his shoulder. "You two care to join us?"

"Another time," Matt answered, as he stopped with his arm still draped around Lindy.

"Good night, Dan," she called out.

"And remember," added Matt, "we're going fishing tomorrow."

Paya smiled and nodded, then waved as he shuffled away with Matheson.

Matt and Lindy continued their slow journey away from the swelling crowd of the curious. They said nothing, only lifted their attention periodically to observe the approaching parade fire trucks and police cars.

"Matt," she asked, anxiously looking up at him, "it's going to work? Keeping Dan out of this?"

"Out of what?" he asked innocently.

"But the arson investigation?"

". . . Will show that two people who've been working with explosives were blown up." He shrugged and grinned. "Happens all the time."

"You sound so sure of yourself," she returned dubiously.

"Happens all the time."

Groaning, she shook her head. "I keep thinking . . ."

"And *I* keep thinking," he said, looking to his left where a remote, isolated corner of Mission Dolores Park suddenly appeared, "about that idea I came up with."

"What idea?"

He began pulling her into the park.

"The one about having a tryst in the bushes."

Stunned, she gasped, "Here?"

"Why not?"

"But the place is going to be overrun with police and firemen any minute."

"It's not my fire they're coming to put out."